# THE DUKE ALWAYS WINS

JESSIE CLEVER

SOMEDAY LADY
PUBLISHING, LLC.

*For my favorite kind of people in all the world -
Librarians.*

# CHAPTER 1

$\mathcal{L}$ady Anna Elmont, the dowager Countess of Wexford, did not mourn her dead husband.

She didn't celebrate the fact that he was dead though. There was something wrong about that, but she did start each day by expressing her gratitude for the fact that her life had taken an unexpected turn.

When Gabriel Phelps, the Duke of Grimsby and Roger's close friend, had come to tell her her husband was dead, Annie had thought it a dream. Roger couldn't be dead. She wasn't that lucky.

But then Gabriel had explained, and it all made a perfect kind of sense.

Roger had died in an illicit boxing match. One blow had been all it had taken. They had thought him fine at first. He had fallen to the mat and got back up. It was all terribly normal. But then he'd staggered against the ropes and slumped. A doctor had been called, something about swelling of the brain, and that was it.

Lady Anna Bounds was a widow.

That was how she thought of herself, as still a Bounds.

Roger's name had never settled quite right on her, feeling not like a union of two people but rather one branding the other as property.

Because she had been his property. He'd always been careful to remind her of that.

She preferred it when people addressed her as Annie when their relationship allowed for it, and then when something more proper was called upon, she insisted on Lady Anna even though it wasn't correct. She just couldn't bear her title, the one she had been given when she married. It was worse when it was extended to include *dowager*.

Roger's heir had moved into the Wexford London townhouse before she'd even had time to pack her trunks, and this finally had caused the scandal Gabriel had feared, the one he had worked so tirelessly to prevent.

The boxing match in which Roger had died had not been sanctioned by the gentlemen's club where it was staged, and the entire thing contained the volatile nature of a bomb. But Gabriel had hushed it up, and suddenly her husband had died of nothing more extraordinary than a fall from his horse.

But then the heir had moved in, a second cousin to Roger, and ordered her from the house. Her parents had been waiting for her, of course, their arms open and ready to comfort her when really she wanted nothing more than to bask in the sudden peace she found inside her childhood home. But it didn't matter how she felt about it. It was still a scandal, and it had taken months to die down.

Still, she heard the whispers.

*The poor widow Elmont, the poor dowager countess.*

It made her sick every time.

There was nothing poor about Annie's situation. In fact, she'd never been happier. Finally she had the chance to discover who she might have been had she not married Roger. That was the thing people didn't understand. She had more advantage as Roger's widow than as his wife, and she planned to embrace every minute of it.

*Finally* she would know who she really was.

Her sister Gwen had given her the idea. Annie could admit that the shock of suddenly being a widow, of being free of Roger, had left her numb for the better part of a year. It had taken something her sister had said, an off-hand comment about how once Annie had been the strong one of the three Bounds sisters, that had reminded Annie of the truth.

She *had* been the strong one.

This then had led to another, far more worrying thought.

How had she let Roger defeat her?

The answer was swift, of course. As his wife, Roger held complete power over her. It didn't matter how strong she was. Roger had had the law, society, and custom on his side. But not any longer, and never again. Annie would remain a widow for the rest of her life. Anything else was unimaginable.

But then the unimaginable had happened. Two dukes were looking for wives that season. Two dukes. In the *same* season. It was unheard of. Annie's mother had clapped with glee—*clapped*—when the day marking the formal end of Annie's year of mourning had arrived, releasing Annie from its clutches. Annie had never seen the woman more excited than when she'd faced the season with three eligible daughters for two eligible dukes.

Then their father had married off Gwen, and that had left only Annie and Eloise, the youngest Bounds daughter. It had been easier to deflect their mother's whims when there had been three of them, but now Annie could feel the noose tightening.

Nancy Bounds, the Countess Stoke Bruerne, mother to

Annie and Eloise, was determined to have a duchess for a daughter, and Annie was determined to remain a widow.

But she would never disappoint her mother, and so she went along with it. She allowed her mother to order new gowns for half mourning and accepted invitations on her behalf. Annie was once again out in society, and she felt the bristle of it at every function.

She hated lying to her mother, although she hadn't technically lied. She had just let her mother believe she would remarry. When in reality, Annie had every intention of getting Eloise hitched to one of the dukes. Poor Eloise. No, Annie couldn't think like that. Her widowhood was too precious for such sentimentality.

If only her mother was the single problem she had that season, but she wasn't. Annie had a far worse problem.

She wasn't a debutante.

She was something much more terrible. An unencumbered widow with a title of her own, social standing, and experience as the wife of a peer.

Annie had the power to stop a conversation dead by merely entering a room, the Marrying Mamas flinging daggers of envy at her with their stares. A game of croquet was suddenly over when she stepped up to the pitch, the participating ladies just as suddenly requiring a bit of refreshment in the shade. A buzzing conversation about fashion and embroidery ceased when Annie wandered by.

No one wished to consort with the enemy, and there was no enemy greater than a woman with much to commend her.

Being a widow was absolutely the best and the worst.

Annie hoped with everything she had left in her that her sister Eloise would snare the Duke of Ardley, one of the dukes on the market that season. With a duke in tow, perhaps their mother would relinquish Annie to the throes of widowhood.

No, it was only Eloise that could save Annie now. Or at least, that had been her hope up until approximately seventeen seconds ago.

Because seventeen seconds ago their butler, Hickinbottom, had presented Annie with a pristine white calling card on a silver tray. It was calling hours, but Mother and Eloise were out. Mother had secured an emergency session with the modiste to fix Eloise's gown as she'd torn it the other night at Gwen's ball. It was only Annie and her chaperone receiving visitors that day, and Annie hadn't expected any at all.

Annie looked up from the card that had so unsettled her to eye her chaperone. Grandmother Bitsy was hardly more than five feet tall, weighed more than seven stones only with her knitting in her lap, and was currently snoring in her chair by the fire. It was nearly June, and the fire was not necessary except Grandmother Bitsy was always cold. Annie had had the windows at the front of the room opened, and that was where she sat with her embroidery hoop, allowing what little breeze there was that day to keep her from wilting like a plucked flower.

She looked back down at the calling card, her heart thumping so loudly it echoed in her ears until a rustling sound broke through the pounding, and she glanced to the side to find her hands shaking, her embroidery needle still clutched in her fingers. She swallowed and stuck the needle into the linen stretched in the hoop before she could injure herself.

"Please tell the duke I am in," she said and pushed to her feet as Hickinbottom left to escort their guest to the drawing room.

Gabriel Phelps, the Duke of Grimsby, had come calling.

She knew she wouldn't escape him. She had not had reason to speak to the man since he'd taken care of things with Roger more than a year ago. It was fitting somehow that Gabriel should go to such measures to quell a scandal, the very last thing he could do for his friend. However, their differences in age, Gabriel being fifteen years Roger's senior, made Gabriel always seem more of a mentor than a friend to Roger. Annie had felt sorry for the duke. He'd always tried to steer Roger on the right path, but Roger had always resisted. It had gotten him in the end.

The duke had neatly covered everything up and then slipped away, the only connection between Annie and Grimsby having disappeared when Roger died. There was no reason for the two of them to engage, and she could admit to feeling a kind of regret about it. The duke had always been kind to her, and in the dark years of her marriage, such kindness was what had kept her going.

But then Gwen had asked for Annie's help in getting Grimsby to accept an invitation to Gwen's introduction ball, a feat which had been certain to pack the ballroom and save Gwen's husband's tarnished reputation. Annie knew she should have called upon Grimsby with such a request, but she hadn't been able to do it, choosing the coward's way by sending him a letter. While she might have missed his conversation, she still felt too unsteady stepping back into the life she had left as if Roger's ghost was lurking there, ready to spring out at her.

But now Grimsby had come. It was the right thing to do really, and he deserved to speak with her. She must remember Roger was dead, and he couldn't hurt her any longer. Besides, they had a chaperone.

Grandmother Bitsy snored with particular gusto then, and Annie frowned.

A part of her had known Grimsby would come. He had complied with her request only two days ago when he'd attended Gwen's ball. The thing had been a smashing success, and even now Gwen was happily on her way back to Yorkshire with a husband whose reputation had been bolstered if not completely redeemed.

The frightened echo of her heart stumbled when she thought of Gwen and her husband. They had seemed…well, happy, a notion Annie only dared hope for. Husbands and wives weren't always happy. It hadn't been that way for her, but she had hoped with all her heart it would be different for Gwen, and it seemed it was.

Annie paced to the opposite side of the room, putting an entire seating arrangement of sofa, chairs, and three accent tables between her and the door.

*Coward.*

The word hissed through her mind, and she welcomed it. She was a coward. Happily. Being a coward meant she was safe.

Her thoughts scattered though when she heard footsteps in the hall. Had it only been days ago when Gwen had reminded Annie of how strong she used to be? Annie's heart galloped. It was easy to be strong when one wasn't so terribly frightened.

The footsteps ceased, and there he was. Gabriel Phelps, the Duke of Grimsby, stood in her drawing room. She had never been sure if Grimsby was handsome or not. His features were of a saturnine nature, and he either appeared terribly serious or as if he were peeling off her clothes with only his eyes, eyes that hovered between gray and blue. The gray that had found its way through his hair only served to strengthen his serious demeanor and was likely why she thought of him as more of a mentor than a friend to Roger.

He wore a navy jacket with dark trousers tucked into riding boots, and momentary panic seized her. He had looked exactly the same when he'd come to tell her her husband was dead.

She didn't dare curtsy, not trusting her legs to hold her. "Grimsby," she greeted him with a nod.

"Lady Anna," he said, his voice steady and deep.

She recalled the first day she had met him. It was her wedding day, and she'd been scared then too but for happier reasons. She had thought it was the beginning of the rest of her life, and she hadn't been able to stop the flutters in her stomach. So when Roger had introduced her to his friend, it had taken her a moment to understand he meant the duke because Grimsby was so much older. It was only later that Annie learned it wasn't so much a friendship but a situation of savior and a person who did not wish to be saved.

Grimsby finally took a step into the room, and she realized she should have asked him to sit. But her mind was a jumble of thoughts, past and present, and they were congealing in her conscience until she couldn't think or act normally.

Grimsby turned his head in the direction of the fireplace. "I take it your grandmother is…well?" he asked, his eyes pinched with concern as Grandmother Bitsy snored ever more loudly.

"Yes, she's quite well," Annie said and forced her hands to relax at her side. "I'm surprised by your visit." She closed her eyes before she could see Grimsby's reaction on his features and summoned the courage to have a normal conversation with this man. She opened her eyes. "Surprised and pleased," she tried again, licking her lips.

Grimsby's expression hadn't changed. In fact, she wasn't sure if he possessed another expression. His face always seemed unfazed by the events around him, remaining quietly calculating as though he were always assessing his opponent. And everyone was his opponent.

"I was surprised as well," he said, taking another step into the room. "Surprised to receive your letter. I hope my presence at your sister's ball served its purpose."

She nodded quickly. "Yes, of course. It most certainly did, and I thank you for it. It truly helped my sister in her introduction to society as the new countess."

"I'm pleased to hear it," he said.

Silence pulsed between them, but he made no further move toward her. He stood on the other side of the seating arrangement, his hands clasped loosely at his back. The stance was likely meant to appear casual, but it only had the effect of accentuating the broadness of his shoulders, and Annie felt uncomfortably small.

Finally he said, "I've come about another matter today, Lady Anna. One I had hoped to address with you earlier this season, but my affairs in Parliament have kept me unusually busy."

She felt a flutter of hope deep in her chest. "Yes, I understand you're working to pass legislation that would mandate the uniformity of drains used in city planning."

She had read as much in the papers, and it was far easier to speak of Grimsby's work in Parliament than anything more personal. Grimsby had a reputation for being a supporter of public works, particularly anything that aided in uniform city planning that improved living conditions for residents. She had gleaned from the articles she had read that he had a passion for factory housing, especially as industry boomed over the last two decades and workers flooded the cities.

For a moment, she thought his expression might have changed, and she wondered if she'd surprised him again. But his features relaxed into the same composed if assessing countenance, and she remembered what he had said.

He wished to speak with her about something. Her blood

cooled. What could her dead husband's friend want with her? Was it something to do with Roger?

Her mind went utterly blank, and she was grateful for it. She needed to focus. Her heart hammered, and her hands shook so much she hid them in her skirts. Roger couldn't do anything to her. Grandmother Bitsy might have been asleep, but her snore was comforting, and Annie pushed thoughts of her husband away.

She faced Grimsby again and even had the courage to raise her chin in silent question.

"Right, the drains bill. It's proving far more complicated than I had hoped. It's hard to prove the merits of hygiene against the bottom dollar for landlords. I thought a more municipal approach might provide relief, but there are still some members of Parliament that are happy to reside in the pockets of rich landowners."

"Aren't you a rich landowner?" The question was out before she could stop it, and she almost bit her tongue.

That was something the old Annie would have asked, the Annie she had been before she learned to keep her mouth shut if she wished to stay safe.

Grimsby smiled though, and her heart stuttered at the way it brightened his face. "I *am* a rich landowner. More by happenstance than actual effort. A title often comes with such weighty history." His smile faded, and he came toward her, his footsteps precise as he passed the sofa and two of the tables. He stopped immediately in front of her, and she feared she might swallow her tongue now.

She had to look up to see his face. He towered above her, and she'd never felt so small, so fragile, so defenseless.

"There are other responsibilities that have fallen on me because of the title, and it's those that I wish to speak with you about today, Lady Anna." He paused, but not, it seemed, in hesitation, but rather as though he were thinking about how best to proceed. "There's a misunderstanding about my intentions that I wish to clear up. I'm not seeking a bride this season."

The words were spoken with such weight it momentarily confused her. Why should it matter to her if Grimsby sought a bride or not? If society had mistaken his intentions for such, it was hardly her concern.

She nodded anyway, unsure. "I see."

"I've already found a bride," he went on, and somehow she must have known what he would say next because her heart suddenly stopped its fearful beat. It stopped entirely.

Yet somehow she managed, "Who?"

This time he didn't surprise her when he said, "You."

* * *

He'd bungled it.

He knew the moment her soft brown eyes—brown with just a hint of hazel tones—rounded, her lips parting the barest of degrees in shock before firming in repulsion.

For of course she would be repulsed. He hadn't explained everything yet, and surely the idea of her dead husband's friend proposing marriage was one of utter disgust.

Gabriel hadn't meant to propose to anyone. He was prepared to let the title go to another branch of the Phelps family. But then Roger had died, and everything changed.

Now here he was, at nine and thirty and proposing to his dead friend's widow. It could hardly be worse, and yet it was almost better. He knew Anna. She wouldn't be a stranger to him, and he trusted her. Surely that accounted for something. They could each live their separate lives knowing the other would be accepting, even supportive. Most importantly, he could protect her.

But Anna would want children. All women wanted children, and he just wasn't sure what to do about that. He couldn't very well tell her he didn't want children. Perhaps they could quietly adopt. A girl. A girl was harmless.

"If you'll allow me to explain," he said when she still didn't speak. "It is time for me to wed. The title requires me to do so, and I would like nothing more than to have you as my wife." The lie stuck in his throat like a fatty piece of meat. He pushed on. "Roger would have wanted it so. Don't you agree?"

Something passed over her eyes then, and he wondered at it. She'd been nervous since he'd entered the room even though they had a chaperone. As if sensing his thoughts, Grandmother Bitsy emitted a sound just then that would make a logging mill jealous. Annie had still been uneasy, visibly so, and he wondered if he reminded her too much of Roger. The thought twisted his gut, but he pressed on. He had to make her see the merit of his suit. It was the only way.

But Lady Anna remained mute, her eyes round, her lips firm.

"You are vulnerable now, Lady Anna. You have acquired certain experience that other men seeking a bride will covet."

Again, her eyes changed, and this time her lips softened. She blinked and broke her gaze from his for the first time in nearly a minute.

"Yes, I know," she said, her voice weak.

He felt the tension ease through his shoulders, and he dared take another step closer to her. "Then you understand the risk. I can't allow you to fall victim to a man with less than honorable intentions."

Her chin came up unexpectedly at this. "Isn't that my father's responsibility?" Her words were forceful, but she looked away quickly, pacing toward the windows behind her.

He watched her retreat, noting the color that had sprung to her cheeks. He was making it worse.

He hadn't had enough time to prepare. When it came to arguing in the House of Lords, he was masterful, eloquent even, orating on topics of uniform drains, proper engineering of street surfaces, the benefits of clean drinking water. He spent days, sometimes weeks, researching a topic until he could speak on it effortlessly for hours, days if the matter required it. Whatever needed to be done to ensure the proper safety laws were passed.

But he hadn't had any warning when it came to Anna. She had surprised him the night of her sister's ball. The moment he'd laid eyes on her he knew he was already too late. She wore a gown of deep navy, declaring the end of her mourning. She might as well have taken an advert out in *The Times* it was so obvious.

He thought he'd have more time. He thought she would enter half mourning and continue to refuse invitations, to remain on the periphery of society for a while longer. But she hadn't. She was there, she was out, and she was in danger.

He had gone immediately to his solicitors the next day to prepare the necessary contracts, and now he was here, asking her to marry him, and he was doing it all wrong. He drew a deep, even breath. He was more than capable of making her see reason. He'd learned the art of it, making a person think something had been their idea.

Yes, Gabriel was very good at convincing people.

"Of course," he said, "I would never suggest your father would fail to keep your best interests in mind. It's only that—"

Anna spun around. "My father made an excellent match for Gwendolyn."

There was something strange about her tone that stopped him. His mouth hung open, his words unsaid as he studied her. Her statement was not a statement at all. Not from the tone of her voice. It almost sounded as if she were trying to convince herself of something.

"I believe he made a very wise and promising match for your sister," he said, holding himself still.

The air between them crackled unexpectedly, and he had the suspicious feeling his marriage proposal was no longer the item being debated. Had he unwittingly stepped into a hornet's nest with his suit?

He watched her carefully as she paced back and forth in front of the windows, stirring the drapes as she passed them.

"My sister appeared perfectly happy while she was here. Didn't she?" Anna stopped, and when she turned her face to him, her eyes were bright.

"Yes, she did," he said, keeping his voice neutral and adding nothing more than what was needed to answer her question.

Anna nodded and went on pacing. "She did look happy. My father can clearly negotiate a suitable match. You mustn't worry that I'll be—" Her voice cut off on a painful sound, and he did move then.

He surged forward, laying his hands gently on her shoulders if only to stop that infernal pacing.

"Lady Anna, I've upset you. I'm sorry—"

"Please don't." Her voice was raw now, as if she were trying to hold back tears, and her eyes had fallen to the floor and remained there.

She was like cold stone beneath his palms. So quickly had she gone from a woman nearly vibrating with agitation to one that was as lifeless as marble, and confusion rocked him.

He stepped back and dropped his hands. Her eyes stayed on the floor, but now he could see her hands curled into fists, her fingernails digging into the soft skin of her palms. He took another step back.

"Lady Anna—"

Her head came up so fast it startled him. "I am not in danger, Your Grace. Your proposal is unnecessary."

"Lady Anna," he tried again. "I promise you I know what gentlemen are like, and they will prey upon you, and I can—"

"They will not, Your Grace, for I will never remarry. I shall remain a widow for the rest of my life."

Her words traveled directly to the center of his chest where they clawed a hole clear to his heart.

She loved Roger. He knew it then without question. She loved him so dearly that she would remain faithful to him even at such an incredible and perilous cost to herself.

Gabriel had never suspected a love match between Roger and Anna. His observations of the Elmont union had been like any other of the *ton*. A quiet companionship that although not riddled with passion at least simmered with quiet happiness. But for Anna to swear such allegiance to a ghost would suggest a different kind of partnership, one for which he had not prepared properly.

"I see." He spoke the words with absolute neutrality. Should he display an ounce of opposition, he knew he would lose her, and he couldn't afford that. The consequences were too dire to even think on. He clasped his hands behind his back and relaxed his shoulders. "I hadn't realized you would intend to stay true to your vows, and I apologize if my actions today have offended you in any way."

He made to turn to the door, but she made a sound then, a strange, strangled sound as if she had meant to say something and had thought better of it when a word was already on her lips. He waited, careful to study her without staring, as if he were merely waiting for her to speak. But really his heart thudded as his mind raced, trying to unravel that sound.

Did she not wish for him to leave? Had she changed her mind about her intent to remain a widow?

This thought he cast aside, never one to give himself so much credit. He had hardly been in her presence for more than a matter of minutes. It wasn't as though he had the power to move her from so ardent a goal with his weak argument in favor of marriage.

Blast. He'd messed the whole thing up, and now she was wary of him. He could see it in the careful distance she put between them, the way she had slid behind a table when he'd touched her.

She had loved her husband, and he had invaded her mourning, pried it open in the most ruthless way.

Damn and blast. What in heaven's name was he going to do now?

He had no further time to think on it because a commotion at the door drew their attention. Lady Stoke Bruerne, Anna's mother, appeared, peeling her gloves from her hands.

"If you insist on playing this game of cat and mouse—" Lady Stoke Bruerne stopped so abruptly at the sight of them, Eloise, Anna's younger sister, plowed directly into her mother's backside as she swept into the drawing room. "Your Grace," Lady Stoke Bruerne said with a hasty curtsy when she recovered herself.

Lady Eloise did not curtsy. She remained where she had caught herself against a chair after narrowly missing her mother, her eyes huge as they blatantly assessed Gabriel, her gaze darting between him and her sister, the glint of protectiveness obvious there. He ignored her and bowed to the countess.

"My lady, I'm so sorry you were not here when I arrived." He gestured behind him to Anna. "I only came to thank Lady Anna for encouraging me to attend her sister's ball the other evening. It proved to be a welcome distraction."

Lady Stoke Bruerne nodded. "Oh yes, it was a rather

lovely evening, wasn't it? I am terribly sorry you find your-self the object of much attention this season, Your Grace."

He smiled. "There is no need for apology, Lady Stoke Bruerne. It is I who have gotten myself into such a mire. One must never hint at one's intentions when one is a duke."

Lady Stoke Bruerne practically fell over the sofa in her attempt to casually make her way closer to them. "Yes, you are quite right." She glanced behind him as if looking for something and gave a cry of surprise. "Oh, would you look at that? It's gone teatime, and I haven't even sent for a tray. Do say you'll be joining us, Your Grace."

Gabriel knew it was hardly past two in the afternoon as he had a clear view of the clock that stood by the door to the hall. He smiled more easily now. "It is I who must apologize now, Lady Stoke Bruerne. My presence is required else-where. But I should hope our paths will cross again this season."

He made the required noises of farewell, careful to keep his tone and attention toward Anna respectfully neutral, before he made his way to the door. He had almost slipped into the hallway when he caught a flash of movement out of the corner of his eye.

He turned just in time to see Grandmother Bitsy snap her eyes shut. He smiled, feeling some of the tension in his chest ease, and left.

# CHAPTER 2

"That was kind of Grimsby to call."

Annie jumped, nearly upending the teacup in its saucer on her lap.

Eloise pursed her lips but said nothing more.

Annie cleared her throat, setting her teacup aside before she could shower herself in cold tea. "Yes, it was."

It had been three days since Grimsby had called. Since he had proposed marriage. *Marriage.* Simply recalling it had the power to send a jolt of fear through her.

It wasn't marriage itself that unsettled her. She had no intention of returning to the state. It was why Grimsby had done it. She was Roger's widow. Roger had been his friend. What was the duke's motive?

But that was it really. She *was* Roger's widow, and Grimsby *had* been Roger's friend. Under normal circumstances, such an offer would be expected. Such arrangements happened all the time in society. Yet the very idea had her mouth going dry and her stomach heaving.

Annie glanced in Grandmother Bitsy's direction. The woman was knitting, but Annie recognized the same lilac yarn the woman had been winding and unwinding from around her knitting needles for the better part of a month and wondered if the woman had only joined them so she might catch any interesting gossip Eloise had to share.

For of the two sisters, Eloise would have gossip.

"I was surprised to see Ardley at Gwen's ball," Annie said now in an attempt to distract Eloise from Grimsby's visit.

Eloise took a generous gulp of tea and nodded in response, unable to actually respond with her mouth full. Annie frowned. If this was how their afternoon would continue, it would prove dreadfully dull.

Annie had suspected Eloise was up to something for the past two months, but she had no proof of her sister's machinations. Clearly they were both avoiding certain topics, and it left rather very little to discuss.

"Grandmother Bitsy," Annie said then. "How is your scarf coming along?"

The tapping of knitting needles stopped suddenly, and Grandmother Bitsy gathered a mass of the lilac yarn from her lap and held it up.

The knitted yarn looked exactly like nothing.

"That's quite lovely," Eloise said before stuffing a whole petit four into her mouth.

This would simply not do.

Annie squared her shoulders and remembered what Gwen had said. Once upon a time, Annie had been strong. Grimsby might have proposed, but she had refused him, and that was that. The matter was settled. There was no need to worry further. It wasn't as though he would propose *again*. Her widowhood was safe.

"Grimsby said he had a lovely time at Gwen's ball and hoped it had proved a success. I should rather think it did. Wouldn't you, Eloise?"

Eloise's eyes brightened, and she swallowed quickly. "Yes,

I do think it was. Do you know I was forced to stand in the gardens for the better part of an hour because there was simply no room on the ballroom floor?" She gestured with an eclair. "That poor Renfield boy had asked me to dance, and we weren't able to make it inside. We spent the whole of the quadrille on the terrace discussing scent hounds." She wrinkled her nose. "He knows very little of scent hounds, and it proved a dreadful interaction."

Grandmother Bitsy shook her knitting needles then. "The Renfield boy? Harvey? He's a good lad. Must be in school now."

Eloise frowned. "Harvey is Renfield's father, Grandmother. I'm afraid you're a generation behind."

Grandmother Bitsy raised her eyebrows and made a soft *oh* with her lips before resuming her knitting.

This time the silence grew until there was a definite buzzing in the air, and Eloise had taken to pairing the petit fours according to their decorative icing, arranging them on the plate according to mauve or peach. Annie wished Gwen were there. She would know what to say.

The thought stopped her.

Roger had done this. Roger had made her incapable of finding things to say because she had put so much effort into learning how to be quiet. It was safer to be quiet, and she'd gotten so terribly good at it. Annie studied her sister, now arranging the eclairs according to length, and felt her stomach turn.

This wasn't her. This wasn't Annie. Annie could talk to her sister. Annie could make conversation. Annie was the bright part of their family. Grandmother Bitsy had once said as much. Annie searched her mind, looking for anything of which they could speak, but her mind was empty. She had spent the past two years trying so hard to do nothing that now she had nothing to give.

She was saved when the doors to the drawing room burst open, and their mother paraded in, arms in the air.

"It's here!" Nancy proclaimed.

Annie felt her momentary relief at the arrival of her mother vanish. "What's here?" she asked.

Eloise's tower of petit fours fell over onto the parade of eclairs. She ducked down, scooping something from the ground while Grandmother Bitsy displayed an incredible amount of interest in the row of stitches she had just placed.

Annie's stomach turned to ice, and her gaze flew back to the door to find her mother standing to one side of it. A maid entered, her arms stretched around a light blue box festooned with a voluminous bow of the palest lavender.

Annie recognized the distinctive blue hue, the silk lavender bow as the mark of the modiste they had frequented since they were small girls, and carefully she placed her hands into her lap, pressing her fingers together to still her racing heart. She didn't wait for her mother's response and instead pushed to her feet as the maid moved to the table below the windows at the front of the room.

Annie watched, her heart beating a staccato in time to the maid's footsteps, until finally the woman set the box down and stepped away. Nancy had followed the maid across the room and now she stood proudly beside the box. She thanked the maid and dismissed her before turning to Annie.

"Eloise and I got you a present," Nancy said, her voice thick with pride.

Eloise's head popped up from under the table where she'd been—pretending, Annie was sure—to search for something she'd dropped.

"Mother," Eloise scolded. "Do not think to rope me into your mischievousness."

Nancy's smile dimmed. "All right, I did this. *I* picked this out for you." She clasped her hands together. "Oh Annie, darling, it's so lovely. It's just the thing to attract a suitor this season." She reached out and adjusted the bow until it lay square against the sides of the box. "Rosemary will be simply green with envy," Nancy muttered, referring to her nemesis, Rosemary Hayes-Martin, Viscountess Bowes. She turned back to Annie. "Come. Open it." She gestured to the box, pride still pouring from her.

Annie didn't move. "I don't require anything else, Mother. You know the modiste finished the necessary garments at the conclusion of my formal mourning period a month ago."

Nancy dismissed this as though it were of no significance. "Those are for everyday wear. This is something special."

Annie didn't like how her mother's eyes glowed at the word *special*. She stood her ground. "A suitor? I thought I was to focus on the dukes this season." Her throat closed on the words as she remembered Grimsby's proposal.

She hadn't told her mother about that because her mother wasn't to know Annie had no intention of remarrying. And now this, whatever it was that was in this box.

Nancy adjusted the bow again, this time making if fall artfully over one side. "Oh come now, Annie. The dukes are a wonderful prospect, but the fact that you have pulled yourself from the depths of your mourning should be celebrated. Any suitor will do, won't it?"

Annie wanted to laugh at this. It had taken very little effort to shed her mourning veil because she hadn't been mourning. She had been relieved that her husband was dead. She shouldn't be celebrated. She should be condemned.

Eloise stood and came around the sofa to where their mother perched beside the modiste's box, nearly vibrating with anticipation. "Just take a peek at it, Annie. I remember how much you loved this color, and it would be so nice to see you in it." Eloise paused, her face folding into a look of confusion. "I always wondered why you never wore the color once you wed. We'd always talked about it when we were girls. About what we'd wear when we had the freedom of being married women." She shook her head. "But you never wore it."

Annie nearly upset her stomach at her sister's words. Before her marriage, Annie had loved all colors. Her life had been bright with hope, and her future lay before her like a rainbow of possibility. Until that first time, only three days after their wedding, when Annie had learned what her marriage would truly be like.

She could remember it perfectly. The excitement she had felt when she'd donned the emerald green walking gown that paired so stunningly well with her dark hair. It showed her off to such advantage, and she remembered the thrill that shimmered through her at being freed from the required debutante's palette of creams, pinks, and pastels. She'd gone to break her fast with her husband, feeling as though the future were wild and unknown before her.

But Roger hadn't felt that way. It was the first time he'd called her a whore, and she'd never worn that gown again. Never wore any gown that would bring her unwanted attention.

She shook her head now. "You know perfectly well color is not suited to the half mourning I am in now. I may be past the required one year of deep mourning, but think of the scandal I should cause if I step out in anything more exciting than lavender." Here she looked pointedly at her mother. "Think of how that will affect Eloise's efforts with Ardley," she said, referencing the duke whose eye Eloise had caught.

Eloise looked away at this, pretending to fiddle with her cuff, but Annie knew better. Something was definitely amiss with her little sister.

Nancy patted the box. "You could do with a bit of scandal,

Annie darling. Come. Just look. If you absolutely hate it, I shall have it refitted for me."

Grandmother Bitsy made a noise then that sounded like a disbelieving snort. Nancy tossed the woman a quelling look before returning her gaze to Annie, an encouraging smile on her lips. Eloise had looked up too now, her cuff forgotten, and Annie could practically feel their excitement.

She drew a deep breath, knowing perfectly well she couldn't disappoint them. There was clearly something in this box they wished her to have, and they had gone to great lengths to secure it.

Resigned, she moved around the sofa. "All right, but I have the final say in whether or not I'll accept it," she said.

When she reached the table, she tugged carefully at the bow, saddened to unravel such a beautiful confection, especially after her mother had arranged it so elegantly. The silk bow slipped away, and Annie lifted the lid from the box, setting it aside. The familiar delicate white tissue was folded inside, and she glanced in the direction of Eloise and her mother. She wondered if their trip to the modiste the day of Grimsby's visit had had anything to do with what she might find inside, and Eloise's torn gown had simply been a ruse.

With one hand she peeled back the tissue, revealing a gown tucked carefully into the box. It was made of fine silk and would be worn off the shoulder, creating a striking look, but Annie knew that wasn't the point of the gown. Nothing about the design of the garment was the point, in fact.

Because the gown was red.

Sinfully.

Red.

She pulled back her hand slowly as if the dress were an adder waiting to strike. "Mother, I can't wear that," she said, her voice steady, but in her head she heard other words.

*Roger wouldn't let her wear it.*

She hated it, the way she could still hear his reprimands even a year after his death. But chasing this thought was another one, a sadder one. She didn't know if she even liked red gowns. Or off-the-shoulder ones. Or ones that showed her neckline. Roger had always dictated what fashions she wore, and then mourning presented its own requirements. And now here she was, left unknowing what she liked in her own gowns. The very idea left her hollow.

"Oh," her mother cooed and stepped up to the box, pushing back the tissue to better reveal the gown nestled within. "Of course you can," she insisted. "You're a widow. You can wear whatever color you want, and this will suit you so nicely."

"Red is truly your color, Annie," Eloise chimed in now. "It will be so vibrant against your dark hair. I can't wait to see you in it."

Eloise was always the optimistic one, and she simmered with it now. Annie remained unfazed. She eyed the red gown. She had been right in thinking it an adder, and she carefully folded the tissue back over it.

"Thank you, Mother, Eloise, but I can't accept this. You know it would cause a stir, and I shan't wish to hinder Eloise's chances with Ardley."

"But what about Grimsby?"

Annie's gaze flew to her mother's face. Her expression was eager with an air of wickedness about her, and Eloise's was no better, playful with glee.

"What about Grimsby?" Annie said, careful to keep her voice modulated, but then her hands shook against the tissue covering the sinful gown, and she snatched her hands back.

Her mother almost glowed now. "He called on you, Annie. That must mean something."

"It means he was my husband's friend. That is all."

She felt guilty for the way her careless words snuffed out

her mother's look of hope. The woman's eyes pinched in concern now, and she stepped forward, taking Annie's hands into hers and squeezing them. "Perhaps you'll think about it. I thought you would look simply breathtaking in it at Marjorie's Summer Solstice Ball," her mother said, referring to the pinnacle of society functions, Lady Marjorie Olmstead's midsummer ball.

"That's still two months away," Annie replied, trying to extract her hands from her mother's grip.

Her mother only tightened her grip, shaking Annie's hands just a little. "Exactly. You'll have plenty of time to think on it." Her mother paused then, her eyes growing watery, sending Annie's heart into a crushing dive. "It's just that I can't help but hope you may find happiness again."

The words were like a dagger directly to her chest, and Annie wanted nothing more than to pull her hands from her mother's grip and run from the room.

Annie knew there were happy marriages. Her mother and father enjoyed one, as did her sister, it seemed. But her mother was wrong about Annie finding happiness. She wouldn't find it *again*.

She'd be finding it for the first time.

* * *

GABRIEL STOOD with his back against a Corinthian column where a panel had been pushed back to connect the two drawing rooms in the London house of Baron Commons. The baroness was hosting a soiree, and so far, the night had been a parade of terrible if passionate poetry delivered by a string of gentlemen each desperate to catch the eye of at least one debutante that season. Gabriel had started the night in a seat near the front of the assembled group, but after several glares from the departing performers, Gabriel had thought it best to filter in amongst the crowd. Lady Stoke Bruerne was correct about the amount of attention he was getting that season, and it wasn't all from the debutantes and their mothers.

He wasn't there to be seen after all. He was there *to* see. Baroness Commons's frequent soirees were a favorite among the *ton*, and he thought Anna and her family might make an appearance. The soiree would provide an opportunity for him to speak with her again, apologize for his blunder earlier that week without drawing undue attention to his actions by calling on her at home a second time.

If he should call on her again, her mother would take note, and he had no desire to get the parents involved at this point. He wanted this decision to be Anna's, and pressure from her parents would not do.

He scanned the room again, noting the gentlemen scattered here and there. Anna wasn't the only reason he was attending the baroness's soiree. If he was to get his bill on uniform drains passed, he needed more support. There were two earls and a marquess he hoped to speak with that night, but so far, he hadn't seen either of them.

A low hum of conversation to his left caught his attention. As he stood with his back to the column that had marked the separation of the two drawing rooms, just to his left was a small corner in which any number of people could have a quiet conversation without interrupting the main festivities. Currently it contained two men, one of which Gabriel recognized as the cousin of the Duke of Ardley. Gabriel had no desire to eavesdrop on a private conversation, and as there was a break in the ill-fated poetry recitations, he could quite clearly hear the topic being discussed, and it seemed not to be going well for Ardley's cousin.

Gabriel made to move, hoping to slip onto the terrace where he knew an impromptu game of whist was underway, stealthily arranged by the Baron Commons for his bored gentlemen friends no doubt, but it appeared the conversation next to Gabriel was tapering off.

"I'm very sorry, my good man, but the answer is still no," said the gentleman Gabriel did not recognize.

With a shake of hands and a wave of farewell with an unlit cigar wedged between two fingers, the gentleman sauntered off in the direction of the terrace.

Ardley's cousin remained where he was, but his shoulders had dropped about two inches. Gabriel took pity on him.

"You must position your argument, so it's rooted in something the man wants," he said, his words nearly drowned out by a round of applause behind him.

Ardley's cousin turned, one eyebrow going up in question.

Gabriel held out a hand. "Gabriel Phelps, the Duke of Grimsby. I'm an acquaintance of your cousin."

The man nodded and took Gabriel's hand into his own. "Yes, I recall we met briefly at the Gracey ball last week. Tucker Ryan, but everyone just calls me Tuck." The man finished shaking Gabriel's hand and then used the same hand to push a lock of tawny hair off his forehead, only for it to fall back into place. "What was that you said?"

Gabriel gestured in the direction of the man who had sauntered off. "I inadvertently overheard some of your conversation. I understand you're trying to raise funds for some kind of scientific endeavor." Gabriel let the sentence hang in hopes the man would provide an explanation.

Tuck nodded. "Yes, a scientific *expedition* actually. I'm looking to study the effects of the aurora borealis on telegraph stations. The best place to observe the phenomena is Svalbard." He grinned self-deprecatingly. "As a man of little to no means, I haven't the funds to get there myself."

"So you're looking for benefactors?"

Tuck nodded again, and he pushed the hair from his forehead again as well. Gabriel was starting to understand the gesture was one more of habit than of actual need. "My cousin invited me to London for the season. He said the prospects were good here." Tuck's expression turned grim. "I'm finding it to be rather unfriendly."

It was Gabriel's turn to nod. "That's likely because you've never needed to win an argument. Am I right?"

Tuck's eyes narrowed. "Yes, something like that." He shrugged. "I'm afraid there isn't much argument involved with a textbook or a glass beaker. I haven't the practice."

"I would advise you to study anyone you hope to approach. Learn their backgrounds, what charitable causes they support, and anything regarding their financial state. What they've invested in, debts, entailments. That sort of thing. Then when you approach them you can pitch your argument in their favor. Make them think it was their idea to support you and not you asking them."

The gentleman appeared as though Gabriel had just given him the formula to turn lead into gold, and perhaps Gabriel had.

"I hadn't thought of it like that. I had hoped the cause itself was interesting enough." He gestured with a hand. "With the Carrington Event still quite recent, I had hoped my expedition would garner interest on its own."

"The geomagnetic storm from the fifties?" Gabriel shook his head. "Most gentlemen I've worked with in the House can't remember what horse they bet on last week, let alone something that happened a decade ago. You would do well to study your opponents before engaging them. I'm happy to provide any insight I might have on candidates you select."

Tuck's lips parted as though he meant to say something but appeared to change his mind as he shook his head. "You would help me like that?"

"Of course," Gabriel replied. "I'm happy to provide assistance."

They were words Gabriel had uttered often enough. He'd even said them to Roger once, little good they had done. Thinking of the man had him wondering about Anna, and he gave the room a quick scan only to stop at a sudden interruption.

"What's this?" a booming voice cut in as the Duke of Ardley himself joined their party with a generous slap to Tuck's shoulder that sent the man bouncing under his cousin's attention. "I hope Grimsby hasn't won your support for his drains bill." Ardley shook his head. "The man doesn't even stop at the members of the House. He'll persuade anyone to buy into his ideas." Ardley was smiling broadly to show he meant the accusation good-naturedly.

Gabriel crossed his arms over his chest. "And why should I stop at members of the House when I'm so good at convincing people of what is best?" He felt a small stab at his words, Anna's refusal still fresh.

He tried to dismiss it. After all, he'd faced such opposition before, and a *no* wasn't a *no* forever. It was just a *no* for right then.

Ardley laughed. "And he's got the confidence to match." He turned back to his cousin. "*Has* he convinced you of his drains bill?"

Tuck shook his head. "No, but I'm keen on it now."

"I've offered to help Tuck here better pitch his expedition to potential benefactors."

Ardley's eyes widened. "You don't say." He clapped Tuck on the shoulder again. "What a boon, old man. Grimsby here is the best debater I've ever seen take the floor of the House. He'll have you in funds in no time."

Tuck's face clouded. "You must allow me to pay you for your expertise, Grimsby."

"Please call me Gabriel. And you must keep your funds for your expedition, or what will have been the point of my aid?" Gabriel shrugged. "Besides there's nothing for which I want." Again that nagging pain sliced through him.

As if sensing it, Ardley said, "That's not quite true, is it? As I understand it, you and I have the same targets on our backs this season. Do I have that right?"

Gabriel frowned. "While it's true I seek a wife, I'm afraid you and I are likely on different paths. I've already chosen a bride."

Both Ardley and Tuck expressed surprise at this in expressions that were oddly similar.

"Truly?" Ardley said. "Who is the lucky lady?"

Gabriel's eyes involuntarily drifted over the crowd again, looking for Anna. "I'm afraid the lady refused my suit," he said instead of answering directly.

"What?" Ardley said ungracefully.

Gabriel met his gaze. "She refused me. I'm afraid I rather blundered it. I thought she would be grateful to receive my offer."

Ardley shook his head, his eyes falling to the floor in disappointment. "Grimsby, my dear fellow, never make assumptions when it comes to women. The odds are never in our favor."

"Did the lady give a reason why she would refuse you?" Tuck asked.

Gabriel felt a modicum of guilt for even discussing the matter, and he had no wish to speak of Anna's private feelings, but he sensed the gentlemen before him were both honorable and might actually be able to help him.

"She's a widow," he said plainly. "I'm afraid she still mourns her husband. She said she wished to remain a widow." He shrugged. "I can only assume she still loves her husband."

Tuck's face clouded again. "Are you sure she's still in love with her husband?"

Gabriel felt a stillness inside of him at the question. "What do you mean?"

Ardley looked to Tuck. "You're thinking of Aunt Sarah, aren't you?" Tuck nodded before Ardley turned back to Gabriel. "Our aunt Sarah was a widow for a good part of her life. She said she valued her freedom too much to ever remarry. Died a happy, independent woman in the arms of her Italian lover who was twenty years her junior."

Gabriel felt the bile rise in his throat at the very idea Anna would take a lover. Would it be more than that? Would Anna allow this faceless lover other things as well? Gabriel didn't know what provisions Roger had made in the event of his death, but Anna must have financial security if she were so adamant in her desire to remain a widow. Would her lover try to take advantage of her?

His gut churned as the past came at him, and he pushed it away. This was entirely different than what had happened with his mother. Everything would be fine. He would convince Anna to marry him, and then she would be safe.

"A happy, independent woman?" Gabriel didn't like the sound of that. Such a notion was wrought with potential danger. How could he protect Anna if she were happy and independent?

Ardley nodded. "Did the lady mention her freedom when she gave her refusal?"

Gabriel felt something shift inside of him, and for the first time, he questioned how quickly he came to the conclusion that Anna could still be in love with her husband. He thought back to their conversation, but the abrupt arrival of Lady Stoke Bruerne and Lady Eloise had made him forget the details.

He shook his head. "I can't quite remember. I only know that she valued her widowhood."

Ardley nodded more assuredly this time. "That's it then. There's only one thing for it."

Tuck also nodded. "Most certainly."

Gabriel felt wholly in the dark. "What is it?"

"You must convince her she's in love with you." Ardley said.

"You mean make her fall in love with me," Gabriel corrected, but Ardley was already shaking his head.

"Love is complicated." He shrugged. "It's nice when it happens, but if you're determined to marry this woman, and she's determined to remain a widow, there isn't time for love. There's only time for the belief of it."

Gabriel blinked. "I'm to make her believe she's in love with me? That sounds terribly deceitful."

Ardley frowned. "You wish to marry this woman, yes? Does it matter how you do so if the result is honorable? She will be a duchess, safe in the wealth and prestige that comes from the Grimsby title. Any lady should covet such a position."

For a moment, Anna's face flashed into his mind, and something strange happened to his stomach, almost like a flutter. Anna was beautiful. He knew that objectively, but there had been something about her face that day in the drawing room when he had proposed, something that seemed to pull at him.

He had to protect her. That was it. When he looked at her pale skin, the fragile look in her eyes, the way her lips parted with uncertainty, he knew to his very bones he must protect her. That was the reason for the flutter in his stomach. He knew what he must do even if he didn't like it.

The ends justified the means, didn't they?

"No," he heard himself say. "No, it doesn't matter." He met

Ardley's gaze. "Ardley, I should like your help in convincing the woman she's in love with me."

Ardley smiled and slapped poor Tuck on the back again. "Excellent. We shall begin immediately."

"Immediately?" Gabriel asked, feeling his objectives for the evening had suddenly grown more complicated.

"Yes," Ardley said, his smile broad. "Is the lady in attendance tonight?"

# CHAPTER 3

Gabriel had only to remember that this was for Anna's safety.

He eyed Ardley now. Roger had been his friend, but their relationship had never been one of true companionship. As such, Gabriel had never felt comfortable confiding in the man. It was more of an acquaintance of happenstance than a true friendship, but it was what Gabriel had always preferred. He likely knew more of Ardley than he did of Roger, and for some reason, he felt he could trust the man before him.

He slid his gaze to Tuck, but the man had already turned his attention elsewhere, likely looking for another potential benefactor.

"I must admit we're only two months into the season, and I've grown bored with what I see," Ardley said before Gabriel could answer. "I rather envy you. You've truly found someone that will suit you?" Gabriel thought he might answer this question, but again, the duke went on. "I had a debutante just the other day show me how she could fold a pocket square. I have a valet for that. Why would I go through the trouble of finding a wife who could do the same? Feels rather redundant to me."

Gabriel waited, thinking another question might be forthcoming, but the duke had apparently truly ceased speaking and was waiting for an answer to his many questions. Even Tuck turned back to their group, and Gabriel wondered if he was used to his cousin's rambling.

Gabriel felt the truth push at the back of his teeth, and once, he would have been happy to speak it. He would have told Ardley that he had planned to let the title go, gleefully allowing it to pass to another branch of the family and entirely out of reach of the vile man who had once tried to usurp its power. Now at nine and thirty, he had been thoroughly content as a bachelor, enjoying the occasional light-hearted affair with a consenting party, and with no plans at all to wed.

And then Roger had died.

He had known widows in the past, ones with whom he'd had some connection through their husbands, but never before had he felt this instinct to protect them. Only Anna had done that to him. Perhaps it was because he felt some degree of guilt for Roger's death. No matter how Gabriel had tried, he'd never been able to reach Roger.

Yes, that must be it. Guilt. No matter though. It still left him with the very real problem of getting Anna to accept his proposal.

"I believe the lady should be here tonight, but I haven't seen her as yet," he said. "We have a shared history through mutual acquaintances, and I suppose that has made my decision easier," he decided to say by way of explanation.

"Is that so?" Ardley raised a single eyebrow in question. "And still she refused you?" He shook his head and turned to Tuck. "I do really think it's the widowhood thing. Don't you agree?" Tuck had no time to respond as Ardley turned back to Gabriel. "Observe, won't you?"

Gabriel watched as Ardley turned, facing out from their little group. Like a compass finding true north, Ardley seemed to have known when a gaggle of debutantes were at that moment traversing the space between the guest seats and the refreshment table.

"Good evening, ladies," Ardley said, affecting a sensual, deep tone, and then…well, the man did something odd with his face, something Gabriel didn't understand.

The ladies tripped over each. In truth. First the one on the right stepped in front of the one in the middle, but the one in the middle had already caught the skirt of the one on the opposite side and together they collided, a fit of taffeta and giggles and dewy eyes. Ardley continued to hold his face in that strange expression, and the ladies giggled harder as they extracted themselves from one another, waving their fans in Ardley's direction as they passed.

Ardley dropped the odd expression as soon as the ladies passed them and turned back to Gabriel, a smile on his face that might have suggested he'd just bested another at a feat of strength.

Gabriel gestured to the duke. "What was that you did with your face just then?"

"He calls it the Wonder," Tuck said flatly.

"The Wonder?" This was growing tedious, but still Gabriel felt something just out of his reach that somehow Ardley had the answers to.

"You put as much sexual tension and heat into your expression as you can, and it makes the ladies wonder just exactly what it is you're thinking about when you look at them."

"And what exactly were you thinking about?" Gabriel asked.

"Corn commodities."

"Ah, prices are up," Gabriel said brightly, suddenly on firmer ground.

"Yes, quite. It will be a good year for my tenants," Ardley said excitedly.

Gabriel stopped him with a hand. "Wait a moment. You were thinking of corn commodities and yet…" He gestured to where the ladies had passed them in a complete fluster.

"Precisely," Ardley said as if Gabriel had figured it out.

It was no wonder Anna had refused his suit. Gabriel had nothing figured out.

"I don't see anything precise about it," Gabriel said, crossing his arms over his chest.

Tuck gestured to his cousin. "That's why you require his help."

Ardley gave that smile again. "Now tell me about your lady."

Gabriel recoiled mentally at the direct question. To be fair, he would have felt the same way no matter who had asked. He didn't know if it was the involuntary reaction honed from years of having to keep himself and others safe or if it was the overwhelming instinct to protect Anna. Perhaps it was a bit of both.

"She's Lady Anna Elmont, the dowager Countess of Wexford," Gabriel said finally.

Ardley's eyes narrowed, and a line appeared between his brows. "Roger's widow? I thought Roger was your friend."

"He was," Gabriel said. "How did you know him?"

Gabriel had known Ardley by reputation before the season had thrust them together, and he knew the duke to be an admirable man, decent in his interactions with people and respectful of giving others the floor in the House. He managed his properties well, and there were no rumors of unseemly behavior. But if he had known Roger, there must have been something about the man that others didn't know. Or that Ardley didn't wish for them to know.

But Ardley waved him off with a hand. "I was partnered with him at that charity game endeavor what's her name puts on every spring. The one to raise money for St. Mary's."

The muscles at the back of Gabriel's neck relaxed. Everyone knew someone from the Marchioness of Lionsley's annual card extravaganza to raise money for the orphanage in the City. It was hardly noteworthy that Ardley should have met Roger there.

"The man *was* good at cards," Ardley said and raised a hand to acknowledge a passing gentleman who returned Ardley's gesture with a nod.

"Roger never missed one of Lionsley's card games," Gabriel said.

"And what of his widow then? You say she refused you. Did Roger leave her comfortable enough to avoid remarrying? If I understand correctly, Roger's death was sudden and unexpected. Had he sense enough to leave a will to allow for his widow?"

Gabriel felt his gut tighten at the mention of Roger's death, but Ardley hadn't been speaking on it in gossip. His expression showed true concern for Anna's wellbeing.

"She's living with her parents actually. Her father is the Earl of Stoke Bruerne. As to her financial situation, I'm afraid I have no further insight."

Ardley began to nod even before Gabriel had finished. "Of course. Met the gentleman myself just the other night. The earl, that is. I've been spending time with his daughter." Here he looked to Tuck. "Ellen, is it?"

Something strange happened to Tuck then. If Gabriel had known the man better, he would have said he looked green.

"Eloise," Gabriel said, saving the man from answering.

Ardley rubbed the back of his neck. "That's the problem

with this whole damn process, Grimsby. Mothers are throwing their daughters at me, and there are so many of them I can't remember their bloody names. I feel like a cad."

Gabriel's estimation of Ardley ticked up a notch. "You must be seeing a far greater number of debutantes than I am."

Ardley waggled his eyebrows. "It's good to be a duke."

There was something about this man that had Gabriel's chest easing in a way it hadn't in years, likely ever, and he thought he could very well form a real friendship with the Duke of Ardley.

"Please, call me Gabriel," he said, and Ardley smiled.

"Then I must insist you call me Liam." He rubbed his hands together. "Now then, let's find your lady and get started." Gabriel made to survey the room to see if Anna and her family had arrived yet, but of course Liam wasn't finished. "Now there are a few things to remember about the initial encounter."

"Initial encounter?" Gabriel interrupted. "But I already know the lady."

Tuck shook his head. "He doesn't mean it in that way." Here he nodded at his cousin. "The man has a system for engaging ladies."

Gabriel was truly baffled now. "A system? Do you mean like a factory?"

Liam seemed to consider this. "Something like that." He brought his hands together as if to accentuate his point. "There is a certain way a man is to engage a lady if he hopes to make a real connection." He moved his head to the side to indicate the room around him. "This—the soirees, the balls, the promenading—it's all for show. It's a gimmick to parade people about in front of one another but prevent them from truly connecting with one another. You'll never win your lady's hand if you rely on such arcane measures."

"But I thought the season was precisely to make such connections."

It was Tuck who answered now. "It's designed to make you think that. Have you ever had a real conversation with one of these debutantes who are so eager for your proposal?"

Gabriel opened his mouth but immediately shut it, shaking his head instead.

"Exactly," Liam said. "Now then, in the first meeting, you must act aloof."

This was nonsense. "I've already proposed to the woman. How am I to act aloof?"

Liam held up a finger. "You proposed using the old system. We're using my system now, and when you engage the lady, you will act aloof. You are nothing more than the dear friend of her late husband. There is no talk of marriage. There are no complicated steps to follow. You are merely there as an old acquaintance come to see how she's enjoying the season. When she answers you, you change the subject to something about you. Do not show interest in what she's saying."

"That sounds heartless," Gabriel protested.

"That kind of notion is precisely what got you into this predicament. The heart has nothing to do with it." Liam tapped the side of his head with two fingers. "It's all about the mind. You convince her here—" He tapped the side of his head again. "And you'll win her here." Now he tapped his chest just over his heart.

"That's manipulation," Gabriel stated plainly, but Liam was already shaking his head.

"That's the game of attraction, my friend. Now you will be alone with your widow. You mustn't engage her amidst the same constructs as you did before, or you will face the same result. No. You must get her alone." Liam's expression turned grim, and Gabriel realized Tuck had started nodding gravely while his cousin said, "But here is where things get difficult. You mustn't touch her." Gabriel had no intention of touching her, and he opened his mouth to say as much, but Liam had already moved on. "You will be tempted to. Such aloneness will have its natural effect, but you must resist it. Touching her will only make matters worse." Gabriel sucked in a breath, ready to end this tutelage when Liam took his arm in a fierce grip. "And no matter what, under no circumstances are you to kiss her."

* * *

THOUGHTS CONJURED by the image of the red gown still haunted Annie as she suffered through another recitation by a gentleman who either had something in his eye or was unusually affixed on Eloise who sat beside her. The poor man winked profusely at her sister, enough so it appeared as though he might be having a stroke. Eloise hadn't even looked up from the program in her lap, her thoughts obviously elsewhere.

Annie might have felt sorry for the man, but she was happy to not have the attention fixed on herself.

The man finished his comparison of a woman's face to an opening rose blossom and left the impromptu stage to a polite round of soft applause.

She took advantage of the break in entertainment to lean over to her mother who sat on her other side and whispered, "I'm off to find a retiring room."

Her mother waved her away with an impatient hand as she resumed her conversation with the baroness who sat on her other side. Annie caught the word *dukes* and lifted her skirts a little higher to escape with greater efficiency. Eloise caught her arm though as she tried to sidle past.

"Where are you going?" her sister hissed.

"Anywhere else," Annie whispered back as she had no intention of locking herself in a retiring room.

Eloise stood at once. "I'd be happy to help you with your hem, dear sister," she said just loud enough for anyone sitting near them to hear.

Annie turned away from the assembled guests before rolling her eyes as her sister continued to hold her hand until they had reached the safety of the cleared area near the refreshment table where guests quietly mingled at the back of the drawing rooms.

Eloise pulled Annie close once more. "If Mother asks, I was with you the whole time," she whispered.

"Same," Annie hissed back and then Eloise was gone, practically skipping through the doors that led to the terrace.

Annie stood there a moment, watching her sister go, envying her easy gait, the way her shoulders squared and her chin lifted as though she hadn't learned to hunch to make herself smaller, less conspicuous.

Hating her own thoughts, Annie slipped through the doors where they had entered and found herself back in the main corridor that would lead to the stairs to the front door. Instead of heading in that direction, she turned the opposite way, moving deeper into the house. She should have exercised greater caution as she was unchaperoned, but she was also a widow, she must remember. Her actions were far less constricted by decorum now, and she could do as she pleased. If only her mind could agree on that without her consciously forcing it to.

After trying three of the closed doors along the corridor, she found what she'd been seeking.

A library.

After checking to ensure she was alone in the hallway, she slipped inside the room, closing the door softly behind her. She leaned back against it, drawing in a deep breath through her nose as she let the tension ease from her shoulders. Thankfully lamps had been lit in the room, and she could make out a seating arrangement just in front of her, a desk along the far side, and shelves encompassing every wall, filled to overflowing with books. The room was decorated in warm, earthy colors, greens and golds and muted reds, and every surface was littered with plump cushions which beckoned a person to select a book and sit a while.

There was something comforting about a library, about the possibilities waiting quietly in each text. A library was a room without pretension or demands, and right now it was exactly what Annie needed.

She straightened and moved away from the door, finding the plush carpets of burgundy, taupe, and navy soft beneath her slippers. She walked clear to the opposite wall and began to peruse the titles there, letting her fingers trail along the leather spines as she read titles like *The Study of Mycology and Its Effects on Hampshire Tree Systems* and *My Summer Along the Nile: A Traveler's Guide to Egypt.*

She paused, her fingers still over the word *Egypt.* The word conjured images of pyramids, sand dunes, and crocodiles, but when she tried to dig deeper, searching inside of herself for…what exactly? A feeling? A reaction? She found nothing. No spark of adventure at the mere suggestion of an Egyptian journey, no repulsion at the thought of getting sand in her petticoats, just…nothing.

She let her hand drop, but she kept her eyes on the title.

She'd been so consumed by the physical aspects of Roger's control that she hadn't considered the mental ones. While he had dictated what she ate, what she wore, and with whom she socialized, it had left her with no choices to make.

And now she *couldn't* make a choice.

When her survival had depended on making the correct

choice, her feelings hadn't factored in, and somewhere along the way she'd lost track of them entirely.

She stared at the gold letters, willing herself to feel something, but there was only a steady blankness inside of her. It was like she had stopped maturing, stopped developing the moment she wed, and now she was left unfinished.

Who was she?

Who was she supposed to be?

Who might she have been?

She was startled from her thoughts at the sound of the door opening behind her. Her heart thumped, her blood racing in the familiar auto-response of fear, and she backed up against the bookcase, her eyes trained on the door.

Somehow she wasn't surprised when Grimsby entered, stepping into the room with his usual confidence and closing the door behind him as if they were forever meeting in strange libraries like this.

"Lady Anna," he said with a small bow. "I beg your pardon. I don't mean to intrude. It's just I saw you leave the soiree, and I wanted to ensure you were feeling well." His brow creased in concern, and she felt something tilt inside of her.

Roger had never asked after her wellbeing, and she wasn't sure how to answer now, with her thoughts in turmoil and her vision of her future blank. For just a brief moment, she wondered if Grimsby had sought her out, had planned to get her alone so he could press his suit, but as soon as the thought came, it vanished. He'd never do that to her. She didn't know how she knew this, but she did.

"Annie," she said. It made no sense whatsoever, and yet right then, she needed this man to call her by her name.

It was odd then. For a moment, the facade she was so used to seeing on Grimsby's face fell away, and for just a second, she thought she saw the man himself, not the persona he had created for Parliament, not the duke he was forced to be. The carefulness about his eyes, the restraint visible in the firm set of his mouth disappeared, and for just a second, he was someone else entirely.

Then something even odder happen. She felt herself falling, her body pitching forward while her feet remained on the plush carpet of the library. For in that small second when Grimsby had transformed, she had found him…attractive. No, that wasn't the word. Grimsby was too severe for such a word. *Beckoning.* That was what she had felt.

But he soon collected himself and said, "Gabriel," and the moment was gone.

This too was strange, that this man should have a given name. Grimsby suited him, with his stern jaw and his unchanging expression. But maybe Gabriel was the man she had seen for that brief space in time.

She smiled, finding the moment entirely too unsettling for anything else. She looked down at her feet, digging her slippered toe into the plush carpet as she said, "I couldn't take another metaphor, I'm afraid." She forced herself to look up, to meet this man's gaze, and was surprised to find it wasn't as difficult as she thought it might be. "I suppose I might not be inclined to poetry." This revelation was a surprise to her, and it settled something inside of her.

It was a decision, an understanding, and she had been so certain she was now incapable of such a thing. Her smile wobbled, but she held firm and even stepped away from the bookcase at her back, feeling untethered but not frightened by it.

Gabriel took a step closer to her. "I hope you don't base such a conclusion on what you've heard tonight. It would be terrible to let this evening's performance influence your feelings about poetry."

"Is that so?" she asked. "Do you have a recommendation

for an author whose work I should consider in rethinking my conclusion?"

His eyes dropped then, and he appeared almost boyish with a one-sided grin as he said, "I might have misled you. I don't read poetry." When he looked up again, his gaze had softened, and for the first time, he felt real to her and not the lofty mentor to Roger he had always seemed to be.

Her eyes studied his face. Who was this man? He was so familiar and yet so different. She had feared him once. No, that wasn't the right word either. Not fear. Respect. She had respected him with a gravitas that came from observing him. The way he so skillfully traversed a room, talking to just the right people, saying just the right thing. Reading about his accomplishments in the papers had made him seem other-worldly. But respect had kept a distance between them that was gone now.

"Well then, I suppose I must keep my conclusion as it is." The light from the lamps was soft, but they were close enough now that she could see there were streaks of deeper blue in his eyes, making them warmer than she had always thought.

This notion alone sent a jolt of realization through her. Both that she should think him warm and that she had stepped so close to him as to ascertain this. She didn't remember moving, but she must have or maybe he had. She didn't know. That feeling of being untethered reasserted itself, and she was suddenly feeling unsure.

Like forgetting to be afraid and then remembering again that she should have been, leaving her to wonder if she were now exposed to danger because she had not kept up her guard.

Because suddenly Gabriel felt like danger, this man who had quietly managed things to keep her from scandal, the same man who had proposed to her. She couldn't forget that.

"Is there something you can recommend I read?" she asked then, even though she wasn't sure why.

Was she speaking to this man about his reading preferences? He'd only come into the library to check on her well-being, and now she'd roped him into a conversation about reading.

"Urban planning reports," he said flatly.

There was a beat of silence, and then…she laughed. The sound was unfamiliar to her, so unused to laughing she had become, but even more, the feeling which had produced the laughter fumbled inside of her as though she didn't know how to keep it going. This lightness. This silliness. This…

What was this?

What was happening inside of her? She pressed a hand to her stomach as though she had upset herself by drinking too much champagne, but that wasn't it. She hadn't had any that evening, and the fluttering in her stomach couldn't have been the bubbles. Yet why did she feel as though she were suddenly drunk? Free from the constrains of her own mind?

"Urban planning reports?" she asked, her voice unsteady with her fading laughter.

He shrugged. "That's all I have time to read these days. I haven't the luxury to indulge in prose."

She could smell him now. Had she stepped closer yet again? He smelled of soap and something muskier like sandalwood. It was the most glorious thing she'd ever smelled. How could she have known a man could smell like this?

"That's a shame," she said or at least she tried to say it. Her voice had gone all strange and breathy. Was something truly wrong with her? Was she ill? That would explain the unsettled feeling in her stomach, but surely that couldn't be it. She'd never felt so wonderful in all her life.

The silence stretched then, and for a horrible moment,

she wondered if he was thinking of her refusal to marry him. But if he was, he wouldn't have bothered to come check on her, now would he? She was being silly, her thoughts getting away from her.

But then why was he standing there staring at her like that, with such heat in his gaze?

Why would he be here at all?

Why…did she suddenly wish he would kiss her?

This thought had the power to scatter the rest from her mind, and the smile that had been on her lips suddenly slipped away as her body froze.

In anticipation?

No, surely it was fear. Surely she didn't want him to touch her.

But she did. She wanted it very much. Did he know that? Could he sense it? Could he—

He kissed her.

Or maybe she kissed him.

She didn't know what was happening, but his lips were on hers, and she was leaning into him, her hands finding his chest, and then—oh heavens, her fingers curled into him, holding him by the shirtfront lest he break off the kiss, lest he—

He pulled back, stepping away completely, severing the sudden and abrupt connection between them. His eyes were wide now and slightly wild, and somehow she knew she wore a similar expression even as her heart raced with exhilaration and the sound of her blood pumping furiously beat in her ears.

"I must go," he said and left, leaving her in the middle of the library wondering if she shouldn't have been the one to run away.

# CHAPTER 4

"I kissed her," Gabriel said by way of greeting as he sank into the chair beside Liam at his club the next afternoon.

Liam blinked, a folded newspaper in one hand and a glass of amber liquid in the other, the epitome of a gentleman at leisure. "That was specifically the one thing I told you not to do," he said.

"I know," Gabriel said, signaling to a passing footman and indicating Liam's glass. The footman nodded in understanding and hurried off. "It's worse than you think though."

"How can it be worse?" Liam asked.

Gabriel met the other duke's eye. "I'm not sure if I kissed her or she kissed me. Whatever happened it was not very aloof."

"I'll say." Liam tossed aside the newspaper. "Did you talk about her interests or were you able to deflect?"

"I spoke of urban planning reports."

Now Liam set down his drink as well. "God save the Queen, you must be joking. I said remain aloof. I didn't say to repulse the woman."

"There's more." Liam didn't speak, but Gabriel found it suddenly difficult to get words out. Gathering his courage, he said, "I enjoyed kissing her."

Liam got to his feet, paced several steps away, and rubbed the back of his neck with one hand before returning to his seat. He dropped into the chair, his body limp like a man defeated. "I warned you about sentimentality, Grimsby."

"I know." Gabriel was given a small respite as the footman delivered his drink. He took a careful sip, letting the burn consume him. "If it's any consolation, I was just as surprised by this development as you are. The lady is my friend's widow. It's dishonorable to have such feelings for her."

Liam did not respond, and Gabriel looked up to find the man eyeing him, a dubious expression on his face.

"What is it?" Gabriel asked, not enjoying how muddled everything was becoming.

"You think it dishonorable that you find her attractive?" Liam shook his head. "I mean this in the most respectful way, Gabriel. The Elmont widow is a damn fine woman. It would be dishonorable *not* to find her attractive."

Gabriel carefully set down his drink. "I find nothing respectful about your statement, Ardley."

Liam leaned forward, elbows to knees. "Look here, Grimsby. From the little I know of her, the dowager countess has everything to commend her. She is not only a superb hostess, excellent dancer, resplendent at conversation, but she's also beautiful. Or have you failed to notice because you're too busy being honorable?"

At the word *beautiful*, Gabriel pictured Annie in the library that night, the soft light casting her features in an ethereal aura. Annie *was* beautiful. He'd always known as much, but he wouldn't have used that word that night in the library. It was far too mundane for how she had looked. Even in her half mourning gown with its simple fabric and plain cut. She could have worn anything and been beautiful. She could have worn nothing…

He picked up his glass and downed the remainder of his drink in one swallow, hoping the burn would kill him. "I haven't failed to notice," he said when he could finally speak again, but Liam eyed the now empty glass.

Gabriel set it down carefully as Liam leaned back in his chair.

"Do you have feelings for this woman, Gabriel?" Liam asked. *No* was the first thing to come to mind, but Gabriel didn't have time to say it as Liam went on. "Because we didn't discuss *your* feelings when I agreed to help you. If you have feelings for the lady, it's going to muddy everything, and I do not wish to be a part of that." The man placed both hands on the arms of his chair as if emphasizing his point. "There is no place in my system for feelings. Feelings ruin everything."

Horribly, Gabriel found himself agreeing with him. Before that night in the library, Gabriel couldn't have said he felt anything for Annie except the need to protect her, but now he felt too many things. It frightened him. He was not a virgin, not at all, but the affairs he'd had in his past were simpler than this. The feelings involved were simpler, being more of the physical kind than anything and found mutually with a consenting partner.

But this…but Annie…well, he didn't know what to feel about her now.

The protective instinct was still there, and he welcomed it. Protecting someone he understood, and it was the safest thing he could think about just then.

"All right," Gabriel said. "So what is it I am to do now? Have I ruined any chance I had of convincing her she's in love with me, so she'll accept my suit?"

Liam studied him for a moment, and Gabriel felt as

though he were back in school under the gaze of a disappointed tutor.

"I think your plan can still be saved, but it will require
extreme measures to repair the damage," Liam eventually
said.

Gabriel sat up. "What kind of extreme measures?"

"You must ignore her completely."

Gabriel waited, but for the first time since their endeavor
had begun, Liam didn't ramble on.

"I beg your pardon?" Gabriel finally said.

Liam waved a hand. "You must ignore her. Completely.
Don't speak to her. Don't accept an invitation from her. And
for heaven's sake, don't kiss her again." Liam looked up as if
searching for something else Gabriel could not do with
Annie, but then he said something far worse. "Ignore her for
at least a fortnight. Hell, a month if you can manage it."

"No." Now the word shot out of Gabriel before Liam
could continue. "She's out of formal mourning. The vultures
have started circling. I just know it. In a month she could be
married to some—" He stopped as he realized what he was
saying. Liam watched him, a curious expression on his face.

"She refused you. What makes you think she'll accept
someone else? Especially in only a month's time," Liam said.
"Unless you think she's already in love with someone else?"
Liam scratched his chin in thought. "We didn't discuss this.
Do you think she refused you because she's in love with
someone else?"

Gabriel recalled the heat of her lips against his, the way
her small hands had clung to him. He swallowed. "I do not
have any reason to believe she's in love with someone else."

As the words left his mouth, it was like razors had caught
in his throat. He raised his head, searching for another
footman to refill his drink.

That was when he saw him.

Gabriel's insides turned to ice, and he stood before he even realized his body would move. It was like an instinct, to gain his feet. He would not face this man sitting down.

The man moved with the same measured stride Gabriel remembered. His footsteps overconfident, boastful, one hand gripping the lapel of his jacket to allow the ruby in his signet ring to catch the light, draw the onlooker's eye, the other hand wrapped around the head of his cane, which depicted a roaring lion figured in gold. Gabriel knew what the cane topper was even though he couldn't see it. Gabriel knew it because the man had beat Gabriel with it once.

"Gabriel," the man said, stopping three feet away. While the man spoke to him, his eyes slid to Ardley, who had not stood at the man's arrival, assessing.

"Belvedere." Gabriel pressed the man's name through his teeth.

Belvedere dropped his gaze to Ardley once more. Gabriel didn't speak. The man might want for an introduction, but Gabriel wouldn't give him so much as the time.

Ardley, however, had his own ideas, as Gabriel could have guessed. The duke made a show of lumbering to his feet, but when Belvedere extended a hand, Liam crossed his arms over his chest and said nothing.

Gabriel still didn't speak, so Belvedere said, "The Honorable Mr. Brogden Belvedere." He held his hand ostentatiously between them, but still Liam didn't take it.

After a weighty pause, Liam said, "Ardley." His eyes narrowed as he gave Belvedere the once over. "Duke of."

Belvedere finally dropped his hand. "Gabriel, it's about your mother. She's sick and needs funds for a doctor."

Gabriel barked a laugh, the sound harsh in the quiet mood of the club. "Hardly. If she needs money, she knows how to request it."

Such a tactic was beneath Belvedere. Gabriel had taught

the man long ago that he wouldn't give in to such a bald-faced scam. If Gabriel's mother required funds, she could procure them from Gabriel's solicitor who would deposit them into an account that only Gabriel's mother could access.

"You would call me a liar." Belvedere sniffed.

"I would call you something worse, but I haven't the energy for it."

Belvedere's lips parted ever so slightly under the bristle of his gray mustache as his eyes slid to Liam as if searching for help.

Liam remained standing, silent, arms crossed over his chest.

Belvedere looked back at Gabriel. "Then I shall tell your mother you don't care if she's sick." Another sniff. "Good day, Ardley." He turned and went back the way he had come, his highly polished shoes soft on the green carpet at his feet.

It was nearly a minute before Liam spoke. "That man means something to you. Something bad."

Gabriel started at the other duke's words. "Why would you say that?"

He didn't answer. Instead he looked down at their feet. For a moment, Gabriel was confused, but then he saw it. Unknowingly Gabriel had stepped in front of Liam's chair when Belvedere had arrived, effectively blocking the parasite from reaching the Duke of Ardley.

"I see," Gabriel mumbled.

Liam slapped Gabriel on the back then much as he'd done to Tuck that night at the soiree, and Gabriel felt a strange warmth pass over him. "I've never had someone play the knight errant for me. Hell, if things don't work out with the Elmont widow, I'll marry you." Liam's face had split into a hearty grin. "Now then, why don't you tell me what that bastard really wanted."

"Is it so obvious I wouldn't simply hand over the funds?" Gabriel asked.

Liam laughed. "I've watched you for years on the House floor, Grimsby. If that man wanted money from you, he would need to submit a request to a three-part committee that only met once a year and then only when Mars was in retrograde and the poles of the earth had reversed."

Gabriel couldn't help his own smile. "Am I really that easy to read?"

Liam only grinned in response and signaled to a passing footman to bring another round of drinks. When the footman had gone, Liam gestured to the chair Gabriel had vacated, and they resumed their seats.

"Now tell me enough about that slimy bastard so I don't fall victim to his schemes," Liam said, crossing one ankle over the opposite knee.

Gabriel considered this. His past was something he rarely spoke of, but Liam seemed sincere in his concern.

"My father died when I was seventeen. He'd suffered through a lengthy illness, and we all knew he would die. He'd had the wherewithal to make arrangements considering I would not be of age when he passed. While I acquired the title, I did not acquire the purse strings. My father had set up an executorship with my mother as the executor. She was to manage the title with aid from my father's solicitors until I turned eighteen, eleven months after my father's death."

"I take it Mr. Belvedere took advantage of those eleven months."

Gabriel didn't see Liam sitting next to him. Instead he saw the drawing room that day his mother had introduced him to the Honorable Mr. Brogden Belvedere. It was a bleak March day, the raw kind that came just before the spring, the kind that made one give up hope of ever feeling warm again. His father had been dead for less than a week, and he still couldn't think of himself as the duke. And now here was a man his mother insisted would help them, would fill his father's shoes.

The footman arrived just in time for Gabriel to take a long drink of the liquor, letting it wash away the sour memories.

"He did," Gabriel said. "And he didn't come here to ask me for money. As soon as I turned eighteen, I cut him off and threw him out." Gabriel shook his head, considered the liquor still in his glass. "No, the Honorable Mr. Belvedere didn't want money. He wanted me to know he's back."

* * *

ANNIE SUCKED in a breath and knocked on Eloise's door.

There was no answer.

Annie looked about her, momentarily confused. It was nearly midnight. Their mother had given them a reprieve from their nightly social obligations, and they had all happily gone off to their own endeavors. She could have sworn Eloise had gone to her room hours ago, but now Annie's knock was only met with silence.

She knocked again.

Nothing.

Perhaps her sister had fallen asleep. Perhaps it was a sign.

Annie dropped her hand to her side. She'd wanted to speak with Gwen anyway. Gwen would know what to do. But Gwen was in Yorkshire with her husband and beautiful baby, and Annie was knocking on her little sister's door in nearly the middle of the night to ask her about kissing.

Oh lud, what had happened to her?

She'd gone into the baron's library to figure out what to do with her life, and instead of finding answers, she'd found a man. What a bloody typical female she was turning out to be.

She tried knocking again but knew her efforts were futile. Still she waited, adjusting the knot of her dressing gown as she stood in the hallway, the tick of the clock down the way her only companion.

The practical thing would be to go to bed, get her rest as nights home were so rare these days. She could do with some proper sleep, but she knew she wouldn't sleep tonight, not with the way her stomach churned at the memory of what she'd done.

She'd kissed Gabriel.

How could she have done that? What was wrong with her? Were her principles so terribly weak?

Her widowhood was a boon, a treasure that could not be treated so cavalierly. And now she'd *kissed* a man. What if they'd been caught?

She pressed a hand to her throat at the thought. How could she have been so careless? Her freedom could have been snatched from her and all because she'd wanted to kiss Gabriel.

Now she pressed the hand to the wall beside her to steady herself.

She *had* wanted to kiss Gabriel. That was what truly plagued her. Only six months into her marriage everything about Roger had repulsed her. When he touched her, she felt only revulsion, her stomach squeezing until she thought she might be sick. But when Gabriel had stood before her that night in the library, her body had been drawn to his as if it were meant to be.

She turned and headed for the stairs. This was all nonsense. She was simply allowing her thoughts to run wild, and it would never do. She needed structure. She needed focus. She needed to remember why her widowhood was important.

Stopping at the top of the stairs, she found the lamp on the table by the landing, her hands finding the match by memory as it was too dark there to see properly. Lighting the lamp, she turned down the wick, not wishing to wake anyone. Carefully she made her way down the stairs, firming her resolution as she went.

She would go to the library and start looking for answers. The book on Egypt she'd found kept floating through her mind. Even though that particular volume hadn't conjured a reaction from her, there were surely others that would. She had only to find them.

Making her way quickly and silently to the library, she found her spirits were already bolstered by the time she set the lamp on her father's desk in the corner of the room. Slowly she eased up the wick, spilling light as far as the lamp would allow, and she took a moment to look around.

She'd always loved their library. It wasn't like the libraries she'd seen in houses belonging to other members of the *ton*. The Bounds library had been lived in, and the clues of such were scattered about the room. The stack of novels Eloise hadn't returned to the shelves and that remained stacked on the floor by the window seat where she preferred to read. The travel memoirs her mother enjoyed were on the low table between the two sofas in front of the window. They lay mixed in with the day's newspapers and an atlas, and this more than anything made her smile. The servants were not to tidy the library. The Bounds family members liked picking up where they had left off in their study, and so the sight of the newspapers still on the table only brought a smile to her face.

Shaking her head free of the thoughts, she remembered why she was there. One could find the answer to anything in a library if one only knew where to look. She turned about and slid behind her father's desk where he kept his science books. If Egypt didn't spark something in her, perhaps science would. Science was interesting, wasn't it? It was at least complex and diverse. There were any number of things that could catch her attention.

But a half hour later, she'd given up. After perusing titles on astronomy, geological formations, and currents in the ocean, she found herself in much the same, dull state. She abandoned science and went to the other side of the room where the books on domestic affairs were kept. She passed by the doors that led out into the courtyard their townhouse shared with the other townhouses along the street. The moon was full and high, and its rays spilled through the sheer drapes covering the doors. She stood for a moment in the moonlight, gazing out at the slumbering gardens before moving on to the books on household management and home remedies.

She'd only taken a step though when something through the terrace doors caught her eye. She almost dismissed it. The sheer curtains meant she couldn't see clearly through the windowed doors, and surely it must have been a trick of the eye. But no. Something was out there. Something moving, taking shape, a form, a—

She stepped forward and yanked open the doors. "Eloise," she hissed.

Her sister tumbled to a halt on the terrace just beyond the doors. Her eyes were huge and bright in the moonlight, her face frozen in shock.

"Eloise Cassandra Bounds, what on earth are you doing outside in the middle of the night?" Annie scolded, suddenly seized by one of those rare moments when she truly felt like the older sister.

Annie expected Eloise to rush forward with an explanation, but instead, she did something rather odd. She looked behind her. Annie lifted her gaze to the yew hedge that bordered the edge of the terrace. There was a small cut through the hedge that opened onto the path that led into the heart of the gardens, but it was dark, shadowed by the tall hedges around it. She returned her gaze to Eloise who had straightened now, a small smile on her lips.

"Oh Annie, you frightened me," she said and walked sedately past her into the library.

Annie gave the terrace and the pathway another look before stepping into the library herself and closing the doors snugly, sending home the bolt before turning to her little sister.

"What were you doing out there?"

Eloise made her way behind one of the sofas, obviously heading for the door and escape. "Just getting some fresh air," she said over her shoulder. "It felt so stuffy in my room."

Annie gripped the knot of her dressing gown sash. "Eloise. It's the middle of the night."

"I know. I should be in bed," she called lightly almost to the door now.

"I thought the same when I knocked on your door earlier."

Eloise stopped, her hand outstretched for the library door. As Annie expected, her little sister turned back at this.

"You knocked on my door earlier?" Eloise's eyes moved back and forth as though she were thinking quickly. "Did anyone else knock on my door?"

Annie tilted her head. "Why would you ask? Concerned you'll be caught?"

Eloise dropped her gaze now and slunk back to the sofa, dropping down upon it as her head lolled back. "I am not good at keeping secrets," she said to the ceiling. "The tax on the body is unbearable."

Annie couldn't stop a smile as she made her way over to the sofa and took a seat next to her sister, drawing her legs up and hugging her knees. "You aren't cut out for it, I'm afraid."

Her sister rolled her head to the side to look at her. "What do you mean?"

"You're too soft for it."

Eloise's head came up at this. "I am most certainly not. I'm tough."

Annie laughed. "Gwen is the tough one. Not you." She considered her sister with her golden hair and her open features. "You're more like a puff of sunshine."

Eloise frowned. "I resent that."

"That doesn't make it any less true."

Eloise straightened now. "Why were you looking for me earlier?"

Annie had been so absorbed by her search through the books, she'd forgotten the blunder that had brought her to Eloise's door, but now it came back to her with full force. Something of her thoughts must have shown on her face because Eloise's expression dimmed.

"Oh Annie, what is it?" she asked.

Suddenly Annie didn't want to tell her, that she'd kissed the Duke of the Grimsby. Once she said it, her sister would start forming ideas, and that was always dangerous. So instead she said, "Have you ever been kissed?"

Eloise sat back. "Of course I have. What's brought this on?"

Annie dropped her feet to the floor. "What do you mean you've been kissed? You're a debutante." She spoke the label as though it conjured all manner of things pure and inno-cent, but after seeing her sister slinking through the garden, Annie doubted such adjectives could be applied to her.

Eloise rolled her eyes. "Debutantes are not all untouched,

Annie. How can we be expected to choose the right husband if we don't see what kind of connection we have with the man first?"

This was entirely confounding.

"Connection?" Annie repeated, the only word she seemed to be able to latch on to.

Eloise nodded. "Of course one must see what kind of connection she has with a gentleman. If there's no initial spark, then how can you expect anything but a cold marriage?"

Annie hadn't kissed Roger before they had wed. They had done all the proper things, the *normal* things contained in a courtship. He called on her, and she reserved dances for him at the balls they attended. He took her promenading in the park, and when the time came, he arranged everything with her father.

But she hadn't kissed him. Was this the problem? Was this the thing that had doomed her marriage? Roger had done all the things she had been taught to expect of a gentleman. How could she have known? She doubted a kiss would have solved it, but it was more about her thinking when it came to the kiss. She hadn't been taught to expect it, so she hadn't even thought of it.

She let her eyes drift about the room, taking in shelf after shelf of books. Each book represented a piece of her future stretching out aimlessly before her because Anna Bounds only did what she was told, and she couldn't think of doing anything else.

"I suppose you're right, Eloise," Annie said now, her voice suddenly soft as her thoughts remained on the books around her. But then an idea did occur to her, and her gaze flew back to Eloise. "Have you felt that spark with anyone?"

If Annie didn't know her sister better, she wouldn't have known to look for the twitch above Eloise's left eye. Her sister was right. She couldn't keep secrets, and at this question, the pale spot above her left eye twitched.

"Oh, just one or two, but it wasn't anything special." She shrugged. "It was just…nice." Her smile was false, and Annie wished to prod her, but she thought perhaps her sister deserved to have her secrets. As long as she didn't get hurt. But then—

"Eloise, is that a twig in your hair?"

Eloise pushed to her feet. "Do you know I think it's time for bed?" She gave an exaggerated yawn. "I'm just exhausted."

"Eloise—"

But she was already through the library door, closing it softly behind her.

# CHAPTER 5

$\mathcal{G}$abriel would apologize.

That was precisely what he would do. Hang Liam and his system. Gabriel was a man of dignity, and right then dignity called on him to apologize to Annie for assaulting her that night in the library.

He only had to ensure he wasn't alone with her when he did it because he was very much afraid he would do it again if given the chance.

That was why when he arrived at Lord and Lady Brocklehurst's garden party that afternoon, he deliberately avoided the viscount's library. He avoided the main house entirely, entering the gardens through the gate at the drive. He would not be found in a compromising position with Annie. He simply wouldn't. He would speak with her in the privacy allowed a conversation held at the periphery of the gathering, and that was all. His conscience would be satisfied even if he was no closer to convincing Annie to accept his proposal.

The only problem with this plan was the fact that Annie was missing.

He'd spotted Lord and Lady Stoke Bruerne almost immediately as he'd entered. They were deep in conversation with the Earl and Countess of Bannerbridge. He'd caught mention of lambing, but the moving crowd of guests had pushed him past them too quickly for him to hear more or anything that might have told him if Annie had come to the garden party with them.

The crowd continued to push him in the direction of a tent that had been erected at the foot of the terrace that led up to the main house. The tent housed Lady Brocklehurst's prized orchid collection, and a bevy of footmen stood sentry as if the blooms were more valuable than the family silver.

After carefully skirting a gaggle of matrons studying the orchids with rapt attention and—was that a pair of opera glasses?—he spilled out of the crowd and into the carefully arranged beds of roses in a spectrum of color ranging from yellow and red to an unusual violet.

Only to nearly collide with the most unexpected person.

"Dowager," he said, the single word catching as he gave a small bow to Annie's grandmother.

The woman was tiny with a familial name that suited her, Grandmother Bitsy, and he wondered if that was how she had acquired the nickname.

"Grimsby, have you convinced Annie to accept your proposal yet?" Grandmother Bitsy gave a wink. "I know you've always thought her a tasty morsel. Perhaps it's time for you to take a bite." She clapped her teeth together then as if demonstrating, and he swallowed, searching for some kind of response that would be even mildly appropriate.

But Grandmother Bitsy did not linger. She raised a hand and a with a soft "Yoo-hoo!" and a wave she was off, waddling through the guests to some other destination.

He stood there, the woman's words rattling through his mind. He did not think Annie a tasty morsel. Why would she say such a thing? It was only recently he'd realized his feelings for her. Surely Grandmother Bitsy couldn't have known. Gabriel didn't know himself.

Had his feelings been so obvious to everyone else? Did *Annie* know?

This was all wrong. This was disastrous. How could he have let his feelings get away from him? He turned, the need to find Annie more urgent than ever, but instead, he nearly ran directly into someone else.

"Tuck," he said, narrowly missing the man as he stepped from the orchid tent.

There was a line between the man's brows, which softened when he spotted Gabriel.

"Ah, Gabriel, it's you." His voice was wary, and his eyes skated away as if looking for something. Or perhaps someone.

"Were you afraid I was someone else?" Gabriel could strangely understand the sentiment just then.

Tuck shrugged. "Take your pick. There are a number of gentlemen—and one vicar, I might add—that I'm afraid I've put off."

Gabriel recalled his promise to help the man, and although the urgency to find Annie pressed on him, he was never one to shirk a promise, and the garden party was an excellent place for Tuck to find a benefactor.

"Ah, I see," Gabriel said. "You've been hunting again."

Tuck cringed, and Gabriel noted it for the sign of character that it was. "Something like that." He scratched at the back of his neck. "I've been through Liam's copy of Debrett's from cover to cover as you suggested, and I'm afraid I'm not better off." He gave that shrug again. "It's given me a list of names and connections that I can work with, but when it comes to nuance, I'm afraid I'm rather lacking in tact."

"Don't lose heart, Tuck," Gabriel said, stepping back to

survey the crowd. "It takes practice and time." He noted several prominent members of Parliament and a vicar. He wondered briefly if this was the vicar Tuck had already approached and kept his gaze moving. "Ah," he said after a few moments. "There you have it."

Tuck turned his attention back to Gabriel. "Have what?"

Gabriel nodded discreetly in the direction of a bench set in an arbor of climbing roses. "That gentleman there. He's on the bench holding his hat in his hands." The crowd shifted then, and Gabriel jerked in surprise. Grandmother Bitsy sat next to the gentleman, and Gabriel was forced to clear his throat as a means of resettling his thoughts.

Tuck shifted ever so slightly. "Yes, I see him."

"That's Niles Crandall, the Earl of Renshaw. The man is perilously kind and utterly broke. He has no heirs, and when he dies, the title will likely revert to the Crown." Gabriel met Tuck's eye. "He's the perfect gentleman on which to practice. You won't lose another potential benefactor, have no risk for failure as the man has no money, and Renshaw will be impossibly kind in the process."

Tuck appeared dubious. "I'm not sure I'm ready to speak to another one."

Gabriel was ready with a bolstering response when luck struck. Lady Eloise stepped from the tent beside them, nearly colliding with Gabriel as her attention was elsewhere.

"Lady Eloise," he said before disaster struck, and she stopped, swaying slightly forward as she brought her gaze around. Why was he attracting every member of this family except the one he wished to speak to?

Her smile was quick when she saw him. "Your Grace, what a pleasure to see you. I trust you are well." Her gaze moved to Tuck beside him, and for just a moment, he thought he saw her left eye twitch, but her smile never faltered, and he thought it might have been the shadows her bonnet cast over her features. "Mr. Ryan, very nice to see you again."

Gabriel recalled the night of the third Bounds sister's ball and knew Lady Eloise must have seen Tuck there, but Gabriel couldn't help but think of what Ardley said about the debutantes blending together this season. Lady Eloise must be exhausted, and yet she continued to exude politeness and even happiness.

"It's an honor, Lady Eloise," Tuck said, bowing with more grace than Gabriel thought the casual air of the garden party warranted.

He turned back to the lady. "Lady Eloise, is your sister in attendance? I should like to ask after her wellbeing."

It was a moment before the woman's eyes came back to him, and when they did, they were unfocused with confusion. They finally cleared as she said, "Annie? Oh yes, of course. You'll probably find her in the Brocklehurst library." She paused, her brow furrowing. "She's spending an awful lot of time in libraries lately." She shrugged. "Perhaps she's facing a slump in her reading material and is looking for inspiration."

This was quite possibly the worst piece of information Gabriel could have received just then. "The library?" he repeated.

Lady Eloise nodded. "Yes, quite. I've heard the Brocklehurst library is extensive. More than likely that's where she's wandered off to."

Gabriel nodded in return. "Thank you, Lady Eloise. Tuck, I assume you're confident in your next steps with Renshaw?"

Tuck looked anything but confident.

"The Earl of Renshaw?" Lady Eloise said, turning to where Tuck was looking. "Do you need to speak with the man? I'd be happy to provide an introduction. He's a dear old friend of my grandmother Bitsy's."

Gabriel hadn't thought Tuck's face could appear any bleaker, but just then, Gabriel feared the man had lost all the blood in his head.

"An introduction?" he managed.

Lady Eloise nodded. "Grandmother Bitsy is with him right now. Let us go over, and I'll introduce you." She was already heading in the earl's direction, gesturing for Tuck to follow her.

Gabriel left them to it, and against his better judgment, took the stone steps leading up to the main house two at a time in search of the Brocklehurst library.

This was a very bad idea. He knew it, and yet he wouldn't stop himself. He must apologize. If he didn't, he was no better than Belvedere, taking advantage of a helpless widow.

The thought had his stomach churning. He hadn't thought of Belvedere since the encounter at his club. The man had purposely sought him out, and Gabriel still didn't know why. He'd made discreet inquiries, of course, but as he was busy trying to convince a stubborn widow that she loved him enough to marry him and give up her freedom, he hadn't truly had the time to suss out the matter.

He slipped inside the house to find the terrace doors were situated at the end of a long corridor that seemed to run the length of the house. The corridor was empty, but he heard voices somewhere along the way and knew guests were likely permitted in the public areas of the house.

Was Annie there somewhere? Was her voice one of the ones he heard? They were too soft to hear distinctly, and suddenly he was gripped with the very real fear she wasn't alone in the library. Had a scoundrel taken advantage of her when she'd sought retreat?

A panic he didn't care to recognize propelled him forward, his stride lengthening as he hurried down the corridor. Doors opened into a drawing room on one side and a billiards room on the other. Both were empty. He continued, and with every step, the voices grew louder. He practically stumbled into a salon, a small room with carefully situated sofas that were overflowing with a mess of ladies. On a low table in the center of the melee he spotted a fashion magazine opened to a lavishly filled spread, obviously the cause of such chatter.

His heart thudding, he stepped back into the corridor before he could be seen.

Where was the bloody library?

He continued down the corridor passing two closed doors and a pair of retiring rooms. It was quieter at this end of the hall, and he thought he might be getting closer. His gaze caught on a set of doors to his right. If he had been walking as quickly as he had been at the start of the corridor, he would have missed it. The door on the right was slightly ajar, leaving a crack of light to appear between the panels.

He stopped, the understanding that this was a very bad idea going straight through him.

He surged forward and opened the door only to be rendered completely motionless, his legs suddenly forgetting how to move.

The room was indeed the library, and Annie was indeed within it.

She was seated at a table directly opposite the door, her head bent over a book opened on the table before her, a book that was surrounded by stacks of other books seemingly discarded as though she had been at her research for hours. But none of this was what had stopped him. No, certainly not. It was what was below that table that had rendered him useless.

She had removed her slippers, and she was using the sole of one foot to rub the arch of the other. The motion was soundless as her silk stockings glided over each other, and a traitorous inferno sparked deep in his belly.

Desire.

It was there so quickly he nearly choked on it.

No, not desire. He would not feel desire for Roger's widow. Protection, that was all it was. The need to protect her was heightened at the sight of her vulnerability, at her unshod feet, at the way her head remained bent over her text.

She hadn't noticed him.

He'd entered the library so swiftly he'd made no noise, and instead of catching her in an awkward position, he was simply being a creep, leering at her without her knowledge.

He stepped back so quickly he nearly fell into the hallway behind him. He brought the door to, leaving it slightly ajar as he'd found it while he gave himself time to find his breath again.

He placed one hand against the doorjamb, but his palm slipped, and he was surprised to find his hands clammy with cold sweat. Dear heavens, what was wrong with him? He hadn't had such a strong reaction to a woman in quite some time. To be fair, he hadn't had time for a woman as his work in Parliament demanded most of his attention. The very thought had his heart slowing as he realized the problem.

He *hadn't* had a woman in quite some time. That was it. It wasn't Annie at all. It was simply the fact that he was going through a drought. Nothing more.

Straightening, he felt his heart calm and breath steady, his resolve once more firm.

He knocked this time before entering, taking careful steps as he made his way around the door. There was only a slight rustle of skirts when he entered to suggest she had slipped her shoes back on, and then she was standing behind the table where he had seen her at study.

"Annie," he said, surprised at how easily her name sprang

from his lips. "I do beg your pardon, but your sister said I might find you here." He closed the door behind him but left it slightly ajar. He might once more be in a library with this woman, but he needn't be entirely alone with her, and especially not behind a shut door. "I've come to apologize."

It wasn't until he'd finished that the look of cloudy confusion on her face registered, and he realized he'd startled her from some deep focus. His eyes drifted down to the pile of books on the table. He was close enough now to see them, and he read the title *Thirty-two Home Remedies Derived From Garlic*. His eyes jumped to the next. *The Home Health Guide for the Happy, Helpful Wife*.

Now it was his turn to appear confused. He looked up to find Annie's expression had cleared.

"No, it's I who must apologize," she said as she made her way around the table toward him.

She wore another simple gown of deep navy, and her dark hair had come slightly loose, a few soft tendrils framing her face. He noted the discarded bonnet on the table behind her and wondered if those beckoning tendrils had slipped out when she'd removed it.

"I should not have kissed you," she said, bringing his attention back to her. "It was unbecoming."

Her words made little sense. "Annie, I kissed you. I've come to apologize."

Her face folded into confusion once more. "What are you speaking about? I kissed you."

He shook his head. "I kissed you. It was the act of a scoundrel, and you have my sincerest apology."

Her lips parted, and he readied himself for another objection when something passed over her face, and the look of confusion returned.

Her next words nearly sent him back out the library door for the second time.

"Gabriel," she said. "Why did you never marry?"

* * *

IT WAS while she was attempting to assert her apology that Annie realized the truth of the situation.

She'd gone to the Brocklehurst library once more in search of answers about her future when Gabriel had discovered her. It was while the apology was on her tongue that she realized Gabriel was *in* the library, the place she knew could help unlock her future. Could Gabriel himself hold the answers for which she searched?

Her discussion with Eloise was still fresh in her mind, the thoughts it had stirred up tumbling one over the other. Annie had never felt a spark, had never known she should be looking for one. She'd simply done as she was told, and the things debutantes were taught did not include any mention of a spark.

She had no plans to kiss Gabriel again, but she knew they would waste time standing there arguing about who had kissed whom and who was therefore responsible for an apology. There was no point in further argument, and Gabriel had information she could use.

He hadn't married. She knew he was nearing forty years of age, and while some men chose the bachelor lifestyle, Gabriel was a duke. He had a responsibility to carry on the title through an heir, and yet he remained unwed. Why? Had he not felt this unknowable spark with someone? Or had he simply been waiting?

She knew the reasons for his proposal had had more to do with protecting her than with obligation to the title, and the questions rampaged through her mind until a single one stood in front of all the rest.

Did he feel the spark with her?

The saints above she hoped not. The very idea had her heart thumping and her stomach tightening.

Gabriel's intentions toward her were completely admirable. He wished to protect her, and although she could understand and appreciate the sentiment, her freedom was too valuable.

But she could get information from him.

For a beat after she asked her question, he stood unmoving before her. She watched him carefully, but he gave no outward reaction to her question.

"You wish to know why I've never married." He spoke the words with the slightest hint of trepidation in his voice, and she found it curious.

"Yes, I do. You're a gentleman, titled—a duke, no less— and your reputation in society is commendable. Yet you are unwed. Why?" She wondered at her forthrightness. Only a year ago she wouldn't have dreamed of speaking to this man in such a way. Much had changed in a year perhaps, but she couldn't help but think it had more to do with the man than with her own change in thought.

She wasn't sure how but in the course of a fortnight she'd grown comfortable around him. That day in the drawing room when he had called on her unexpectedly, had proposed marriage even, seemed so far away. She'd been scared then. She knew that now. Frightened of what he would ask of her, but she knew now with distance that the fear had been of her own manufacturing.

There was nothing about Gabriel that was demanding. She wondered now why she had placed him on a pedestal so many years ago when she'd first met him. Putting him up there had granted him an insurmountable edge that had seemed lofty and impenetrable, and she realized in doing so she'd lost a friend. It saddened her now to think of the time they had lost.

Her thoughts should have been dangerous, but she couldn't think about them like that. Not now.

His lips parted, but he closed them without speaking. And then, he did the most peculiar thing. He closed his eyes and let out a breath that sounded terribly weary and so unlike him.

"That is a very long explanation, I'm afraid." He looked about them. "Would you mind terribly if we had this conversation somewhere else? The rules are more relaxed for widows, but I still don't wish to risk someone finding us here."

*Alone.*

He didn't speak the word, but he didn't need to. It hung in the air between them along with what they had done that night in the baron's library.

Annie shuffled back a step. "You're right. I'm sorry. I wasn't thinking." She shook her head, Roger's voice suddenly there again.

This boldness was still new to her, and it was so easy to let Roger intrude, to let his voice ring in her head, hurtling questions at her she didn't want to hear, questions that only served to undermine her confidence.

*Who do you think you are? Rather high and mighty for a nobody like you. Know your place, whore.*

"I'm sorry." She was repeating herself, but Roger's voice was getting louder in her head. "I'm sorry, Gabriel. I shouldn't have bothered you. Please forgive me."

She made to move past him, picking up her skirts to flee. Her blood pumped hard, and a ringing had come into her ears. It seemed impossible. Only seconds before she had been so sure, so steady, so…at ease. But then something had triggered Roger's ghost, and he was back, hurting her.

She needed to run like she hadn't been able to when she was married. She had been Roger's property, and property couldn't run away. But now she could. She could run, and she did.

Only Gabriel grabbed her arm, his hand slipping into her bent elbow as she hurried past him, and that was when it happened.

Roger's voice reached a crescendo, and her body moved on instinct, her hand going up to shield her cheekbone, her head ducking low as if this would lessen the sting of the blow. It hurt so very much when he hit her there, his fist striking bone so her face felt as though it would explode, her teeth inadvertently snapping down on her tongue until there was blood. So much blood.

Silence.

It was complete and absolute as reality came back to her, as she remembered where she was, as she recalled who she was with, as Roger's voice faded away again, and—

As she realized the secret of which she had just let go.

She dropped her hand, lifted her head, and turned to find Gabriel. Perhaps he hadn't seen, didn't know, didn't comprehend—

He'd let go of her, taken a step back, and his eyes were wide in understanding. It was too late.

"Gabriel—"

He held up a hand, cutting her off. And then he spoke, his voice unlike anything she'd ever heard from him before. There was a steeliness that rocked her, a hardness that sent her heart racing, a softness that was lethal as he said, "He hit you."

Gabriel didn't need to say his name. They both knew of whom he spoke.

Roger.

Roger had hit her.

She shook her head, the words coming forth involuntarily. "Not often. I swear. It was only—" What was she saying?

Why was she defending him? She snapped her lips shut, willed her mind to focus.

Gabriel backed farther away from her. His eyes had narrowed now, his jaw tightening.

Something compelled her forward, something made her go after him. "Gabriel, I—" She was reaching for him, she realized. Her hands outstretched in front of her as if she could convince him of something if only she could touch him.

She dropped her hands, dropped her excuses. That was what they were. She wasn't defending Roger. She was defending herself. How could she have let him hit her? How could she have let him treat her like that?

She raised her chin. "He manipulated me." The words came slower now, firmer. "He convinced me I was worthless. That I deserved to be treated like that. He wouldn't let me see my sisters, my mother and father. He isolated me, so the only truth I knew was the one he fed me." She had to swallow, the words suddenly sticking in her throat. She thought she should feel something, anything. She'd never spoken of what her marriage had really been like, and she thought telling someone her secret for the first time would conjure a maelstrom of emotion, but she was oddly hollow, as though the only parts left of her were numb. "I realized after he was dead, after I had returned to my family, what he had done. How he had convinced me of my unsavoriness."

Gabriel's face changed, like dangerously thin ice his expression cracked, the grimness splintering but not shattering. Was he judging her? She suddenly didn't care. Like a dam broken, all of the things she had kept inside of herself for so long were suddenly freed.

And she wanted all of them gone. The regret, the guilt, the recriminations. They would only weigh her down, and it was time to sweep everything clean.

"That's what all of this is about." She gestured to the table of books now behind Gabriel. "I've spent so much of my life doing as I was told and listening to the lies of others that I never got the chance to find out who I was." The next words were harder to say as she studied his face, wondering how low she had sunk in his estimation. "That's why I can't marry you, Gabriel. My widowhood is my only chance. My only chance to see who I might have been had I been given the opportunity."

There was silence then. She'd said everything she could possibly say. Now it was up to him to cast his judgment. She was ready for it. There was nothing he could say that could be any worse than what Roger had said to her. That numbness crept over her again, like iron this time, clamping down any fear that might try to rear its head.

But Gabriel didn't sentence her. He didn't repeat the names she heard in her head, the ones that told her she was weak, that she was a coward. He did something else entirely.

"Why didn't you tell me?" The words were pushed between gritted teeth, and at first, she thought she heard him wrong.

The question was unanswerable, and it left her speechless.

"Tell you?" She shook her head, trying to give herself time to gather her thoughts. "What do you mean?"

He retraced his steps to her now, his eyes never leaving her face. "Why didn't you tell me?" he repeated when he stopped directly in front of her. "Why didn't you tell me what he was doing, Annie? Why didn't you come to me? I would have stopped him. I would have—"

She touched him before she knew she was going to, her hand going up to cup his cheek. She needed to touch him, as though her fingers could draw the anger she saw in his eyes, pull it from him so it couldn't hurt him anymore.

"Oh Gabriel," she whispered. "There was nothing you could have done."

Her words were true even as they hurt her to speak them. Roger had taught her not to trust another story, not to believe in hope. Even if Gabriel had found out, there was nothing he could have done because she wouldn't have believed in anything else.

She watched her words hit home, and his eyes changed again, darkening, and then there it was.

Her worth.

It was reflected in his eyes, and it took her breath away. He'd already left her speechless, and now he'd made her breathless with a simple look.

She *mattered* to him.

Not in the way a friend would care for a friend either. This was deeper, unfathomable, and she saw all of it play out in his eyes.

This, right then, was far more intimate than the kiss they had shared. This was the very thing Roger had convinced her didn't exist, and yet Gabriel did it so easily.

He cared for her.

Slowly she withdrew her hand, feeling the first tendrils of fear claw their way inside of her. It wasn't a fear of Gabriel. That was impossible. She knew that now. No, the fear was worse than that.

The fear that Gabriel was becoming to matter to her too.

She took a step back, and finally he broke his gaze from hers.

"We've been here too long. Someone will be looking for you." His words belied no emotion, and her stomach tightened with worry, but he was right.

Someone might notice they were both absent from the party and wonder where they were.

He retrieved her bonnet from the table and handed it to

her. Although when she tried to take it from him, he didn't let go.

"Gabriel?" There were so many questions in that word, in the sound of his name leaving her lips, and yet she couldn't have asked a single one of them.

He didn't respond. He only moved his hand, sliding it along the rim of her bonnet until his hand covered hers. A power like nothing she had known swept through her, something strong and vibrant and fiery.

A spark.

But then he released her and stepped back. "You should go," he said.

And she did, turning to the door. This time she didn't flee. She didn't pick up her skirts and run. She walked to the corridor, closing the door behind her, only not quite. Something stopped her, something made her look back, and she wished she hadn't.

Gabriel had sunk to one of the sofas, his head dropped into his hands, and her heart splintered at the sight of him, her past and her future tumbling together like broken shards of glass, and she knew it would be impossible to gather them back up without getting hurt.

She turned away and left him.

# CHAPTER 6

Gabriel did not want to be there.

In fact, he might even wager he'd like to be anywhere else in the world, but he couldn't have stopped himself.

He sat there, watching the front door of the townhome he rented for his mother as the rain sluiced against his carriage window. He watched it, knowing eventually he would need to gather the courage to get down from the vehicle, walk up the stone steps, and lift the brass knocker, allowing it to fall and alert the occupants he had come. But for now, he sat in his carriage like a coward.

The afternoon in the Brocklehurst library hung around his neck like a heavy chain. He didn't try to remove it. It was his burden to carry, and there in his carriage, the rain beating down around him as he avoided seeing his mother, the chain felt heavier than ever.

Roger had abused Annie.

He understood it, and yet he couldn't make it make sense in his head.

Beautiful Annie with the wide expressive eyes, the shy

smile, and the gentle touch. How could anyone have hurt her?

Anger burned inside of him. Anger and something else, something more aggressive, but there was no outlet for such aggression. Roger was dead, and that rendered Gabriel's emotions pointless.

This more than anything was what stopped him from stepping from his carriage. The idea that his emotions were pointless, that he'd failed even before he'd made an attempt.

But Annie's revelation alone had driven him this far. Now he must summon what was left of his patience and will himself to move forward and call upon his mother.

He hadn't forgotten Belvedere's visit. He had thought to push it to the side, not allow himself to rise to the man's bait, but then he'd learned the ugly truth about Annie's marriage, and he suddenly couldn't ignore it, his own past and Annie's combining into a mess in his mind, and the idea that his efforts were futile, the damage having already been wrought, propelled him forward.

Belvedere had returned from the Continent where Gabriel had driven him, and there could be only one reason for his return. He wanted something from Gabriel, and the man had always gone through Gabriel's mother to get it. He owed her no loyalty, not after what she'd done when his father had died, yet his own moral code propelled him forward.

The memory of that day in the drawing room came back to him without warning. His mother making the introduction, Belvedere stepping up, leaning forward with his hands pressed to his thighs as though Gabriel were a child and not a young man of seven and ten.

He snapped open the door and jumped into the rain before the memory could progress. He climbed the stairs two at a time, and within seconds, his knock was answered, the butler ushering him in.

Gabriel waited in the drawing room where he'd been shown, standing in front of a fire he could not feel. Rain dripped from his boots, dampening the carpet at his feet. He watched it, the colors woven into the carpet growing muted with damp, and his mind wandered.

How long had Roger been abusive? Was it from the very start of the marriage or had it come later? How often had he hit her? What other kind of torture had he inflicted on her?

He reached out and gripped the mantel over the fireplace, letting the thick wood cut into his palm, as he forced the questions from his mind. He'd never ask them of her. He would never make her relive it, and so the questions were futile, taking space in his mind when they did not deserve to.

"Gabriel."

He turned about at the sound of his name and found his mother standing in the doorway of the drawing room, her hands folded neatly in front of her. Elizabeth Phelps, the Duchess of Grimsby, was nearly seventy now, her face marked by the lines of time. He couldn't remember when her hair had gone white, but she wore it as she always did, parted down the middle and wrapped in a twist pinned low on her head. Even from this distance, he could see the glint of the gold band she still wore on her left hand.

"Mother," Gabriel said, stepping forward. "I've come with news, I'm afraid."

He didn't visit his mother often. Relations between them had been strained since the day he'd come of age and banished Belvedere from their lives. It had been easy once his mother had ceased to be the executor of the title. Belvedere no longer had an avenue of power to clutch at the title, and Gabriel had suddenly been the one in charge. Belvedere's plan had been unclear, and even now Gabriel couldn't surmise what it might have been. The only explanation for the parasite's confidence in acquiring the pseudo-control of the title lay through Gabriel's mother, and this had left things unsettled between mother and child.

Now his mother's face lightened, deepening the lines around her eyes and mouth as she might have smiled. "Are you to be wed finally?"

It took all he had to stop the wince his mother's words invoked.

"No, Mother, I'm afraid it's not that," he said, unable to refute her question entirely because to do so would be to admit he must give up on Annie. "I'm here on another matter."

He watched his mother's face fall, but he had already steeled himself for it. He would never marry if he didn't marry Annie, and now that prospect appeared grim. Yes, he hadn't protected her when she'd needed it, but now he understood the reason why she guarded her widowhood. The idea of forcing her to give up her freedom was like putting a freed bird back in its cage. He simply couldn't do it.

But he was used to disappointing his mother, and the tight expression on her face was familiar to him instead of jarring.

"Belvedere has returned," he went on, hoping to get through this as quickly as possible. "He claims you are ill and require funds for medical treatment."

His mother laughed softly and moved farther into the room, drifting slowly over to the fireplace. "Oh Gabriel, as usual, you must have misunderstood. Brogden wouldn't have asked you for money, not for my sake."

It was always like this when he broached the subject of Belvedere with his mother. She defended the man to the last degree and took his word over her own son's. Gabriel had again grown shockingly used to this behavior, and he didn't hesitate to continue.

"He did ask for funds, Mother. He approached me at my club in the presence of other gentlemen, which was unseemly. I'll not have him do it again."

His mother stood in front of the fireplace now, holding her hands out as if to warm them, but she turned her head back to him at this. "Would you like me to tell him as much the next I see him?"

Her words cut through him like the sharpened blade of a guillotine, but again, he gave no outward reaction. So Belvedere had been there, to see Gabriel's mother again. Perhaps the man had been back before, perhaps his mother visited him on the Continent, perhaps they exchanged letters, keeping their relationship going through all these years. The details of it didn't matter. The point was Belvedere wanted to ensure Gabriel understood the man still had control of the duchess.

But why?

Gabriel did not change his posture. He drew a single even breath. "There's no need," he said. "I shall tell him myself."

His mother returned her gaze to the flames. "I had thought with time you would come to see how foolish you're behaving, Gabriel. Brogden is no threat to you, and yet you treat him so harshly." She turned now, her eyes meeting his. "Your father would be so disappointed in the man you've become. You're so unlike him." She took a step toward him. "Your father was a fair man and kind, two qualities you do not possess. Brogden was right."

A river of emotion coursed through him then, and with a single heartbeat, he squashed every single one of them. This was his mother's favorite game, convincing him of something that wasn't true yet something that would grant her power over him. But Gabriel knew the truth, not just his mother's lies. The Duke of Ardley himself had rained praises down on him only that week, and his mother's accusations fell off of him like dead leaves falling from a branch.

Annie had used the word manipulation.

He opened his mouth to rebuke his mother's statement and stopped.

Annie had used the word *manipulation.*

She'd only had Roger's accusations and no one else. No one else to refute the lies she'd been given.

Something shifted inside of him then like a window left open in a room, forgotten until a draft slammed the door shut. He would get nowhere with his mother, and now that he'd made it clear he had no intention of bending to Belvedere's demands, he needn't linger.

There was somewhere else he had to be. Someone else who needed him.

"Right, I must be off," he said and turned for the door, just catching the look of shock on his mother's features as he slipped into the hallway toward the front door.

"Gabriel!" she called after him.

He took his overcoat and hat from the footman at the door, not bothering to slow down for his mother's sake. He heard her rustling skirts and the slap of her slippers on the marble floor, but he wrenched the door open when the footman did not move, his eyes fixated somewhere behind Gabriel where he imagined his mother was striding to catch up to him.

"Gabriel," she called again, more sternly than panicked this time.

He held the door in one hand and turned only his head to look at her. "Yes, Mother? Was there something else?"

"You're just leaving?" she asked, her voice a note higher than usual.

"Yes, I am," he said and plunged into the rain, shutting the door behind him.

He threw himself into his vehicle, and his driver had the carriage in motion as soon as the door snapped shut. Gabriel shook the rain from his overcoat, his thoughts already miles ahead of him.

He had felt that surge of anger, defensiveness, inadequacy, and worst of all, hopelessness. He was a grown man, and still his mother did not believe him, and in that moment in her drawing room, he firmly believed she never would. The idea was over-whelming and complete, and if he hadn't had years to get used to it, hadn't known how others viewed him in starkly different ways, he knew it could so easily dictate his next moves.

But he had had years of experience; he had had others commend him for his character.

Annie hadn't had such luxury. She had been married only two years, and what had she learned in those two years? The very thing she had told him. She had learned to believe the truth Roger gave her.

Recrimination rose in his throat like bile, and he thought he might be sick. It was his fault. He had tried to guide Roger as soon as he had learned of the man's unsavory habits at one of the Marchioness of Lionsley's charity games. He had gone out to the terrace for a spot of fresh air between rounds and inadvertently stumbled upon Roger with another young man Gabriel didn't know. Roger had stopped talking as soon as Gabriel had arrived, but he'd heard enough of the exchange to know Roger had been threatening the younger man.

Gabriel recalled being tired that night, tired of the demands of society, tired of the obligations of the title, and tired of having to deal with hot-headed young men like Roger. He'd taken Roger under his wing then, done his best to steer him right, even got him a membership in his boxing club, thinking the exercise would help sap some of the anger Gabriel saw inside the man.

It was the boxing club that would be his end.

When Roger died, Gabriel had blamed himself. It was impossible not to. He'd tried to help the man, and his actions had only led to the man's death. For the first time in over a year, the weight of that guilt wasn't so heavy. It wasn't gone. He doubted it ever would be, but it fit differently on his shoulders.

Because he could finally help. He could do something about Roger's death, and it didn't involve marrying the man's widow.

The driver made excellent time in returning them to the Grimsby townhouse as there was little traffic, likely on account of the rain. He vaulted from the carriage now, gesturing to his driver to take the carriage back to the mews as he wouldn't be needing it any longer that day. He must think. The rules were different for widows, he knew that, but how different? He didn't know, and he must figure it out if he were to make any progress.

He didn't wait for his butler to open the front door, and soon he was stripping off his sodden coat and hat. He'd taken two strides down the corridor to his study when he registered his butler's urgent voice calling his name.

"Your Grace, I do beg your pardon. I tried to stop her, but she insisted on seeing you."

Gabriel turned to face his butler, Rives. "What is it? What's happened?"

The man was making no sense. Rives was getting on in years, but he wasn't that old. He was a good, loyal servant, and Gabriel couldn't believe the man had lost his senses, but his words were confusing.

It was his housekeeper, Mrs. Featherstone, who

answered, stepping into the foyer from the hallway that led to the kitchen.

"There's a lady, Your Grace. She arrived at the kitchen door not more than a quarter hour ago. She insisted on seeing you." Mrs. Featherstone looked him directly in the eye while Rives struggled to even remain still. Gabriel couldn't blame him. This was an unusual turn of events and a bit alarming that a lady should call on him, and it was *especially* unusual that she should arrive at the kitchen door as if she didn't wish to be seen.

Mrs. Featherstone's words righted themselves in his head, and before he could draw another breath, he said, "Where is she?"

"She insisted on waiting, so I put her in the library, Your Grace. I had a fire lit, and I was just about to send up a—"

Gabriel waved off the rest of the woman's explanation and turned in the opposite direction, taking the stairs up to the main floor at a fast clip. The library was on the floor with the rest of the public rooms, and his legs seemed entirely inadequate as it took far too long to reach her.

But finally he was in the right corridor, through the right set of doors, and—

Annie stood in his library.

* * *

ANNIE OWED HIM THIS.

Seeing him like that in the Brocklehurst library had shifted everything for her. It wasn't a sweeping change. She didn't suddenly realize all of her past mistakes and the way to right them. It was more subtle than that. It was like the dark lifting, and finding the truth of the things that had only been shapes in the night. It had been there all along. She had only to learn how to see it.

She had thought Gabriel had been Roger's friend, but she saw it differently now. The look that had gripped Gabriel's features at her inadvertent revelation had not been disbelief. It had been disappointment. It was so obvious to her now. Gabriel *had* been trying to save Roger. Everything Gabriel had ever done for Roger, all of it, it was meant to reform him somehow. Every introduction Gabriel had managed, every opportunity, even introducing him to that boxing club, it had all been to help Roger. It seemed strange, that last one, but the boxing club had gotten Roger out of the gaming hells.

So she had shown up at the kitchen door of Gabriel's townhouse in the pouring rain requesting entry. Of course she had been denied, but she'd persisted, Gwen's words echoing in her ears. Annie thought it was likely the poor woman who had answered her ring, a small woman with sharp features, had simply taken pity on her. The rain had been coming down in torrents, and Annie was just plain soaked. Her cloak was helpless against the onslaught, and the woman had pulled her inside and taken the garment, whisking it off into what had appeared to be the laundry.

Annie didn't care if she never saw it again. She only had to get to Gabriel. The woman came back, explaining His Grace was not in, but she could wait. Annie had expected Gabriel's home to be like any other home of a duke, but what she was not expecting was his library where the woman showed her to wait.

The carpet onto which she stepped when entering the room was likely ruined for the time she had stood there, ogling the space around her. Gabriel's library was a two-story, soaring room with bookshelves requiring brass library ladders. A circular staircase in the far corner gave access to the gallery above, and she had to resist the temptation to march straight over to it and climb up. She had already invaded his home. It wouldn't do to poke around his library.

Not that she thought he would mind.

She settled for standing on the tiles before the hearth, both to dry herself with the heat of the flames and to contain the small puddle that formed everywhere she moved. From her vantage point by the fire, she took in the towering shelves of books, the deep tones of the maple furniture, the plush drapes that shut out the world beyond, leaving one free to get lost in all these books. There was a desk tucked into the alcove made by the circular, wrought iron staircase. It was littered with papers, stacks of books, and piles of post. It was as though Gabriel had just stepped away from his work there. She felt as if she were prying directly into his personal affairs, and she was forced to look away.

It wasn't long before her gaze caught on something else. Something far more intriguing than any book. There was a single sofa in the middle of the room, and it faced the only window on that side of the library as the rest of the wall was taken up by bookcases. It wasn't the lack of other sofas or chairs or the single window in the range of bookcases that drew her attention. It was the cushions of the sofa that did. Each one had a defined area of wear, clearly indicating where someone had lain upon it, lain upon it so much as to have left his mark. Without warning, her mind put Gabriel there, reclined on the sofa, his long legs stretching the length of it as he reached for her—

"Annie."

She jumped, the heels of her slippers clicking against the tiles at her feet. It was a full second before she could regain her composure enough to turn to the door and the man standing there, and then, composure regained, she surged forward. "Gabriel, I'm terribly sorry to invade your home like this, but I must explain." Roger had convinced her of mistruths for two years, and she was done allowing others to think things that weren't true. The need to explain everything to Gabriel, to ease his burden, to take away the defeat she had seen cloak him the day he had learned her secret was more than enough reason to break every rule propriety held for her.

"You mustn't apologize," Gabriel said, and she realized they'd done it again.

He had come to her while she had gone to him, and they had met in the middle of the room, directly in front of that damn sofa with its tantalizing imprint. It was odd, this kind of synchronization with another human being. She hadn't even done this with her sisters.

She eyed Gabriel now, wondering when it was this duke had stopped being an icon and had started being a man.

But then he touched her again, his hands warm and reassuring on her shoulders, and she wondered how she could have ever thought of him as anything else.

"Did anyone see you?" he went on. "My only care is for your reputation."

She shook her head. "I snuck out. My parents think I'm in bed with a headache."

Gabriel dropped his hands. "You snuck out?"

She couldn't stop the smile. "I got the idea from my sister. I caught her one night sneaking back into the house. She said she had been taking the air, but she had a twig in her hair, and I knew she—" Annie sucked in a breath. "I probably shouldn't be telling you this."

"Probably not," he agreed, crossing his arms over his chest. "But please continue."

"I think she's been meeting someone, in secret." She thought she would feel guilty betraying her sister's secret, but instead, she felt a rush of exhilaration. "I think she might be in love with him."

"Why do you think that?"

"Only love would make someone do something so careless," she said before the reality of their current situation dawned on her, and she felt a lick of awkwardness.

She wasn't in love with Gabriel. Not at all. There wasn't anything awkward about her decision to come to his home, unchaperoned, in the middle of a rainstorm that seemed to block out all the rest of the world. No, there wasn't anything untoward about it in the least.

"Indeed." Gabriel dropped to the sofa beside them, relaxing back into it, and every drop of blood drained from her head. "Who do you think it is?"

He was so at ease that she couldn't help but feel at ease too, and soon she found herself sinking to the sofa. "I haven't the slightest notion," she said. "I only know it's not the Duke of Ardley."

"What makes you say that?" His expression displayed obvious interest, and it occurred to her that Ardley could very well be Gabriel's opponent in the game to find a bride. The thought sent the blood roaring back into her head, and she felt dizzy. It didn't matter that Gabriel should marry someone. Of course he should. Why should she have such a strong reaction to the mere thought that he wouldn't be marrying her?

She went on, hoping the pull of gossip would distract her. "Because whenever my mother mentions the duke, Eloise changes the subject."

"Wouldn't that make it even more likely that it *is* the duke?"

She blinked. "I hadn't thought of that."

Gabriel raised both eyebrows. "Perhaps your sister's found a love match with the duke."

She scoffed. "Not likely. Everyone knows the duke is the worst kind of flirt."

Her eyes widened as she realized what she'd said, and before she could stop it, her hand went to her mouth, her fingers covering her lips as if she could take the words back. She was acting as though she were gossiping with her sisters, and that was hardly the case, but there was something about Gabriel that put her at ease. Too much at ease.

"A flirt? The Duke of Ardley." She couldn't decipher the expression on his face then. It was a curious mix of disbelief and surprise. "How do you know the Duke of Ardley is a flirt?"

She shrugged. "Everyone knows. The rumors insist he has some sort of system for managing ladies."

Gabriel surged to his feet so quickly, she nearly fell off the sofa in surprise.

"May I get you a drink?" he asked over his shoulder as he went to a cart in the corner. "I believe Mrs. Featherstone is sending up a tray in case you're hungry, but I can at least get you something to drink for now."

While the question was polite and casual, there was nothing relaxed about his stride as he ate up the carpet, and she wondered if he were suddenly trying to get away from her.

She glanced at the windows that broke up the bookcases along the far wall and watched the endless sheets of rain. "A drink would be lovely. But—" She nearly swallowed her tongue as words she didn't realize she was going to say tripped against her teeth. Gabriel hesitated, looking over his shoulder at her. She pushed to her feet. "Only I shan't like sherry or brandy. I don't care for either. I know a lady should, but I don't. And I don't want one now. I'd like…" She fumbled suddenly with her skirts, her fingers twitching as she tried to arrange her thoughts. "Well, quite honestly, I don't know what I should like, but I know I don't like sherry and brandy."

"Should you like to borrow a book to help you in your

decision?" His mouth lifted on one side as he looked about the room at the stacks of books that surrounded them.

It was a beat before she realized he was teasing her, and then when the realization struck, she laughed. The sound was terrible, like the bleat of a goat, as her laugh was so unused, but this only made her laugh harder.

"I think I'll take a different approach," she said when she got herself under control again. She wove between two tables littered with newspapers to where he stood at the cart and looked down at the myriad liquor decanters. "I should like you to choose something for me."

He pulled a decanter from the middle of the cart and held it up for her. "A smooth whiskey, I think. A mild flavor on which to build your new palette."

She nodded. "That sounds awfully exciting."

He pulled the stopper from the decanter with a soft pop. "You did say you were looking to your future."

His words brought back the reason for her visit. "Yes, about that…Gabriel, I should explain. About Roger…"

He handed her a glass, a small amount of the whiskey sloshing in the bottom. "You don't need to explain, Annie." He met her gaze as he spoke, and she felt something warm blossom in her chest. "I don't require an explanation, and you shouldn't feel obligated to give one. What happened is yours and not anyone else's."

She took the glass from him, momentarily at a loss for words. "But I want you to know you mustn't blame yourself. There was nothing you could have done—"

"I know." He was pouring himself his own glass, and so she almost didn't hear him as he wasn't looking at her.

"You know?" There was such conviction in his voice, but…how?

He put the stopper back into the decanter and replaced it on the cart before picking up his glass to face her. "I know.

Even if I had discovered what Roger was doing, I likely couldn't have helped although I would have tried. Roger would have convinced you of anything to keep you under his power, and I don't think I could have said or done a single thing that would have penetrated that." That warmth in her chest began to spread, and a strange tingling erupted in her fingers. She feared she might drop her glass without having taken a single sip. His expression darkened then, but somehow she knew it wasn't for her but rather for him. "I'm afraid I have experience with such manipulation, and I know too well how overwhelming it can be. I'm only sorry you were made to suffer under his control."

Something inside of her stilled. She had always imagined Gabriel as invincible. He was older and wiser, and this had made him seem impenetrable in her mind, but seeing his face just then, she knew it wasn't true. Something had hurt him, deeply, and she reached out a hand before she knew what she was doing, touching his wrist as if by touching him she could draw more of the hurt out of him.

"Oh Gabriel, I'm so sorry," she said. "No one should experience such manipulation."

He gave a shrug and indicated her glass. "I've had many years to grow used to it. Now try your drink."

His words rang true, and she knew he wasn't trying to deflect her question by returning to the whiskey, but rather he was used to whatever had happened to him, and it was almost as though he were weary of speaking of it.

She took a sip from her glass, not wishing to cause him further discomfort by pressing the subject. Her eyes widened as warmth flooded her mouth, and smooth flavor filled her senses.

"Oh, that's quite good," she said, peering at her glass as if it held something more valuable than gold. "I think I like that," she mumbled to the glass, and Gabriel laughed softly.

"I may have corrupted you, Lady Anna," he said when his laugh died away.

She looked up and met his gaze and wished she hadn't. The weariness she had witnessed there earlier was gone, and instead she saw only heat. Her body tightened, remembering their brief kiss, the feel of his lips against hers that seemed to have happened an eternity ago.

She blinked and looked away before she could get her body to move. Slowly she made her way to the windows, taking another sip of her drink in hopes the alcohol would unwind her nerves.

This couldn't be happening. Not now. Not with Gabriel. It was all in her head. Her sister had done it. Eloise had been the one to point out the idea of a spark. Before that, Annie had been perfectly happy remaining alone in her widowhood.

Perhaps it was the setting, the dimness of the library with only a few lit lamps, the soft rain at the windows, the whiskey…

She turned about only when the window was at her back. Gabriel hadn't moved, his glass seemingly forgotten in his hand.

"What was it that happened to you?" she asked, desperate for anything to put space between them, to cool the heat that still lingered low in her belly. "You mustn't speak of it if you don't wish to. It's only…" She licked her lips, feeling so much inside of her topple over. Gabriel. The whiskey. This spark that unexpectedly ignited between them. These were all things she hadn't counted on, but then once upon a time, she thought the things she could count on would keep her safe. Perhaps it was better to embrace the things she hadn't anticipated. "It's only I had hoped we might be friends."

She had never spoken more frightening words.

Her widowhood was like a cloak that covered her

completely, kept her apart from the kind of human connection that could break her, hurt her. But now she'd reached through it. To him.

And she'd never felt more vulnerable in her life.

Gabriel watched her. She was too far away now to see the color of his eyes, and she wondered if they had darkened from blue to gray or perhaps lingered somewhere in between. She inhaled and exhaled, counting her breaths, and wondered when it was she should retract her statement, feeling suddenly unsure.

*Know your place.*

Roger had convinced her she wasn't worthy of friends, and now his voice came back to her in the quiet. Instead of listening to it, she took a drink of the whiskey, letting its warmth travel down her throat, fill her belly, and eradicate the echo of her dead husband's voice.

"My mother formed an attachment with a vile man who tried to usurp the power of the title from her while it was in executorship before I came of age." Gabriel's voice was devoid of feeling, and again, she felt more than knew just how long he had had to carry his reality.

She had been about to take another sip of her whiskey, but her hand dropped away at this. "Your mother…what?"

"She fell under the power of a man who wished to wield control of the dukedom. As I was only ten and seven when my father died, I inherited the title, but the estate affairs were held by the executor until I came of age. The executor being my mother. This man thought to take advantage of her, and he did so for nearly a year, but I came of age and had him physically removed from our lives."

There was a danger in his voice she'd never heard before, and once she might have been frightened by it, but as she stood there, the muffled sound of rain, the warmth of the whiskey lingering on her tongue, and the smell of leather and paper, she couldn't help but be thrilled by the strength in his tone.

She swallowed, her throat suddenly dry despite the drink still in her hand. "Physically removed him?"

"I threw him from the front door," he said, nodding his head to indicate the front door of the house in which they were standing. "I think he might have broken his arm. I didn't remain to find out. I told every lender and solicitor in London of his underhanded dealings and ruined his reputation. He was forced to flee to the Continent."

The thrill that had bubbled inside of her erupted into a flood of desire. She took a large swallow of the whiskey, willing her rampaging emotions to cool. But then—

"Gabriel, when you asked me to marry you, were you trying to protect me from—" She paused and met his gaze. "What was the man's name?"

"Brogden Belvedere." His tone was flat as he said the name.

"Oh heavens, he sounds like a villain in a Gothic novel. How dreadful."

A smile tugged at the corners of his mouth at this, and she realized she liked making him smile. For two years, he had been the composed, older gentleman, dashing and distinguished with the gray that shaded his dark hair. She thought he held all the answers, but now she was coming to understand he was human after all.

"And yes," he said quietly. "I was trying to protect you from the Brogden Belvederes of this world."

She didn't know what overcame her then, perhaps it was her own weariness, her own wish to stand firmly on her own two feet, to not feel so afraid all the time. Whatever it was, she set down her glass on the table under the window at her back and marched over to Gabriel, extending one hand in front of her when she reached him.

"I'd like to strike a bargain with you. Should I be approached by any villains from a Gothic novel, you shall be the first person I inform. Do we have an agreement?"

He eyed her hand, that smile playing at his lips again. "Yes, we do," he said and took her hand in a firm handshake.

He smiled now, and it lightened his expression, easing something in her chest their serious conversation had brought on. She let go of his hand and looked about the room.

"I haven't failed to notice you have a robust library here, Your Grace," she said, indicating the stocked shelves, the gallery above.

"Hmm, yes," he said in a stuffy, scholarly tone. "I have an impressive collection of books on the migratory practices of the short-eared owl. Would that interest you?"

She met his gaze, feeling her own smile tugging at her lips. "I don't know," she said. "But I'd love to find out."

He set down his own glass and made a show of offering her his arm. "If you'll allow me, my lady," he said.

She took his arm and let him lead her away.

# CHAPTER 7

*S*he woke slowly, one muscle at a time, each coiling in sequence as she tried to remember where she was.

And more importantly, who she was with.

Because she was not alone.

Her eyes flew open even as she willed her body to remain still, to not wake this person who slumbered beside her, his chest rising and falling under her hand, his arm tucked securely around her back as he cradled her. She didn't feel fear or trepidation. She felt something far worse.

She felt safe.

*Gabriel.*

Her head lay nestled in his shoulder, and she could see her hand directly in front of her, the one that lay on his chest, and she watched it rise and fall with every breath he took. The sight was hypnotic, and it soothed her. Soothed her entirely too much as her eyes began to close again, but she willed herself to remain awake, to recall what had happened.

She remembered their conversation, the revelation he had made about his mother, the death of his father, and the man who had tried to usurp power from a near child. She remembered far too much about the migration practices of a short-eared owl, and—

Now she let her eyes close.

The *whiskey*.

How much of the stuff had she drunk? What had it done to her?

They had been on the sofa in front of the window. She blinked her eyes open, taking in the fall of heavy curtains across the room, and the windowpanes that were now black with night. Oh heavens, how long had they been asleep? Was her family missing her?

No, she must concentrate. She'd worry about her family later.

The whiskey, the short-eared owl, the sofa, and...

She remembered feeling sleepy, the song of the rain against the window and roof, Gabriel reading from the text about migratory bird routes, his voice deep and comforting in its recitation, the glass of whiskey in her hand as she leaned back into the sofa, and then—

Nothing.

She must have fallen asleep. How embarrassing. What would Gabriel think? That she found him so utterly boring she couldn't remain conscious? That was hardly the truth. She had never felt the kind of peace that enveloped her. Never. Not even after Roger had died. Not even after she had returned to the cocoon of her family.

Nothing had felt as good as being with Gabriel Phelps.

Oh heavens, she was in trouble.

She could feel her widowhood as if it were a glass sphere she held in her hands, and she'd nearly let it slip through her fingers. How could she have done this? How could she have let Gabriel get this close? How could she have been so care-less with the thing that was most precious to her?

She stared unblinking at the dark window across from the sofa, listened to the faraway tick of a clock muffled by the sound of Gabriel's deep breathing, and let her mind transport her to another line of thinking.

Widowhood gave her freedom. Freedom from the constraints of marriage, yes, but freedom for something else.

She let her gaze shift then, traveling up the length of his chest, higher to the chiseled line of his jaw, the dark stubble that covered his cheeks, and—

Oh lud, he was even more handsome when he was asleep.

She studied him, his expression so relaxed it took her a moment to realize how carefully he must hold himself when he was conscious. The idea pained her.

What was he protecting himself from? This Belvedere that had so recklessly ended his childhood? Or was it something else? Something he wouldn't let her see?

Overcome by her emotions, her fingers moved of their own volition, traveling up his chest, skating along the open collar at his throat until finally they brushed the stubble along his jaw that beckoned her. She kept her touch light, not wishing to wake him, only to enjoy him.

Because while widowhood gave her freedom from marriage, it also gave her the freedom to take a lover.

Her stomach churned as soon as the thought entered her mind. Hadn't she asked this man to be her friend mere hours earlier? Why now was she thinking of him as so much more than that? It was only the whiskey, the rain, the coziness of the library. It wasn't real, and she could jeopardize something that was so very important to her if she acted on this sudden burst of feelings.

She made to withdraw her hand when his eyes opened.

Her fingertips hovered at his jaw when his gaze met hers. His eyes lingered on her, searching or perhaps simply waking. She wondered what he saw in her eyes because there was no hesitation as he turned his head and kissed her.

It was like coming home.

The rightness of it overwhelmed her, the perfectness of it suffocated her, and she wanted nothing more than to stay right there for eternity.

He captured the hand that lingered along his jaw, pressing her palm against his cheek as his lips claimed her.

Desire shot through her, strong and unquestionable, and tears erupted behind her closed eyes in response. She had never dreamed to feel this kind of yearning, had almost feared it, and now that she should experience it, it seemed like a miracle. All too quickly the tears vanished, and she could think no more of how lucky she might have been because Gabriel turned them, rolling her onto her back even as he plucked cushions from the sofa, tossing them heedlessly around them as he made more room for him to cover her with his body.

Oh Lord, it was glorious. To have his weight against her, to have him hovering over her, to have his lips—

"Ah." The sound escaped her, unable to hold it back as heat flooded her, her body tingling to life as if it had lain dormant her whole life, waiting for him. For— "Gabriel." His name was forced from her lips as he kissed the sensitive place behind her ear.

There *was* a place behind her ear that was sensitive, that sent a bolt of lightning clear to her toes when he laid his lips there. What else was there that she didn't know? What other secrets was her body keeping?

For a fleeting moment, she remembered the rumors, the ones debutantes traded so easily. The idea that a woman could enjoy the love act as much as a man, that a woman could find release. Annie never believed it, knowing it to be a lie after she had wed, but now...now...

With every touch, with every caress, with every kiss, Gabriel made her doubt.

Could she find release in the love act?

She didn't want to think about it. She only wanted to feel, and when he kissed her again, his lips hot against hers, she arched into him, wanting to feel all of him pressed against her. He took advantage of her arched back to slide his hand around the curve of her hip, delving, exploring, lifting her further against him until her breasts were crushed to his chest.

She'd never felt such exquisite torture. The clothing that separated them had suddenly grown barbs that dug into her skin, and she wanted it off. She wanted to touch him, feel his skin beneath her fingers as she had when she caressed the stubbled line of his jaw. Suddenly she wanted to know everything she didn't know.

But he had moved, his lips tracing a path down the column of her neck. His efforts were thwarted by the high collar of her mourning dress. Never before had she wished she were wearing that red gown. Her eyes flew open at the thought, momentarily distracted, understanding penetrating the sensuous haze that enveloped her.

For Gabriel, she would wear that red gown.

The thought sped through her, and with it came a surge of strength she had thought had long deserted her. Thinking of Gabriel gave her strength. Not fear or confusion or disbelief. When she thought of Gabriel, she remembered who she had been before Roger had hurt her.

"Gabriel." His name came out twisted now, so wrapped in emotion she almost couldn't speak it.

He lifted his head. Her hand went to his cheek, his brow, wanting to wipe away the concern she saw there.

"Gabriel, I want you to touch me." His eyes darkened, and somehow, impossibly, his gaze narrowed until she felt like the only thing in the world. "I want to…find release." Those were probably the wrong words. She didn't know the right ones, only what she had gleaned from girlish rumors, but when Gabriel's eyes darkened further, from blue to cool gray, she knew he understood.

He cupped her face, his touch impossibly gentle. "Annie, have you never felt pleasure before?"

Too much emotion clogged her throat, and all she could do was shake her head.

Again there was no hesitation, and her heart soared with it. He didn't treat her as so many had treated her in the past year. As the poor Wexford widow. His hands moved over her as though there was nothing poor about her, his mouth claiming her as something precious, fiery, and alive.

*Alive.*

That was what she felt as his mouth chased his fingers, as they unbuttoned each of the small, cloth-covered buttons of her bodice, marching down the length of her neck, her chest, lower, until the lace edge of her chemise stopped him. He pushed one side of her gown to her shoulder, his teeth scraping her collarbone, so she came up off the sofa, her fingers curling into his back, wishing he'd shed his shirt when he'd removed his coat and cravat earlier in the night.

Heat was building inside of her with every touch of his lips, and something pulsed deep in her belly. She didn't know what was happening, didn't know her body could feel like this. But somehow she knew it could only happen with Gabriel. The way his body seemed to cocoon her, shelter her, at the same time he drew her out, teased her, beckoned her. The way his hands seemed to know her body even though he'd never touched her. Not like this.

His hand moved along her hip, traced the contour of her thigh, even as his lips reclaimed hers. She was lost, lost to his touch, lost to his kiss, lost to the passion that pulsated between them.

But then he stopped.

She opened her eyes, apprehension cooling her body. "Did I do something wrong?"

He didn't answer her. His eyes studied her face as if he couldn't quite believe she was there, and something inside of her broke. How could he look at her like that? As if she were the most incredible thing to happen to him?

She was nothing, and yet he could make her feel like everything with a simple look.

"Annie, I need to know you're sure about this." His tone was so serious it squeezed her heart as if what she wanted meant everything to him.

She reached up and, wrapping her hand around the back of his neck, drew his lips back to hers, telling him what mere words could never do as she let his body overtake her.

His hand skimmed down her thigh again, but it kept going this time, reaching, exploring, lifting the hem of her gown until she felt his touch on her knee, toying with the lace at the top of her stocking, and then higher.

"Gabriel," she moaned against his mouth, her back arching.

He tore his mouth from hers, lowering his head to the pulse in her throat, pressing a hot kiss there as if it could assuage the torment he had conjured inside of her.

His fingers drifted up her inner thigh, his touch so light she wondered if she dreamed it, but she couldn't have dreamed it. Not the way her body sang for him, danced for him, moved for him. Only him.

Finally he touched her in that place where she ached, and she couldn't stop the moan that erupted from her throat, couldn't stifle it with his kiss. She let it come, her hands curling in his hair as he pushed the other shoulder of her gown down, loosening her bodice, exposing her to him and his greedy mouth. She ached everywhere and all at once, and she wanted him to touch her again, there, but his hand retreated, teasing, coaxing.

"Gabriel, please," she whispered, suddenly afraid he would know just how much she wanted him, just how much she wanted him to give her pleasure.

He touched her again, and again, his fingers escaped, her body reaching for him, her hips coming up to chase after the desire he could cull forth with just the brush of his fingers against her.

But even as his fingers teased her, his mouth tormented her. Her chemise proved no barrier, and with her bodice loosened, he pushed it down, releasing one breast and then the other. She thought she'd feel shame, embarrassed, shy, but she felt none of those things. She felt wild and freed, and she—

"Gabriel," she pleaded. "I want you to…I want you to…"

His head lifted, and his quiet gaze was on her, studying her, watching her, sending that hum of electricity through her.

"Gabriel, I want you to touch my breasts," she said before she could lose her nerve. They felt heavy and full, and she knew the only thing that would make it better was him. His hand cupping her, lifting her, stroking her. Kissing her.

"Like this?" He took his hand out from beneath her skirts, and she whimpered at its loss, but with a single finger he touched one taut nipple, and pleasure shot through her.

"Gabriel." It was the only word left to her as her eyes closed against the pleasure that tore through her.

"Or like this."

Her eyes flew open as his hand disappeared, and his mouth—that beautiful, hot mouth—descended on her, sucked her nipple, licked her, the roughness of his tongue branding her skin with sultry fire.

The pleasure was too much, the ache at her very center too great, but he seemed to know that. Perhaps because he had done it on purpose, driving her desire higher and higher until he knew just when she was about to break because that was when his devilish fingers found her again, stroking her sensitive nub. His fingers moved easily against her and in her as she was so very wet for him. He'd done this to her. He'd made her body do these things.

But then he pressed his lips to her ear and whispered, "Take your pleasure."

That was when she shattered, the very moment she realized in giving her body to him, she'd given herself freedom.

# CHAPTER 8

"An expression as foul as the one you're wearing can only have been caused by a woman."

Gabriel looked up from where he had been contemplating his empty glass and why there wasn't more alcohol in it when Liam's voice pulled him from his thoughts. Thoughts filled with the sounds Annie made when he'd driven her to pleasure, the way her body seemed to fit so perfectly against his, the way her laugh always seemed to surprise her.

Not wishing to analyze any of the emotions he had been wading through in the three days since he had sneaked Annie out of his townhouse, he simply stated, "We're friends," adding, "We shook on it," when Liam and Tuck did little more than stare at him.

He and Annie had done far more than that, but neither of these gentlemen needed to know. Gabriel wasn't even sure he believed it had happened. He had sworn to protect her from men who would take advantage of her, and what had he done?

Given her pleasure just as she'd asked.

He swallowed, something too warm and enjoyable spreading through him at the memory.

"You…what?" Liam asked, but Gabriel knew better now than to answer. "Did you hear nothing I said? I was very specific about not engaging with Lady Wexford. Did you not understand? I thought my instructions were clear. You were to avoid her at all costs."

"She snuck into my house. The library to be exact. I cannot be held responsible."

Liam did not speak at all, and Tuck was looking anywhere but at Gabriel.

They stood in a corner of the Tyntsfields' drawing room, trying desperately not to hear the musicale going on at the other end of the connected rooms. Gabriel knew the Marquess and Marchioness of Tyntsfield had numerous daughters to marry off, but subjecting members of the *ton* to such torture seemed an odd way to go about it.

"I don't know what I should even say, Grimsby." Liam shook his head. "And I always know what to say."

Gabriel shrugged. "I suppose I'm an utter failure at convincing a woman she's in love with me."

Liam's gaze narrowed. "Did you try kissing her again?" He shook his head once more. "No, don't tell me. You'll probably tell me that instead of kissing her you introduced her to the finer points of tapestry weaving."

"It was the migratory patterns of the short-eared owl actually," Gabriel murmured, hoping the truth didn't show on his face.

He'd done a lot more than kissed her. He'd tasted her. Hell, he'd *supped*.

"Heavens above, someone save me," Liam practically gasped in mock horror as Tuck tried to stop a laugh.

The other man sobered enough to say, "Did you really do that?"

Gabriel nodded. "I did. I have an excellent collection of books on migratory bird practices."

Tuck crossed his arms. "You don't say. You wouldn't happen to have anything on migration routes to Svalbard?"

"I'll look into it," Gabriel said, and Tuck nodded, pleased.

Liam held up a hand. "I will not stand here and listen to another word about migratory bird routes." He faced Gabriel squarely. "What is your next step? Surely you must have thought of a way to repair the damage you have wrought."

Gabriel swallowed, finding it suddenly difficult to speak. "Well, that's not quite all of it."

Liam signaled a passing footman and plucked a flute of champagne from the man's tray. After downing nearly half the glass in a single swallow, he said, "All right. Proceed. I'm ready now."

"We fell asleep." He stopped there. Ardley and Tuck didn't need to know the rest, but Gabriel was pitifully out of his depth here and needed help.

It was at that moment that the music stopped, and a sad applause started at just the right moment to drown Liam's strangled bark of surprise.

"Saints above, I cannot do this." He made to push past Tuck and out of their little corner, but his cousin shoved him back.

"You can't abandon him now. He clearly needs you," Tuck asserted.

But Liam shook his head. "There's no helping this man, and I shall not have my good name impugned."

"Just listen to him." Tuck held up his hands in a gesture of trust, and Liam stopped his attempt at escape.

He turned back to Gabriel. "Out with it."

Gabriel waited, but surprisingly Liam said nothing more.

"We were going through the books on migratory bird

practices, it was raining, we'd had a couple of glasses of whiskey, and..." He let his voice trail off.

To be honest, he couldn't recall how that part had happened. The rest of it would be branded on his mind until the end of days.

They'd collected the books on migratory bird practices and spread them out on a table by the sofa. He read aloud from one while Annie perused the rest of the stack, flipping idly through the pages. It was difficult to concentrate, he remembered that much. Watching her in the lamplight, her face relaxed, the lulling melody of the rain cocooning them.

He had been telling the truth about the whiskey. After she had discovered she enjoyed the stuff, she'd asked for another glass after studying the table of contents on a particularly thick volume detailing the habits of the male short-eared owl and had drunk down nearly all of it.

He remembered laughter too. So much of it as he read aloud the dullest text he'd ever encountered on how the shape of the owl's wing was critical to its ability to travel long distances. The author had taken four pages to state a fact that was terribly obvious, and this had made Annie laugh as he had turned page after page.

He'd never had such a wonderful afternoon in his life.

How they had come to fall asleep together on the sofa was beyond him, but he supposed it was inevitable.

It was probably because Annie had removed her shoes. Again.

He wondered if that was a ubiquitous habit of hers or something she only did in libraries. It didn't matter really. Her shoes had come off, and she'd drawn her legs up onto the sofa, curling into the corner opposite him, arms wrapped around her bent legs as she listened to him. Her hair had loosened, and tendrils of her dark tresses framed her face.

He'd never seen her look more beautiful than she had that afternoon, and he hated himself for thinking it.

She was a widow, vulnerable and unschooled in the more sensual endeavors available to a widow, and she should not have been sitting on his sofa like that, and they damn sure shouldn't have fallen asleep.

Not that the migratory patterns of the short-eared owl were stimulating reading material, and the rain had been soothing, and the whiskey…

He could keep enumerating the excuses, but he couldn't deny what had happened after they had fallen asleep.

She'd ended up in his arms. This he rather remembered. Her head had slumped against the cushions awkwardly, and he had reached to straighten her only…well, she'd simply come into his arms.

What was he to have done about that? She was asleep or at least asleep enough to have responded only instinctually, her arms reaching for him as he'd tried to adjust her against the pillows, and then quite simply she was holding him, her head on his chest, and he'd felt like the luckiest man in the world.

It was his turn to signal a passing footman and pluck a flute of champagne from the tray, swapping it for his own empty glass, but emotions, all of them, rammed in his throat and he thought if he took a sip he would drown.

He had no business naming what he felt. He had no business even feeling it.

He was no better than Belvedere.

He banished the thought as soon as it came. He was *not* Belvedere. He simply wasn't.

"I probably would have fallen asleep as well," Liam said. "Don't take it personally, old chap."

"I would hardly have fallen asleep," Tuck interjected. "The

idea that such a small creature could traverse such extensive landscapes and survive year after year only demonstrates the incredible tenacity of the natural world." He pushed his hair out of his face only for it to flop forward again. "Utterly fascinating."

Liam only stared at his cousin for a moment before turning back to Gabriel. "How did you leave it then? I assume some sort of maneuvers were attempted to remove the woman from your home without damaging her reputation." He gave Gabriel the once over. "Or yours for that matter. I've heard nary a whiff of scandal, but such behavior does put your reputation in Parliament at risk, I should think."

Gabriel sipped his champagne instead of answering. Maneuvers was an interesting word. There had been plenty of those. When he'd gotten her gown set to rights, it was still raining, and it had aided in camouflaging her escape. He'd ordered his butler to hail a hackney and had it brought around to the back entrance where he'd snuck her into the conveyance under her cloak. It had all been terribly easy, but Liam was right. He'd risked both of their reputations that day.

And he didn't care a single bit.

"I'm not sure I can help you anymore, Grimsby," Liam said now. "I've never befriended a woman in my life."

This tugged Gabriel from his thoughts. "Never?"

Suddenly Gabriel recalled what Annie had said about the duke's reputation.

Liam looked as if he'd eaten something sour. "Heavens, no. The creatures are highly intelligent, strong willed, and elusive. Why ever would I get myself so entangled?"

Gabriel considered this. "You hold a lot of respect for women, and yet you have a system devoid of emotions for dealing with them."

Liam met his gaze directly. "Of course. How else do you expect me to survive?"

Gabriel looked to Tuck, but Tuck only shrugged.

"One day you're going to fall in love, Ardley, and I only hope I'm there to witness it," Gabriel said.

Liam laughed, throwing his head back as the humor gripped him. "If I fall in love, I will be sure to save you a seat in the front row, Grimsby." He slapped Gabriel on the back then, rocking him forward on his feet. "Now then, what are we going to do about your…friend?" The word stumbled out as though Liam found it difficult to say it.

Gabriel discarded his champagne flute on the tray of a passing footman. "I'm not sure there is anything to be done. She discovered my true motivation for asking her to marry me, and we came to an agreement."

Liam's lips parted, and his eyes widened, and Gabriel felt everything he had been fighting to keep together slip out from his grasp. His mother and Belvedere, Annie, it all had moved beyond his control somehow, and he knew if he tried to wrest it back it would only be a waste of energy. He had made a deal with Annie, and he would respect it.

"An agreement?" This Liam said as if it were worse than *friend*. "What sort of an agreement?"

Gabriel shrugged. "Just as I've told you. We're to be friends and nothing more. But she did agree to allow me to help her should she ever find herself in a vulnerable position."

He wondered if that were still true. Things had changed between them physically, but did that change how she felt about her widowhood? Was he even thinking of it? It wasn't as if he *wanted* to marry. Did he?

"Vulnerable position?" Tuck asked. "Do you truly think someone will try to take advantage of her?"

Liam spoke before Gabriel could. "Ah, my cousin the

scientist. He always has his nose in a book instead of sniffing out the fairer sex as he should be." Now he slapped Tuck on the back. "Of course widows are vulnerable," he said, and then paused as if thinking of something. "Say, we should get you a widow. It would help work out the frustrations you're having with finding a benefactor."

If the light had been better, Gabriel would have said Tuck turned a violent shade of pink at his cousin's pronouncement, but the man looked away, pulling at his cravat, and said something that was only garbled as he continued to tug at his collar. Liam laughed and turned back to Gabriel.

"The poor boy has never been good with women. He'll die a monk, I swear."

Tuck turned back at this. "I'm no monk, cousin. Of that I can assure you."

Liam raised an eyebrow. "Is that so? I wouldn't have guessed it."

"I take it things with Renshaw didn't go well the other day," Gabriel said, hoping to deflect Liam's interest in Tuck's romantic affairs.

Gabriel expected to hear a recitation similar to the ones he'd heard before from the young man, but instead, Tuck's expression turned quizzical. "Not at all," he said. "In fact, it went better than I'd ever anticipated. I'm going for a walk with the man tomorrow. He wishes to show me the Serpentine."

Gabriel nodded, feeling not a small measure of pride. "I'm glad to hear it."

"Say, old chap," Liam interrupted. "Is that the Wexford widow going into the garden?"

Gabriel turned in time to see a woman slip through the open terrace doors opposite them. He only caught the back of her, but he'd recognize that dark hair anywhere.

"It is," he said, straightening his jacket. "I wonder where she's going."

Liam turned in the direction of the impromptu stage, and Gabriel followed his gaze to find the musicians had broken for an intermission.

"I suppose now would be a good time to practice being the lady's friend, don't you think, cousin?" Liam looked to Tuck.

Tuck raised both eyebrows. "I should think so. You could ask her if she has any more thoughts on the short-eared owl. I, for one, should like to—" His gaze traveled somewhere over Gabriel's shoulder and again, Gabriel was fairly certain the man turned pink. "Would you please excuse me?"

He was gone before they could say anything further. Gabriel looked to Liam, but Liam was already turning away.

"I see a gaggle of debutantes I haven't winked at this evening. If you'll excuse me, Grimsby," he said and left Gabriel alone in the middle of the room.

Perhaps they were right. He headed in the direction of the terrace doors, but he resolved not to ask Annie about short-eared owls or any other migratory bird for that matter.

* * *

Out of all the social events her mother was forcing her to attend, Annie enjoyed musicales the least.

It wasn't that the performances were awful, even though they often were. It was reminder of what she herself had endured when she'd first debuted. Every time she saw a poor debutante, fresh out of the schoolroom, likely no more than ten and seven, she remembered what it had felt like to be on a stage, vying for the attention of a man, pinning all of one's hope on securing an advantageous match.

She'd caught Roger's eye almost at once.

She swallowed and pushed the memory away and hoped these poor girls—for they *were* only girls—had a better outcome than she'd had.

It was too hot for the gown she was wearing, a heavy damask with long sleeves and a collar that ran tightly up the length of her throat, and at the first intermission, she excused herself for the beckoning call of the gardens and the relief she might find there.

The Tyntsfield townhouse—the Marchioness of Tyntsfield had four daughters all out that season, poor woman, and all were tone deaf it seemed—was one of the newer homes in Mayfair with a shared courtyard like the Stoke Bruerne house. The hour was late, the moon already high in the sky, and she used its light to find her way to a more secluded spot between two yew hedges. Carefully she slipped the two topmost buttons of her gown free. The sudden night breeze against her neck might as well have been an Arctic blast for how comforting it was. She even gave in to an indulgent sigh.

Momentarily she thought of the red gown with its off the shoulder neckline and billowing sleeves and yearned for just a moment to be in it instead of her half mourning gown of modest tailoring, which only meant the wearer might suffocate in it. The Summer Solstice Ball drew nearer, and for the first time, she could picture herself wearing that gown. She could also picture Gabriel taking it off of her.

She nearly choked at just the thought. She couldn't wear that gown. She knew that, and yet the thought was not as persistent as it had been the first time she'd seen it, and for a moment, she let herself indulge in the idea of it. Of Lady Anna Bounds wearing a sinfully red gown.

Of watching Gabriel's eyes grow dark at the sight of her.

She touched her body, her hands pressing flat against her stomach as memory assaulted her. Gabriel had given her pleasure, yes, but he'd done more than that. He'd shown her a passion that was already inside of her, lighting the path to her own sensuality. Her body vibrated with possibility now, the numbness of her mourning seemingly forgotten.

And she wanted more. More of Gabriel, more pleasure, more life.

The breeze shifted and on it came a whiff of gardenia and lilac. She didn't know how much time had passed, but it was enough. She made to do up the buttons at her throat so she could return to the drawing room where the guests had assembled but heard a noise at her back.

Swinging about, she remembered to drop her hands from her throat at the last moment. The two buttons felt like a target, and she wondered if whoever was coming would see them, witness her indecency, and louder than ever Roger's voice was in her head, calling her those names, those words she'd never heard uttered before her marriage. She shook her head, physically hoping to dislodge his voice. It was dark, and she was in shadow. No one would see her gown, not in such detail.

The sound grew clearer, and she realized they were footsteps, a heavy tread with a slight hitch on one side as if the person were promenading rather than simply strolling. Annie held her breath, which was ridiculous, but she couldn't seem to unfreeze.

And then he was there.

It wasn't until the man had stepped free of the hedgerow that she realized she'd been expecting Gabriel. But the man before her was not the Duke of Grimsby, and for the first time since hearing the noise, Annie was afraid.

"Lady Wexford," Miles Davidson, Viscount Overby cooed, his voice dangerously low.

Annie took a step back, which was the worst thing she could have done because it only pulled her deeper into shadow. If anyone passed by, they would think she had been waiting there for Overby.

"Viscount," she murmured now. Was that even her voice? Why was it so weak?

Overby was slightly younger than her father, somewhere in the middling years where some men took on a doughiness. Overby could have opened a bakery. His stomach strained against his waistcoat while his trousers had given up, slouching down until several inches of his shirt showed between waistcoat and waistband. The rolls of his neck fell over his crumpled collar, and his cheeks shook slightly with his lecherous smile.

"Would you like some company?" His eyes moved up and down her person as though she were horseflesh, and he was deciding whether or not to add her to his stable. "A lady like you shouldn't be..." His eyes met hers. "Alone," he said, licking his lower lip with his sloppy tongue.

Her stomach churned, and her hands shook, but somewhere deep inside her, she heard a voice telling her to run. Except she couldn't move. She was still frozen. She couldn't even make her voice work. She could scream for help. She could simply walk away. Overby wasn't even that close to her. Escape seemed so easy and yet so impossible.

Gabriel had been right. Gabriel had been trying to protect her.

*You deserve this, whore.*

She was too late. Overby came toward her now, one lugubrious step at a time. She watched his feet move over the flagstones of the garden path, her heart thumping dangerously at each one.

"You don't know what kind of creatures are lurking out here in the dark, Lady Wexford." He was close enough now that she could smell the tang of alcohol on his breath, the sickening scent of cologne, far too much of it really as if

Overby hadn't bathed in some time and was using the scent to mask his odor. It didn't work. The aroma of stale sweat and tobacco smoke lingered around him like an aura, and Annie thought she would truly be sick.

She needed to move. She needed to get out of there. She needed to scream. For Gabriel. She needed Gabriel.

*You're no better than a dollymop.*

No.

No.

No.

She was not a dollymop.

She moved, sidestepping the viscount until her back was to the path back to the house and the viscount was effectively pinned in the copse of yew hedges.

"You're entirely correct, Viscount. One can never trust the creatures one encounters in the dark." Her voice was steadier now, but her heart still pounded. "Good evening, Viscount." She gave a nod of her head in farewell and turned toward the house, but Overby's words stopped her.

"Roger was right about you." The words were spoken with a phlegmy snarl, but she heard every one of them like a trumpet blast in her ear.

"I'm sorry?" She shouldn't have spoken. She shouldn't have responded. She should have just fled.

But...Roger? What was Overby talking about? Roger had spoken about her? To this man? To whom else?

Overby wiped a hand over his mouth, the gesture making a revoltingly wet sound. "Roger always said you were a cock-teaser. That's why he had to keep his thumb on you. If you had just been a good wife, he wouldn't have had to do that, now would he?"

She couldn't think. Overby's words seared her mind, rendering her dumb and frozen once more. Had Roger truly said such things to the viscount? Annie swallowed, bile burning her throat. She knew her husband, and because of that, no doubt lingered as to whether or not Overby was telling the truth.

She really was going to be sick. She could feel what little she'd eaten at dinner coming up. The tremor in her hands had spread to her arms. She had to move, but her feet wouldn't respond.

The next she became aware Overby had shifted, stepping closer to her once more until the scent of stale sweat and filth overwhelmed her.

"If you had been my wife, I would have taught you to behave." Overby's voice was nearly a whisper now, and he was so close she could feel his breath against her cheek. He did something then, his eyes dropping as he moved, and suddenly he was pressed against her, all of him, his protruding belly, his beefy hands, his—

He shifted again, and this time he made a noise of wet pleasure as he pressed his erection into her unmoving hand. "There's a good girl," he whispered. "Now how's about I pick up where ol' Roger left off? I'll teach you how to do a man right."

That was when she slapped him.

Her hand shot out as if it were controlled by someone else, her palm making contact with the puffy cheek of the viscount with a resounding smack. Someone screamed—it was probably her—and the viscount fell backward, the surprise of being slapped and his likely drunken state finding him upended in the yew hedge.

There was noise then, a lot of it. Footsteps. Running footsteps. The crack of glass and something metal—maybe a serving tray—the echoing ring of it against stone. Something crashing through the hedges.

And then people were there. The guests from Tyntsfield's musicale, all of them, too many of them. How could all of these people be standing there, in the garden, all at once? She studied them, the gentlemen, holding back their wives, daughters, sisters. Keeping them safe or preventing them from gawking? Some held flutes of champagne as though they had thought the musicale had moved outside while others appeared in a state of dishabille, shawls clinging to one shoulder, hats gone askew as their wearers had stampeded to the garden to see what the commotion was all about.

For an instant, she thought it funny, the spectacle before her, until she realized why they were there.

While she studied them, they were *staring* at her. At the spectacle she had made by slapping Overby.

Two footmen had plunged into the yew hedge in an attempt to rescue Overby. Only his pudgy legs were visible as he pedaled them in the air in an obvious attempt to extract himself. He was saying something, yelling something really, but his words were garbled by the hedges and the instructions the footmen were trying to give him so they could free him.

She didn't comprehend any of it. Her eyes had found the palm that had struck Overby, and she stared at it as though it were no longer connected to her body.

She'd never hit a person before.

All the times Roger had tortured her with those horrible words, she had dreamed of what she would do to him if given the chance. But she'd never done anything because at the heart of it, Roger was right. As his wife, she was his property, and he could do anything he pleased to her.

So she'd never fought back. She'd never even tried.

But Overby wasn't her husband, and she was not his property, and the vile beast deserved what he'd gotten. She dropped her hand finally, taking in the sight of the viscount emerging from the hedge, a yew branch stuck in his hair, his jacket torn across one shoulder, and his collar come loose so that it stuck him in his meaty jowl.

For one precious moment, euphoria filled her veins, and triumph swept through her in waves. And then she remembered the gathered guests, all come to gawk at her...at her...

Downfall.

Reality crashed into her like a runaway locomotive. She had assaulted a peer, a man whose word reigned above hers. He could say anything as no one had been there to witness the truth of it. Overby could claim she had slapped him when he had refused her advances. He could twist the truth around and lay the blame at her feet. Just as Roger had always done.

The injustice of it suffocated her, and she opened her mouth, ready to declare her innocence when a warm hand touched her shoulder, and she was being moved, drawn against a comforting chest, a solid arm wrapping about her.

At first, her brain somehow connected the arm with her father, but her father had never been demonstrative in his affection, and he most certainly would not have behaved so in front of the crowd that surrounded her.

But once again, reality intruded, and she realized who it was that held her.

Gabriel.

Where had he come from? What was he doing? Why was he holding her like this? It was improper. People would talk.

Oh heavens, people would already talk. She was *ruined*. Worse, Eloise was ruined too just by being her sister, and this finally broke Annie. She crumpled against Gabriel, his arm the only thing holding her up.

Overby's voice broke through her stampeding thoughts. "You wretched girl! How dare you treat me with such disrespect?"

She didn't move under Gabriel's arm, only her eyes turned to the viscount to find the footmen attempting to pull yew twigs from his jacket. He gave them no heed and somehow managed to flop backward. He sat on the flagstone path, his trousers having fallen to his thighs, and his waistcoat popped free of its buttons.

"To think I tried to act the gentleman when you—"

"I'd watch my words carefully if I were you, Overby," Gabriel said, his deep voice vibrating against her back. "You are speaking about my betrothed."

Resistance surged through her like a drowning person scrambling for the surface.

*Betrothed.*

No. She had said no. She had refused Gabriel's offer. What was he saying? She was not his betrothed. They were friends. Friends. She'd never had a friend. What was he saying?

But Overby had gone quiet at Gabriel's words, and the tension emanating from the crowd turned from her to the viscount slumped on the ground.

*Betrothed.*

So small of a word and yet it meant everything. Because Annie knew what Gabriel had done. He'd saved her. He'd claimed her as his, and as a future duchess, she was nearly untouchable. But the truth of it was far worse than that.

By saving her, he had also condemned her.

# CHAPTER 9

$\mathcal{W}$ith the help of Gabriel's connections, they were married quickly and quietly by special license.

Annie's mother had wished for an elaborate ceremony, but Annie had been able to dissuade her, knowing her mother's intent was only to find an excuse to rub the fact that her daughter had snared one of the dukes in the face of her arch nemesis, Rosemary Hayes-Martin, Viscountess Bowes. Explaining that she'd already had a grand wedding ceremony, Annie had been able to deflect attention once more to Eloise, who had yet to experience such pageantry and wouldn't her marriage to the Duke of Ardley be quite a spectacle. It was like passing a dish of cream under a cat's nose.

Her mother's attention deflected, Annie and Gabriel were wed in the drawing room of Stoke Bruerne House. There was no wedding breakfast. Annie did not even procure a new gown for the affair, preferring it all be done with efficiency if only to salvage what remained of her nerves.

She was married.

Again.

The one thing she swore never to do. Her widowhood had been so precious, and it seemed, fleeting. It grated on her. All she had done was go into the gardens to get a bit of fresh air. Something so innocent, so normal. And yet her life had been ruined because of another's actions. It was unfair, cruel, and for the first time in her life, she wished to cause another physical pain.

Overby had taken away her freedom.

No, Overby had only been the messenger. Roger had planted the seed long ago to cause her downfall. Overby's words still echoed in her mind, the things Roger supposedly told him.

Was it true? Had Roger smeared her name? Had Roger convinced others she could be treated so vilely?

It simply wasn't fair.

Until Gabriel had put his arm around her and made his pronouncement, the gathered guests had lain the blame for the affair squarely at her feet. Annie knew that. It had been in the way their gazes had zeroed in on her, the way their bodies had crowded round, ready to pass judgment.

But that hadn't been the worst of it. The worst of it had been the loss of her friendship with Gabriel. For now she was his wife. His *wife*. Was it only a fortnight ago that she'd spent the best afternoon of her life in his library? She'd never laughed so much, been so at ease, felt so much…hope.

So much…pleasure.

She closed her eyes against the memory, unable to bear it any longer. She no longer knew if they were friends at all or what their marriage might be like. Would he even want her now that he'd been forced to marry her?

There hadn't been time to talk to him. There hadn't been time for anything. The past week had been a series of closed doors, hushed meetings, and talk of contracts. There hadn't even been time to write Gwen, to tell her what had happened, not that there would be time for her to make it to the wedding ceremony, coming all the way from Yorkshire. But suddenly Annie wished her big sister were there.

Once more she had packed her trunks and left the sanctuary that was her childhood home. Her mother had been tearfully delighted, waving a handkerchief as Gabriel escorted Annie to his waiting carriage as if her mother were treading the boards in some melodrama. Father had hardly noticed, his nose already back into his papers as he turned in the direction of the library. Grandmother Bitsy clutched Eloise's hand and murmured something about how it was nice to see Annie had finally accepted Gabriel's proposal.

This had caught Annie's attention, but they had already reached the carriage, and there was no time to question her grandmother. She had wanted to ask Gabriel about it, but the carriage ride to Grimsby House was much like the rest of their hurried conversations over the past week. Annie was to meet the servants upon their arrival, tour the house—she'd only seen the library after all—and get settled while Gabriel had an afternoon meeting about his drains bill.

It had all happened so fast. One minute a widow, the next a wife.

Mrs. Featherstone, the housekeeper, was indeed the diminutive woman with the sharp features who had met Annie at the kitchen door that long ago rainy afternoon. Seeing the woman now as her mistress instead of the crazed woman banging on a duke's door in the middle of a storm was awkward to say the least. But Mrs. Featherstone was clearly a good housekeeper as she did nothing but curtsy in greeting and offer to show Annie the silver.

She wondered at it now, how swiftly her life always

seemed to change, as she listened to the first silence she'd heard in days as she lay huddled under the covers of the Duchess of Grimsby's bed.

For that was what she was indeed doing.

Hiding.

Under the covers.

Like a child.

Only she wasn't a child. She was a bride, and this was her wedding night, and she knew what would happen.

And she *wanted* it.

Roger had only frequented her bed a handful of times in their marriage. He had repeatedly accused her of disgusting him, and she thought this had likely saved her from the agony of having him touch her, violate her.

But now as she lay there, the new Duchess of Grimsby, she was hiding from her own feelings.

She wanted Gabriel to touch her again, like he had that afternoon in the library, and yet she felt shame for wanting him. He'd already married her. She knew the true intentions of his proposal, and she felt she'd trapped him now in a decision he had never wished to make, and even after all of that, she craved his body.

Somewhere in the mix of her emotions she remembered he'd never answered her that day when she'd asked him why he hadn't married. Things had gone awry, and the question was left unanswered. It made sense she would only think of it now that she was married to him, and she couldn't help but wonder if it had something to do with his mother and that Belvedere man.

Was there something in his past that had prevented him from marrying? Had she driven him to a life he didn't wish to lead? Suddenly huddled under the covers, she felt very close to her husband in more than the physical sense.

She had wanted more than anything to be friends with the man, and she was heartbroken to think it may no longer be possible. Now that she was his wife there were certain things she would need to do and say, ways she was supposed to act. The very idea that she could be his friend was absurd. Duchesses were not friends with their husbands. That wonderful afternoon they had spent together would never happen again, and she thought she might cry for its loss.

The duchess's room in Grimsby House was comfortable and tastefully decorated. She wasn't sure why she had been dreading it, settling into her new home, but she found the furnishings of good quality, the decor subdued and welcoming. It almost felt…peaceful.

She shoved the covers away, her thoughts so tangled she pressed her palms to her forehead as if the pressure itself could stop the rambling, waffling between wishing to be friends with her husband to wanting to spend hours in this very bed with as few pieces of clothing between them as possible to wondering how their marriage would be as they were both coming to it with reservations. If only she could talk to Gabriel.

As if summoned by her thoughts, a knock broke the silence at exactly that moment. Instinctively she pulled the covers over her head. She lay cocooned in the dark, her eyes squeezed shut before she realized how ridiculous she was being. She threw back the covers and sat up.

"Come in," she called before she could think better of it.

He entered, and it wasn't until he stood inside her room that she realized she was bracing herself. She felt the tension coiled along her shoulders, the stiffness in her neck as she sat poised against the headboard of the bed. It all became startlingly clear when Gabriel entered because her husband was still fully dressed.

She felt the first stirring of apprehension. Quickly she

sorted through her memories, recalling her first wedding night. Roger had come to her in his dressing gown, and he'd worn nothing underneath, prepared to consummate the marriage.

But Gabriel still wore his boots and even his jacket. She clutched at the covers again, pulling them only up to her chest this time.

"Gabriel." His name was both question and greeting, but she realized too late he wasn't looking at her.

He was eyeing the furniture spread about the foot of the bed, and before she knew what he was about, he'd bent over and begun to push her unpacked trunks into a neat pile in the corner.

She was out of bed before she realized all she wore was her nightrail, but her husband's behavior was too odd to ignore.

"Gabriel, my maid didn't have time to finish unpacking me. She was..." But she realized her words didn't matter because now her husband had moved on to the chairs before the dormant fireplace.

He was all but refitting the room as if she weren't standing there nearly naked on their wedding night.

When he had all but cleared the carpet that lay in the center of the room, he straightened, tugging at the cuffs of his shirt as he surveyed his work.

"That should do," he said and then began to remove his coat.

She backed toward the bed, her feet moving involuntarily.

Did he wish to do the act...on the floor?

"Gabriel." Once again his name was a question, but again he ignored her as he placed his jacket over one of the chairs he had pushed to the side and began to roll up his shirtsleeves.

The alarm which had begun to simmer inside her bones

at her husband's entrance reached a near boil now, and suddenly the mattress struck the backs of her thighs, and she couldn't retreat any farther. If she'd had presence of mind, she would have snatched up her dressing gown as added defense.

But she wasn't thinking because now her husband had removed his cravat and undone his collar, and standing there, halfway dressed in the candlelight, he was the most magnificent thing she'd ever seen.

His forearms were sinewy with muscle, and she was mesmerized by them. She hadn't been given such luxury that afternoon in his library, the luxury to gaze upon him. Their library now, she supposed, and she indulged, her eyes roaming over his body as if he were a work of art meant only for her pleasure.

Her husband was beautiful.

Just as the thought settled into her stomach, he turned toward her and formed a fist with each hand.

Fear overrode every emotion, and she scrambled up on the bed behind her, heedless of how it might look, of the show she was giving him as her nightrail rode up, baring her to him. None of it mattered. The instinct to flee was too great, and she pawed her way across the slippery bedclothes, falling to her elbows time and again, and time and again, getting back up to get farther away from him.

Her husband.

Her owner.

The man who could hurt her—

"Annie, stop." His voice was low and calm and cut through the tumult that was her mind more readily than a shout ever could.

He hadn't come after her.

He stood at the foot of the bed, in the clearing he'd made on the carpet, his hands hanging at his sides in loose fists.

"Annie." He said her name again, his voice still even and unhurried. "I'm not going to hurt you. You know that."

She did know that, but how did he know she knew? Again that strange tingling erupted inside of her, and it was as though she could see an invisible connection between them, something unworldly that connected the two of them, something she'd never had with anyone else, and again, she regretted the loss of the friend she had hoped to have in him.

"Then...why?" she asked, unable to articulate the questions rampaging through her mind.

But he understood her. Of course he did, and he said the very last thing she expected.

"I'm going to teach you how to throw a punch."

* * *

He hated how she retreated from him, scrambling across the bed as though any escape was good enough even though the very walls of the room kept her contained.

He was, however, still a man, and as her nightrail rode higher and higher up her legs in her retreat, he'd been forced to look elsewhere. The glimpse of her unshod feet had nearly undone him, and the expanse of bare leg that had been afforded him was too much even for his steely control. The pattern of the carpet had become terribly interesting just then.

He would not make a repeat of his transgression. He had to protect her, and that was why he was here.

When there was no length of bed left for her retreat, he'd finally gained her attention, assuring her he had no plans to ravage her. Although the sight of her nestled amongst the pillows, her thick, dark hair in a loose braid over one shoulder beckoned him.

He frowned. Deeply.

He had to be stronger. No matter how she begged—God, how she mewled—for him to take her, he couldn't. He had to protect her.

When he'd found her that night in the Tyntsfield garden, everything had seemed so easy. He had wanted to put his fist directly into Overby's face and put the guests on the first ship bound for the Arctic. Those emotions had been too much, and he'd done what was sensible instead.

He'd stated his intention to marry her.

And now here he was. He'd done what had seemed right, and it had made everything more difficult. How was he going to keep from touching her again now that he had *married* her?

"I'm going to teach you how to fight back in the event there's ever another Overby in your life. As your husband, I will do everything I can to protect you, but I know there will be times when I cannot be there, and it will ease my mind to know you have something on which to rely for defense." He pointed to the carpet at his feet. "Come here and assume a fighting stance."

She only blinked, her beautiful brown eyes wide with…it wasn't fear. The fear had abated the moment he had stated his objective. No, this was something different. Puzzlement? Concern? Or was it…curiosity?

"Annie." He spoke her name as if it could release her from whatever had mesmerized her, and it worked as she relinquished her grip on the bedclothes and slipped off the mattress to patter across the floor to him.

Heavens above, he could see her ankles. He swallowed and snapped his gaze to her face.

"I slapped him." She nearly whispered it as she reached the end of the bed, her feet stilling on the carpet.

"I thought as much," he said, a smile lifting one side of his mouth. "I wondered how he ended up in that hedge."

The past fortnight had been filled with negotiations and meetings with officials to obtain the special license when all he had wanted to do was talk to Annie, to find out what had happened that night in the garden, to discover if she was all right. But there hadn't been time for it. He'd never accomplished something so quickly in all his life, and still it had taken too long and had demanded his time and attention when he had wanted to give it to someone else entirely.

"Gabriel, he tried to…he tried to…" Her words seemed to cram up, repeating them over and over as if eventually they would come free.

"I know, Annie," he said. "I know what men like Overby want." Something passed over her face then, and he wondered if there was something else she wished to tell him, but then her expression cleared, and she stepped around the bed to stand in front of him.

"Right," he said. "Stand here." He pointed to the spot directly in front of him. "Which is your dominant hand?"

She blinked, those huge eyes boring into him. "Dominant hand?"

He held up his right hand. "Dominant hand. The one you write with. Which is it?"

She mimicked him, holding up her own right hand. "This one." Her voice was hardly more than a whisper, but he pressed on.

"I'm going to put you into position," he said and reached forward to grasp her shoulders, pulling her left one forward. "Move your left foot in front of the right and soften your knees until you are stable."

She was pliant under his touch, allowing him to move her into position, and he was bolstered by the change in her, thinking maybe she had come back from wherever she had disappeared in her head. When she had her left foot braced in front of the right, he let go of her.

"Now, you make a fist like this." He showed her his own fist with the thumb over his curled fingers.

She curled her fingers without a word, tucking her thumb inside. He reached slowly forward so she could see his every move and gently pulled her thumb from the nest of her fingers, placing it carefully along the folded digits.

"Like this," he said. "So you don't break your fingers."

Her brow furrowed at this. "Will I be in danger of breaking my fingers? I shouldn't think I'm quite that strong."

She was teasing, he realized, and something inside of him shifted, like a stuck window finally coming free to let in the fresh air.

"I would never dare to underestimate you, Your Grace." A smile tugged at his lips. He was enjoying this far more than he thought he would.

When he had found her that night in the garden, pure terror had coursed through him at the sight of Overby struggling in the hedge, Annie backing slowly away. Having only just learned the truth of her marriage, his usual protective instinct when it came to the widow had been on high alert, and he knew at once that he would need to teach her to defend herself.

He just hadn't realized he would enjoy it quite so much.

He let go of her hand and backed away. "Now punch me."

She dropped her hand immediately. "I will not."

There was that smile pulling at his lips again. "Not to inflict pain. That will come later. Right now I want to make sure you have the proper mechanics of the thing." He stepped forward again, indicating he would place her back into position.

If this had been an average wedding night, they would be assuming entirely different positions. As soon as the thought entered his mind, he hated himself for it. He was nearly twenty years her senior. While other gentlemen of the *ton* had no qualms about wives excessively younger than themselves, Gabriel couldn't help but feel like the wolf and Annie the prey. He mustn't harbor such carnal thoughts about her. He'd already trespassed too much, allowing himself liberties with her body because she'd asked. God, she'd *asked* him to pleasure her. He had to stop thinking about it, or he was going to get hard from the sheer memory of it.

But distracting himself proved to be difficult, seeing her like that in only her nightrail, the thin material draped over her body. He knew she wore no corset, and for the first time, he was seeing every true, soft curve of her. He forced himself to focus on moving her elbow.

"You want your forearm and elbow aligned like this, so you don't break your wrist," he said, moving her arm to demonstrate the arc of a punch. "And always follow through. That is where the power will come from. Don't simply make contact with your opponent. Move your fist directly through him."

"You assume I'll only be punching men, then?"

He stepped back, dropping her arm. "Are there women you'd like to punch?"

"Several," she said without hesitation. "All of the ones who excluded or disparaged my sister."

He didn't need to ask which one for it was obvious. Gwendolyn's smallpox scars had made her an outcast. It had been so clear even Gabriel had been aware of it. It was why he had responded so readily to Annie's request that he attend Gwendolyn's introduction ball. Saints, that seemed like a lifetime ago.

"Perhaps this is a bad idea. I had wished to teach you how to stomp on the arch of a man's foot and then kick him in his most vulnerable area, but I feared you wouldn't have time to get your skirts up for such a maneuver. But perhaps such a tactic would spare the women who unknowingly trod upon a tigress's toes."

Her fist, which had been hanging half-heartedly in the air where he had left it, floated down to her side as if forgotten. "Do you truly think me a tigress?"

"Of course," he said quietly.

He wanted to say more, but he stopped himself. He wasn't sure how much she was ready to hear. After discovering what she had endured, he understood perfectly why she had refused his proposal, why she had insisted on remaining a widow. She had been so adamant because in her mind it was the only way to keep herself safe. That was the only explanation. The danger was still too new and fresh to her, and he wasn't sure she was ready to understand the courage she must have possessed to have survived such a marriage. He could only imagine she still blamed herself. It was in the way she had so quickly defended Roger when she realized what she had revealed that day in the Brocklehurst library. No, she wasn't ready yet. But hopefully one day soon she would be, and he hoped he would be the one to tell her.

She studied his face for another moment, and then her expression hardened. This time she raised both hands, her fingers already curled into fists as she squared off in front of him.

"All right then," she said. "Show me how it's done."

And so he did. They practiced punching and follow through, the angle of the elbow to wrist and fist, the power that came from the shoulder. Eventually he was forced to retrieve a pillow from the bed when she gained the confidence to put strength behind her punch. Again and again, they went through the mechanics of it. Her stance grew steadier, stronger, and he tested her, trying to push her from her position, but she held fast.

Soon he moved on to showing her how to block a

responding attack with her left arm while she regained her footing to punch again. With every maneuver, every repositioning, every punch, she grew more relaxed, and by the time he called an end to their practice, she no longer hesitated to move her body into the correct position, the movements coming naturally.

She protested, as he expected, and he held up a hand. "You should get your rest. I thought you might wish to accompany me tomorrow on some Parliament business."

He didn't think her eyes could grow any rounder than they had when he'd first suggested she learn how to throw a punch, but they did just then, and he thought he might get lost in them forever.

"Accompany you?" She licked her lips and swiped at her forehead with an arm as a light sheen of sweat had appeared there.

He forced his eyes away and retrieved his jacket from where he'd discarded it earlier. "Yes, I thought you might like to tour some factory housing that's recently been erected under the building requirements I am lobbying for in the House." He faced her now that there was some distance between them. "You still wish to discover who you might have been, yes? I thought seeing how others live might help you in your quest."

Her lips had parted, and now her eyes moved over him, the uncertainty he had seen so readily in her earlier returning. But the uncertainty was over something else as she stepped quickly toward him.

"But we're married now," she said, shaking her head.

"What does that matter?"

A darkness passed over her eyes then, and he felt the weight of her past close in on him like he hadn't before. He tossed his jacket aside and took hold of her shoulders once more.

"Annie, I would ask something of you. Only this one thing." He paused, and she nodded, but she didn't speak. "I would ask that you not think our marriage will be like your first one. We are equals in this union, and I expect you to pursue the interests that matter to you. I hold no expectations for you. None. I've lived many years without a wife, and I've been perfectly fine for it. You have things you wish to accomplish, and it would be my greatest honor in helping you to achieve them." He let go of her and straightened. "Now then, would you like to accompany me?"

She was quiet for so long he feared he had lost her to the past, but then lifted her chin. "Are we still friends?"

The question was unexpected, and it broke his heart nearly in two at the way her eyes pinched together, at the way her voice strained as if her very existence depended on his answer.

He didn't know why he did it. Maybe it was the night, their wedding night, the weight of tradition bearing down on them, clouding his thoughts. Maybe it was just her. Beautiful Annie. *His* Annie. He took her face in his hands and kissed her. Softly. Slowly. Completely.

When he eased away, he whispered against her lips, "We will always be friends, Annie."

He let go of her, his fingers trailing along her cheeks as though he unconsciously wanted to keep touching her until there was too much distance between them, making it impossible to feel her creamy skin under his fingertips.

Her eyes fluttered open, her expression soft with wonder. "Yes, I should like to accompany you," she said, her voice suddenly thick.

He smiled, wondering how he had come to be married to this woman. He picked up his jacket once more and headed to the connecting door to his rooms.

"Good night, wife," he said, the smile still lingering on his lips.

"Good night, husband," she called after him as he quietly shut the door between them.

As he walked away he couldn't help but think as far as wedding nights went, that was surely the oddest one on record.

# CHAPTER 10

*O*n her way down to break her fast the following morning, Annie's muscles were sore, her shoulders and back ached from the exercise of the night before, and she feared she was half in love with her new husband.

This seemed entirely impossible. The very thought should have sent her fleeing, but it didn't. Not at all. It settled on her like a warm puddle of sunshine on a spring day. It was just too easy to love Gabriel Phelps.

He seemed to understand her in ways she didn't understand herself. It was more than that though. At times, she wondered if he could *feel* what she felt. The whole of her first marriage had been spent feeling as though she were little more than property. But it wasn't that way with Gabriel. She felt human again. No, something more precious than that. It was in the way he had looked at her in the Brocklehurst library. She *knew* she was precious to him.

And then he'd kissed her. He could have taken more; he could have taken everything. She was his wife now, and he had certain rights. But he hadn't. He'd taken just enough to keep her yearning.

She nearly fumbled on the last step at the thought.

Did he still want her? Or was she chasing rainbows to think someone like Gabriel should want her like that? It was all so terribly confusing.

He was her husband, and she had spent her wedding night with him learning how to punch. It had been glorious. The power she had felt, the rightness of it, when she finally understood how to hold her elbow, how to align it just so with her wrist so her strength flowed through it. That was it really. He had shown her the strength she already held inside of her.

For the first time in years, she felt hope as she stepped into the breakfast room of her new home. It was funny how hope made one feel lighter, and she nearly skipped to the sideboard to fill her plate. This was so much more than hunting for answers in a library. She would finally do something about her future.

It was odd to think she had snuck into Grimsby House only a few weeks ago, and now here she was as its mistress. It was a well-furnished home although it had felt austere in places, and she wondered if this was because Gabriel had been a bachelor for so long. The house had simply not been lived in. As she sat down with a plate of eggs and sausages, she wondered what changes would be wrought in the house from her presence alone.

She had just tucked into her breakfast when she heard footsteps in the corridor. Her fork hovered in the air above her plate as her heart stuttered. She had met the staff the previous day when they'd arrived after the wedding ceremony, but she couldn't help but feel like the woman who had been forced to sneak in the back door. Rives, the butler, had been nothing but cordial to her. Mrs. Featherstone had been all smiles and quick nods, but it needn't matter. She knew there would be a period of adjustment. There always was, and she simply needed to stop being such a ninny about it.

When Gabriel appeared in the door, her heart slowed, and a smile came automatically to her lips.

"Good morning, Gabriel," she said, pouring herself some coffee from the urn on the table and gesturing to Gabriel to see if he wished for some.

He nodded in response as he made his way to the sideboard. "I trust you slept well."

She finished pouring him a cup and set it beside the place at the head of the table. "I slept very well, thank you. I had a great deal of exercise unexpectedly yesterday."

He gave her that one-sided grin as he filled his plate. "I hope it didn't overtax you."

"Not at all," she reassured him before getting to the day's plans. "Where exactly will we be going today?"

"The East End."

He said it so casually she had nearly taken another bite of her eggs when her fork clattered to her plate.

"Where?" she managed even as she reached for her cup to ease her suddenly constricted throat.

"East End. New housing has gone up for the ship builders that use modern design to meet hygiene standards not seen in most housing of its kind."

She forgot entirely about her breakfast and held only her warm cup between both hands as her husband joined her at the table and tucked into his meal. "The East End?" she said again. "Are you sure it's safe?"

He paused to meet her gaze. "I should think so. I've seen how you are with a punch. I don't think we have cause to worry." He smiled his one-sided smile again, and while it usually reassured her, it did not in this case.

"But the...crime," she said when she couldn't think of another word.

He took a sip of his own coffee before replying, "Crime is prevalent in the East End, yes, but so is disease and over-crowded housing conditions. If we can improve one, shouldn't it stand to reason that it may improve the others?"

She set down her cup at this. "Do you really think so?"

"It stands to reason if a man has food on his plate and a roof over his head, he has no need to steal, doesn't it?"

She couldn't meet her husband's gaze then. Roger had had everything, and yet he still did terrible things. But any improvement must help surely.

She looked up to find Gabriel watching her carefully. She noticed that about him, the unhurried way he did things. A part of her wondered if it was his age. The brashness and hurry of youth had worn off of him. Gabriel had already fought the battles a young man thought he should, the battles that had always tormented Roger, and there was a quietness about him that soothed her. She never felt rushed around him, not even now when she knew he expected an answer from her.

She shook her head. "I think bad people do bad things, and there's nothing to stop that."

She never would have dared to defy Roger like that, but this wasn't Roger, and she was proved right when Gabriel smiled.

"Then I think we'll just need to see who is right," he said.

A little more than an hour later, their carriage was greeted by a Mr. Timmons, a man likely to be around forty years of age with riotous dark hair that had gone gray in spots and appeared to not withstand the taming of a comb. He wore round spectacles that accentuated his slightly bulging eyes, and his suit was freshly pressed if worn at the elbows and cuffs.

"Your Grace," the man said in a pristine voice that suggested he had a mother on which he doted. "We at the

Merchant Shipbuilding Company wish to thank you for your interest in our enterprise and welcome you to the Sagamore Housing Unit." He spoke with eyes downcast, as if his speech had been prepared in the pavement at their feet.

It was clear the man had gone to great lengths to ready himself for the Duke of Grimsby, and Annie couldn't help but smile, already appreciating the man's obvious pride in his position. Although it was clear he had never before been given such an important task, and he was displaying obvious signs of nerves.

He gestured then to the brick edifice behind him. It was new, the bricks a bright red hue and the smell of concrete and sawdust still thick in the air even though they were blocks from the docks. "If you will allow me, it will be my honor to show you just how the Sagamore was built with the latest advancements in mind."

With this Mr. Timmons ushered them up a set of small concrete stairs that led to a freshly painted door in a bright and promising blue. It was only when she stepped inside that Annie became aware of the noise, or rather the lack of it. When Gabriel had said they were to visit the East End, her mind had immediately conjured images of crowded streets, deplorable odors, and an aura of confusion of bodies and sound.

She peered back over her shoulder and then again inside to where Mr. Timmons stood in the middle of a yawning corridor that appeared as though it stretched on forever under a neat row of shaded lamps that hung from high on the walls. Her glance behind her afforded her a better view of the street as she was slightly elevated now. There was only the odd gentleman or lady passing by, and down at the corner, a gaggle of children scurried past. She had pictured a surge of human activity, but the area was terribly vacant. She turned back to her party to find Gabriel watching her.

"You've observed something, Your Grace," he said.

She realized with a start he was encouraging her to speak up. When he had proposed she accompany him, she had planned to stay silent. She swallowed, remembering what he had asked of her the previous night, that she not think of their marriage as being like her first.

She raised her chin and met Mr. Timmons's gaze. "Where is everyone? It seems quiet. Is it always like this?"

Mr. Timmons's eyebrows rose up behind the gold frames of his spectacles. "Ah, yes, that is because the buildings here are still new. This area has been under construction for several months, and I think the locals have learned to skirt the area." He raised a hand above him. "All of the rooms in this building have not yet been let. New tenants will be moving in at the first of the month." He smiled, but his eyes moved between her and Gabriel as if judging to see how his answer was accepted.

"How many units do you have in this building?" Gabriel asked, and Mr. Timmons began to recite a string of facts and figures he had, again, clearly memorized.

With this, Mr. Timmons began their tour by moving along the corridor. They were shown one of the unoccupied flats at the back of the building. It consisted of three rooms: a kitchen, a parlor, and a bedroom. The flat was small but adequate. Still, upon viewing it, Annie couldn't help but feel as though the walls were closing in on her. Mr. Timmons indicated an entire family would occupy one flat, but Annie wasn't certain how an entire family might exist in such a place. Thinking of being trapped in those three small rooms with just her sisters was terrifying enough. But an entire family?

They made their way to the back of the building where a door let out into the yard. A row of privies were built on one side and on the other, a line of hand pumps for fetching water. Mr. Timmons launched into an explanation of the use of drains and cesspool linings that were employed to ensure clean water for the tenants from the wells opposite, but Annie had stopped listening.

The well farthest from the door was occupied by a slight woman, a real scrap of a thing that could be no more than ten and eight. She was using all her strength to push the handle of one of the pumps down, but it didn't budge, and certainly no water appeared.

Annie sensed Gabriel behind her, but she raised a hand to assure him and went to help the woman at the pump.

"Have you tried priming it?" she asked as she approached, and the poor waif jumped, startled. Annie held up both hands as the woman spun about, her hand at her throat. "My name's Annie. I've just come to offer my help." She gestured to the water pump. "Have you tried priming it?"

The woman's lips parted as if she meant to speak, but she stopped suddenly and shook her head instead.

Annie indicated the pail of water sitting at the base of the pump. "You use this to prime it." She bent and retrieved the water before sloshing it into the pump. She reached out a hand. "Give me your bucket."

The woman's eyes had grown impossibly round in her face, and for a moment, Annie feared the poor woman would faint. She silently handed Annie her bucket. The water pump handle resisted at first, but with the help of the priming water, it soon began to move. The woman's bucket was filled in little time, and Annie refilled the priming pail, placing it back where she'd found it.

She straightened, a soft smile on her lips when she noticed there were tears in the other woman's eyes. Annie hesitated. "What is it?"

The woman shook her head. "How did you know how to do that?" She nearly whispered the question, but even then,

Annie could detect the Irish accent the woman was trying desperately to hide.

Annie smiled harder now to put the woman at ease. "My little sister played a terrible joke on me once with a water pump. Shot water right into my face." Annie laughed at the memory. "I suppose that's what little sisters are for, aren't they?"

The other woman shook her head. "I haven't a sister. Nor a mother." She gestured at the water pump. "I never learned how to do things like that." The tears fell down her cheeks now, but the woman's shoulders were rigid, and Annie knew comfort would not be welcomed. Still she didn't move as the woman clearly had more to say now that she'd spoken. "My da was a butcher. I can dress a cow just as clean as anything, but I can't fetch water from a well." She paused then and sniffed, the sound generous and wet, and ran the sleeve of her gown under her nostrils. Annie noticed then the grime that streaked the woman's sleeves and apron, the greasy yellow hair that fell from beneath her cap. "My da did his best, and Mrs.—" Here the woman cut off, sending a wary gaze at Annie. "Well, the neighbor lady, she's who took care of us. I helped my father in his shop from sunup to sundown. There wasn't time to learn things like this." She gestured at the water pump, her long fingers red and raw. "There wasn't time for learning how to cook and sew and do the things a lady ought. And now me husband—" Her words cut off abruptly, and the woman flashed a wary glance in Annie's direction.

Annie had servants to do things like fetch water and likely the other things this woman was thinking of but not saying.

"Do you know how to read?"

The woman's sadness turned quickly to anger. "Of course I do. What do you take me for? An id'it?"

Annie raised her chin. "Then you're luckier than most.

Because any question you might have can be answered with the right book."

The woman's mouth pursed with that anger that simmered just under the surface, and her eyes narrowed. "What you take me for? I ain't got coin for a book."

"That's what lending libraries are for. Have you ever been to a library?"

The woman's anger disappeared as quickly as it had come, and her lips parted in what could only be shock. "Yer daft, lady. Me? In a library? There's no time for such things."

"A library will give the answers you need to better your life. Don't you think you should make the time for such an endeavor?"

The woman's eyes fell to the bucket of water at her feet before rising slowly back to Annie's face. For a moment, Annie thought she might have gotten through to her, her eyes were searching instead of pinched, but then her lips thinned, and she cried, "Yer daft!" again before snatching up her bucket and disappearing into the building.

Annie watched her go, but she couldn't relinquish the urge to help the poor woman.

* * *

GABRIEL WATCHED Annie with the woman at the water pump while he half listened to Mr. Timmons. The man had described the very same system Gabriel supported in future worker housing from the design of the cesspool to prevent contamination of the water well to the design of the three-room flat to provide adequate space for an entire family instead of the cramped single rooms seen elsewhere.

He should have been paying the man greater attention, but the discussion between Annie and the unknown woman seemed to have increased in tension. It was lucky the woman picked up her bucket and stomped away as he'd been very close to going over there to see what was the matter, which was precisely not what he wished to do.

Having been married for all of a day, he was doing his best not to dictate to his wife when he felt the urge to protect her stronger than ever. She was his *wife*. The very word set off an instinct inside of him he didn't even know he possessed. For so long he pictured his future as solitary. He'd never fathomed the idea that he would have such strong emotions when it came to being wed. Perhaps it wasn't the married state itself but rather about Annie in particular. Whatever it was, the need to exercise greater care when it came to his wife was obvious.

Annie stood by the water pump for several seconds after the other woman had left before she joined them at the line of privies along the opposite side of the yard.

Mr. Timmons had just finished explaining the regular cleanings the privies would receive, and Gabriel took the opportunity to address his wife.

"Is everything all right?" he asked.

She nodded vaguely, but her attention was on the other man. "Mr. Timmons, would you be able to tell me who that woman was? The one at the water pump just now."

Mr. Timmons pushed up his spectacles with a single finger. "Well, I believe that to be Mrs. O'Hara, the wife of John O'Hara in flat three on the main floor." He smiled and rocked back on his feet as though he had successfully answered the question asked of a tutor.

"Was the woman unwell?" Gabriel asked then, feeling that spike of concern once more.

Annie shook her head. "No, it's just...well, she seems to be in need of aid. She had some questions about domestic affairs, and I should like to return with a book that may be able to help her. I just wished to know who it is I am to seek out when I come back."

The muscles along Gabriel's neck tightened at the idea that Annie should wish to return here, so close to the docks, but he tempered his response. "A book?"

Annie nodded quickly. "There are several books on domestic affairs that should help the woman, and it would be my pleasure to assist her."

A book seemed harmless enough, and he felt the tension coiling inside of him ease somewhat. He indicated for Timmons to continue their tour then, and the man led them back into the building to show them the upper floors. The building contained three separate staircases to provide multiple ways of egress should there be a fire. This was in addition to the emergency chute located at the back of the building.

Gabriel was impressed, and having concluded their tour and once more standing on the pavement in front of the building, he asked, "Can you provide me with a report on the costs of the added safety and cleanliness features? It would also be helpful to have a statement from an executive of the shipbuilding company explaining why such measures were taken."

Mr. Timmons was already nodding before Gabriel had finished. "The Merchant Shipbuilding Company believes a healthy worker is a productive worker. All future housing will contain such measures as to provide a robust level of living."

Gabriel eyed the brick building, thinking robust was rather overdoing it, but it was a step toward progress. He thanked Timmons again and helped Annie into their carriage.

"Have you always wished to help people?" she asked as soon as the carriage rocked into motion.

"Help people?"

She nodded in the direction they had just come from. "Helping people through your work in the House. Through legislation that will provide better and cleanlier housing."

"I suppose I've never seen it as helping people," he replied. "I've always just thought of it as doing what was right and necessary." A shadow came over her features then, and he involuntarily took her hand into his. "What is it?"

She looked out the window before answering, "It's nothing really. I just worry I'll never find what it is I'm supposed to do in this life." She looked back at him. "You're very fortunate to know what it is you want."

He knew of what she spoke, but his mind traveled in an entirely different direction.

He wanted her.

He pushed the thought aside, wondering if he would ever grow used to its burden.

"Yes, I suppose I am," he muttered and looked away because it was the only thing he could do.

How could he have let this happen?

How could he have let his emotions run away like that? He had sworn never to marry, never to carry on the Grimsby title. He glanced briefly in his wife's direction, but her gaze lingered out the window, her expression showing she was lost in her own thoughts.

Could he have her without letting her consume him? He didn't think it possible and turned his gaze away from her and his mind away from his troubling thoughts.

He watched London roll past them, coffee houses and pubs turning to townhouses and sprawling parks as they traveled into Mayfair. He willed his driver to go faster, for the horses to be swift and deft, cutting through traffic ahead of all else.

He had to get out of that carriage and away from his own

thoughts. He would take a lover. That was the only solution. He couldn't risk anything else, and yet why did taking a lover repulse him?

They reached Grimsby House after what seemed an age, and he alighted before the tiger could open his door, reaching back for Annie. He kept his hand firmly on hers as he helped her down and let go as soon as propriety allowed it.

He turned in the direction of the house to find Rives had already opened the door to admit them, but something had caught Gabriel's eye as he had turned about.

He shouldn't have looked back. He should have taken Annie's arm and proceeded directly into the house, but of course that wasn't what happened. Turning back, he saw immediately what had caught his attention.

Belvedere.

And his mother.

Icy cold dread poured through him, and his hand snatched out, latching onto Annie's arm to pull her behind him before he took another breath.

Belvedere and the dowager duchess strolled arm in arm down the street as if they hadn't a care for propriety and custom. It was as though they were too happy to flaunt their relationship, and Gabriel supposed the *ton* must have grown used to it.

Except Gabriel hadn't.

Until a month ago, he had thought Belvedere safely ensconced on the Continent. Gabriel had been so embedded in his Parliament work as to not have concerned himself with society gossip or the movements of his own mother. He realized now he should have been paying greater attention.

"Gabriel," his mother said when she reached him. "How perfect. Brogden and I were just coming to call on you."

Did Annie's arm tense under his grip or had he imagined it?

"Mother," he said, purposefully ignoring Belvedere.

His mother's gaze moved to Annie, who somehow knew to stay behind him as she huddled against his shoulder.

His mother's smile then was cold and wicked. "I had heard you were wed, Gabriel, and I take it this waif of a child is your bride." Her gaze moved back to him. "I can't say I'm surprised you married so beneath you. I suppose at some point you were forced to take whatever lady might have been willing. Don't you agree, Brogden?"

Belvedere made a phlegmy noise deep in his throat, and the bristles of his mustache vibrated as he said, "Yes, I quite agree, Elizabeth. It's clear she's no duchess. How disappointing you continue to be, Gabriel."

He had been too focused on Belvedere, too tense in his desire to protect Annie to realize what she was about to do, but before he could understand, she'd tugged her arm free and moved in front of him.

"Gabriel, we have that meeting this afternoon about the horticultural society charity dinner. We mustn't be late. And I must get the linens in order this afternoon or we'll never be able to decide…"

He wasn't paying attention to her words. He was paying attention to what she was doing, to the expressions that evolved on the faces of Belvedere and his mother as Annie stepped between him and them, her chatter incessant and distracting as she took his arm and simply led him away.

She gave no cutting remark. She didn't even look at them.

It was as if they…didn't exist.

She marched them up the stairs, talking without cessation, and only when Rives shut the door firmly behind them did she turn to face him.

"I take it that man was Brogden Belvedere. The man you

told me about. The Gothic villain?" She raised an eyebrow as she shed her gloves and bonnet, handing them to Rives.

Gabriel couldn't help but look behind him as though he expected his mother and Belvedere to knock at any moment. "Yes, it was," he said, turning back to his wife as he slipped out of his overcoat and hat.

Rives collected them before floating silently away down the hall, leaving Gabriel alone with his wife.

Annie poked at her hair, adjusting pins as she studied her reflection in the hall mirror. "What a dreadful man. Has he always had that deplorable mustache?"

He watched her, his heart slowing painfully at the domesticity of the scene before him. His wife, fixing her hair after removing her bonnet. The quietness of that moment sent a jolt through him like electricity, and he was forced to look away.

"Yes, I'm afraid he has. I'm not sure he has the sense to shave it." He picked up the morning's post which had been left on the small table in the foyer and began to sort through it, anything to distract him from the tumult occurring inside of him.

"And that woman, she's your mother?" Annie paused, but Gabriel sensed her thought wasn't finished. "She looks familiar. I must have met her somewhere."

It was a moment before he realized Annie had stilled, her gaze on her reflection, but her eyes had gone unfocused as if she were thinking of something else.

"What is it?" he finally asked, his hands pausing in the act of opening an envelope.

She shook her head and turned about. "It's nothing." She met his gaze. "I have some letters I should like to return, and if we have no further obligations for the day, I should like to get settled. It would be lovely to have a chat with Mrs. Featherstone as well. I'd like to understand how the household is currently run," she finished.

He gestured to the mirror with the half-opened envelope still in his hand. "What was it you were thinking just then?"

She shook her head. "It was nothing really."

Her hand was on the balustrade of the stairs when he said, "Annie, please. Tell me what you were thinking."

She hesitated even as he persisted, and he watched her as she seemed to think. Had Roger done this to her? Had he made her reluctant to speak her mind? In the past several weeks, he had come to realize Annie had an unusual awareness of the world around her, and her insights were painfully truthful.

She turned just enough to look at him, her hand still on the balustrade. "Well, it was the way that man spoke to you." She shook her head. "He sounded as though he were your father. Why would he think he had the right to speak to you like that? How terribly bizarre." She shook her head again and continued her way up the stairs.

He let her go, the post forgotten in his hands.

# CHAPTER 11

It took Annie a week to procure the book in question and another three days to convince Eloise to accompany her to the Sagamore to deliver it to Mrs. O'Hara.

The bookshop on Oxford Street where she'd gone to purchase the book claimed to be regularly sold out of *Mrs. Beeton's Book of Household Management,* and Annie supposed that was likely true. She'd stumbled upon a copy in Lady Brocklehurst's library, which had seemed rather odd at the time. Lady Brocklehurst had a battalion of servants to manage her household. Why she would require a book on the subject seemed redundant.

The shop owner had promised Annie a copy in the next shipment, however, and when it arrived, Annie had coerced her sister into accompanying her to retrieve it. When she would have returned her sister to Stoke Bruerne House, she'd simply instructed her driver to take her to the Sagamore. As he'd taken them for their tour the previous week, the man was familiar with the route and didn't hesitate to take the direction.

Eloise, on the other hand, was less than pleased.

"You said we were going shopping." She crossed her arms and glared at her sister as the carriage rocked along.

"We did go shopping," Annie pointed out. "And now we are doing a good deed. This poor woman has had no one to instruct her on the necessities of managing a household, and now she finds herself wed without a clue as to what to do."

Eloise did not uncross her arms. Instead, she added a frown to her tableau. A deep one. "I don't see how this should involve me being kidnapped and dragged into the crime capital of the city."

Annie wrinkled her nose. "That's rather dramatic."

Eloise's grin was quick. "It was rather, wasn't it?" She glanced out the window. "Where is it we're going?"

"The Sagamore. It's worker housing for the Merchant Shipbuilding Company."

Eloise returned her gaze to Annie. "And Gabriel is all right with you going? Unaccompanied?"

"You're accompanying me," Annie noted.

Eloise's frown returned. "You know that's not what I mean. It's dangerous in the East End. What if something should happen?"

Annie felt heat spread to her cheeks. "Well, actually, Gabriel taught me something with which to defend myself."

Eloise's eyebrows disappeared into her fringe. "He did?" She hopped off her bench and with a flourish of skirts, flounced down next to Annie. "What did he teach you? You must tell me everything."

Eloise's eyes were far too bright, and Annie was forced to glance out the window to collect her thoughts.

"On our wedding night, Gabriel taught me how to punch a person."

Eloise was speechless.

This was rather concerning as Eloise was never speechless.

She blinked, her eyes owlish, before finally muttering, "He did…what?"

"Taught me how to punch." Annie held up her fist to demonstrate. "You put your thumb here. Align elbow to wrist and the power comes from the shoulder."

Eloise's brow winkled. "Is this because of the incident with that viscount?" The wrinkle vanished as realization seemed to dawn. "Oh Annie, was Gabriel acting the knight errant that night in the Tyntsfield garden?"

Annie swallowed, feeling the complexity of the answer to Eloise's question. "Something like that," she decided to say.

Eloise smiled and hooked a hand through Annie's cajolingly. "Tell me everything. What else happened on your wedding night?" She did a funny thing then with her eyebrows that was far too suggestive for Annie, and she couldn't help but laugh.

"Oh, it was nothing so exciting, sister. I assure you. Gabriel is quite the gentleman."

*That kiss.*

It still haunted her, far more than the things they had done in the library, and she hoped her cheeks hadn't grown red with the memory of it.

Eloise's expression melted. "Oh." The word was quiet, disappointed, and she sat back on the bench, her demeanor deflated as her arm slipped free of Annie's.

"What is it?" Annie felt a tightening in her stomach.

Eloise gestured weakly with one hand. "It's just Gabriel has always seemed so dashing, so distinguished." She shrugged. "I guess I had always hoped he might sweep you off your feet." She met Annie's gaze directly. "I do so wish for you to have a grand romance, Annie. After everything you've been through." She shrugged again. "I suppose you'll need to show him how you wish to be treated. To be more romantic."

Annie's eyebrows shot up now. "Show him how I wish to be treated? Whatever are you talking about?"

Eloise's tone was bland. "You'll need to romance him. That much is obvious." She sat up as if having a sudden idea. "Perhaps it's because he was a bachelor for so long. He probably isn't sure of how to go about it." She tapped Annie on the shoulder. "That must be it. You must show him how to do it." Eloise nodded as though she had figured out how it was the planets moved around the sun.

"I must initiate a romance with my husband?" Annie shook her head. "But we're friends."

Eloise blinked at this. "Friends? Truly?" Her smile was whimsical. "Oh Annie, that's wonderful. But don't you wish for a little romance? A little adventure?"

"Certainly not." She folded her hands in her lap, gripping her skirt as if the very mention of the word would catapult her into turmoil. "I like how quiet our relationship is. It's a partnership."

Eloise's expression turned sour. "Partnership? Are you playing at cards or are you married?" She patted Annie's clenched hands. "It's all right, dear sister. Adventure isn't for everyone."

While Annie may have felt a degree of apprehension at the idea of adventure, it still smarted to hear her sister say it might not be for her. But if she were being honest, she truly did enjoy the quietness of her marriage. She'd only been married a little more than a week, of course, and that was hardly enough time to determine how one might carry on, but there was an easiness to her existence with Gabriel that felt comforting.

Still, Eloise's words bothered her a lot more than she thought they ought.

"I met his mother," Annie said finally, bringing Eloise's gaze around from where it had strayed to the window.

"His mother?" Eloise scooted closer somehow. "Did she say why she didn't attend the wedding?"

"My assumption is she didn't attend the wedding because Gabriel didn't invite her." She pursed her lips in thought before saying, "I think their relationship is rather cold."

Eloise's brow puckered in thought. "No," she breathed. "Gabriel? He's quite literally the most thoughtful, kind gentleman I've ever had the honor of meeting. How could he have a poor relationship with his mother?"

"I think it's because she treats him terribly and has formed a connection with a gentleman who reminds me of a Gothic villain."

Eloise's mouth formed a silent *oh*. She shook her head. "Perhaps you're destined for adventure yet."

Annie shook her head now. "Hardly. But his mother seemed familiar to me somehow. Elizabeth Phelps. Does her name sound familiar to you?"

Eloise thought a moment before saying, "I'm not sure. Maybe I would recognize her face, but her name isn't familiar to me."

Annie let the thought linger in her mind, mulling it over as she tried to recall where it was she'd seen Elizabeth Phelps before that day on the pavement outside Grimsby House.

They fell into companionable silence then, and Annie watched the buildings grow thick as the carriage rumbled into the East End, letting her mind wander back to Eloise's earlier comment. Did Annie wish to remain only friends with her husband? Or was that what she had convinced herself she wished for when she had been so keen to protect her widowhood? But for a moment, hadn't she considered Gabriel as a potential lover? It was all so complicated, and now Eloise's comment bounced around inside of her, wreaking havoc.

Thankfully they reached their destination before Eloise could make any more life-upending comments, and collecting the wrapped book from beside her on the bench, Annie alighted before the tiger could open her door. She stood on the pavement and peered back into the carriage where Eloise hovered.

"Aren't you coming?" she asked.

Eloise's gaze skated left and right outside the open door, but she didn't step down from the carriage.

"What are you doing?" Annie finally prodded.

"Checking for murderers," was Eloise's quick reply.

"Eloise." Annie pursed her lips and tried to assume the perturbed look at which their mother excelled.

"You can never be too careful," Eloise muttered as she stepped down.

The Sagamore was quiet as it had been on the day of their tour, and their footsteps were loud in the corridor as they made their way to flat number three. A fragrant aroma filled the space around them, something yeasty with just a hint of spice, and above their heads came a scraping sound as though someone were moving furniture. Annie wondered if more of the residents were moving in.

They reached number three, and before Annie could second-guess herself, she knocked purposefully on the door.

No reply came.

Annie knocked again.

The door opened with a whoosh, and a blast of steam billowed out, driving Annie and Eloise back from the door. Mrs. O'Hara's face appeared in the cloud, red and damp as if she were in the midst of something particularly taxing.

"What d'ye want?" she bellowed, her Irish accent thick.

Annie watched recognition dawn on the woman's face.

Her lips snapped shut, and her eyes narrowed, her expression closing.

"Mrs. O'Hara," Annie said quickly, stepping forward before the woman could close the door in her face. "I've brought you this. It's *Mrs. Beeton's Book of Household Management*. I thought it may be of some use to you."

Mrs. O'Hara eyed the book as if Annie were offering her a lovely but poisonous flower. The woman's yellow hair had frizzed from under its cap, wet tendrils clinging to her temples. When Annie was sure Mrs. O'Hara would close the door in her face, she snaked out a hand and snatched the wrapped parcel.

She tore the brown wrapping with little ceremony and stopped when the title of the book became visible. Her eyes moved once up to Annie's face and back down to the book before she surged forward, driving Annie back to avoid being trampled. Eloise grabbed her arm as they came up against the opposite wall of the corridor, and Mrs. O'Hara stepped into the hall, shutting her door behind her.

She turned to them. "Follow me."

She didn't ask who Eloise was, and Annie felt it wasn't the right moment for introductions. Exchanging a glance with Eloise, they linked arms and followed Mrs. O'Hara down the corridor. They reached the central staircase where the woman began to climb, and Annie and Eloise had no choice but to follow.

The second floor was much as the first had been. A line of doors marched down a lengthy hallway. All closed, all quiet. Mrs. O'Hara seemed to have a destination in mind and stomped down the length of it until she stopped and knocked on one of the closed doors. The door eased open cautiously a moment later, and Annie saw only a pair of dark eyes through the crack between door and jamb.

"This is the lady I was telling you about," she said,

throwing a thumb over her shoulder in the direction of Annie. Mrs. O'Hara held up the half-wrapped book. "She brought me this."

The wary pair of eyes traveled over the cover of the book before looking up and landing squarely on Annie's face. Eloise's grip on her arm tightened, and Annie willed herself to breathe.

What had she done? Had she overstepped? Had her need to help put not only herself but Eloise in danger as well?

But then the door swung open, and a woman stepped into the hallway. She was nearly a whole head taller than Mrs. O'Hara with bright red hair pinned up in a straggly mess atop her head, which only accentuated the height difference. She wore a drab gown of brown and mossy green that stopped just short of the tops of her boots.

"Lady, can you help me?" she said, stepping forward as if Mrs. O'Hara weren't standing there. "It's me mum you see, she's got the arthritis real bad like, and some days it keeps her in bed. I ain't got the time to care for her. I've got little ones. Three of 'em. I need something that will help me mum." She shook her head despondently. "I can't take care of everyone and still have tea ready when me man returns from the yard." Her eyes pinched. "There must be a book about remedies and such. We can't afford a doctor and certainly none of that fancy medicine he would be like to prescribe. Please, lady. Can you help me?"

Annie stood, baffled that this woman should plead so earnestly for help from her. Her. Lowly, nobody Annie. But she wasn't a nobody. Roger had told her that, but it wasn't true. She shook her head as if to force those thoughts from her mind for good.

"I would be happy to help you. A book on arthritis remedies? That's what you require?"

The woman's broad face softened, the pinched look

easing. "Oh that's right fine, lady. I'd much appreciate it." She held up a finger as if indicating they should wait, and in a single step she reached the other side of the corridor to tap on the door there.

It opened after several seconds, and a small woman with mousy brown hair emerged, pushing her smudged spectacles up her nose as she surveyed the crowd in the corridor.

"This is Molly. She's lookin' to learn to read and all. I thought I could teach her if I had something to work with. You know. One of thems books that talks about letters and such. The ones they use for children." She laid one arm awkwardly around the woman called Molly as the poor woman only came up to the red-haired woman's bosom. "Reading will do her good, it will. Can you help her too?"

Eloise's grip tightened unbearably on her arm, but Annie only patted her sister's hands as she smiled and said, "Of course."

* * *

"I'm not sure whether congratulations are in order or not."

Gabriel looked up from where he'd been staring into the fire, happily ensconced alone in a small sitting area of his club with a glass in one hand and an unread newspaper in the other to find the Duke of Ardley peering down at him as if he were a hound that wouldn't hunt.

"If I'm honest, I'm not sure either," Gabriel mumbled.

"It's that bad then, eh?" Liam said, taking the seat beside him. "I figured as much and thought I should find you as soon as I was able. I'm sorry I wasn't able to attend the wedding." This last bit was said with a marked note of sarcasm that tugged a smile to Gabriel's lips as no one besides Annie's family members had been invited.

"I blame the hasty circumstances on one Viscount Overby."

"I take it the viscount was the very thing you were trying to protect your widow from, was he not?"

The question was heavier than it would have appeared to an outsider, and Gabriel admired the duke's handling of words.

"Quite," Gabriel answered. "But in this case, the lady defended herself with stunning verve."

"Except she shouldn't have been called upon to do so."

Gabriel cut a swift glance at Liam, feeling the weight of his words more than his earlier question. He was coming to understand the Duke of Ardley was like a river, deep and always moving so one could never claim to know the man. One moment he was giving his all in a round of flirtation that had Gabriel considering taking the vows of a monk if only to heal from the display, and the next he prodded the very heart of an issue with but a handful of select words. If he were to have a true friend, he was glad Liam was it.

"I'm afraid you're right."

Liam nodded. "It is not my place to pry, but what I know of the Widow Wexford is favorable, and I shouldn't like to think she has found herself trapped once more by marriage. Is she faring well?"

This was a question Gabriel feared he couldn't answer. In the few weeks of their marriage, he'd done everything he could to stay away from her. Her with those damnable eyes that made him want to swim in her gaze forever. Her with that laugh like audible sunshine. Her with that touch that proved she was something angelic. How was Annie? She was a damn sight better than he was.

"She's taken on a charitable endeavor that has kept her busy, and I think it's proving good for her spirits." He met Liam's gaze directly. "Meanwhile I am a terrible mess."

"I had that figured as well." Liam sat back in his seat, propping one leg on the opposite knee. "If you'd care to speak of it, I am happy to listen. If you'd like companionable silence while you lose yourself in whiskey, I am happy to go along with that as well."

Gabriel eyed him. "Don't you have better things to do?"

Liam pulled his pocket watch from his waistcoat and glanced at the time. "Not for another three hours."

"What happens in three hours?"

Liam tucked his pocket watch back into his waistcoat. "The sisters Mallory promenade along the Serpentine every afternoon during the season."

"You prey on innocent sisters promenading?"

Liam shook his head. "In this case, I'm using them to invoke the feeling of jealousy."

Gabriel raised an eyebrow. "Jealousy?"

Liam's lips firmed momentarily. "It's a particularly difficult case."

"Flirting can be difficult?"

"There have been times when I've never found anything to be more challenging in my life." He made a gesture with his chin for Gabriel to go on. "Now then tell me what's happened. All of it."

So Gabriel did. He told Liam everything from what really happened in the Tyntsfield garden to teaching Annie how to throw a punch on their wedding night. He even told Liam about their run-in with Gabriel's mother and Belvedere.

The only thing he kept to himself was his growing desire for his wife and his fear his self-control was waning.

Liam's gaze grew more and more narrow as Gabriel relayed his story until finally he said, "Belvedere came to your home? How very odd."

Liam's words and tone were strangely reminiscent of

Annie's own sentiment that day, and it had Gabriel's attention.

"Odd how?"

Liam shook his head slightly as if working out his own thoughts. "It's rather strange behavior, isn't that? The man should seek you out at the very home from which you'd ejected him nearly twenty years previously." He paused to meet Gabriel's eye. "It was the same home, yes?" Gabriel nodded, and Liam went on. "Any other person would have seen such an ejection as cause to never return to such a place, but the fact that Belvedere felt comfortable approaching the house—nay, he did so flagrantly on the arm of your mother, no less, is like the dog who has already felt the cat's claws willingly going in for another swipe." Liam shook his head. "That's nothing less than the behavior of a bully."

"A bully?"

Liam dropped his foot and sat forward. "You said Belvedere attempted to gain access to the title while it was under control of the executor, your mother. Do I have that right?"

Again Gabriel only nodded.

"But you've been the duke now for twenty years, under which the lands and monies are controlled by you. The man has nothing to gain, and yet he comes back." Liam's brow had wrinkled to such a degree Gabriel was concerned the man might think himself into a stupor.

"I believe he has been carrying on an affair with my mother for the entirety of the twenty years," Gabriel supplied when Liam had been deep in thought for several seconds.

This tugged the man from his haze. "An affair? This is a summation on your part, I take it."

Gabriel nodded. "I've based it on my mother's behavior and understanding of Belvedere. She seemed to know he was in London before I did, and their behavior on a very public street would suggest the lack of newness about their situation."

"I would agree," Liam murmured. It was a moment before he brought his hands together and sat back. "Then there you have it. Belvedere is nothing more than a common bully."

Gabriel blinked. "A common bully?" The word bully did not usually conjure the reaction he felt for Belvedere, and he found the application of the word to the parasite rather weak.

But Liam was quick to nod. "The man stands to gain nothing by tormenting you. He seems merely to take plea-sure in the act itself. Therefore one can conclude the tormenting is the thing he seeks."

"Belvedere is a bully." He said the words as if by saying them he could believe them. "Annie thinks he treats me as if he's my father."

He couldn't stop himself from stirring the pot. Belvedere had been his parasite alone until mere weeks ago, and he could feel the easing inside of him when he spoke to others who were familiar with the man. As if by merely speaking of him, Gabriel was sharing the burden of Belvedere's existence.

Both of Liam's eyebrows rose. "Interesting. A clever observation on the part of your dear wife. What is it that has caused her to draw such a conclusion?"

Gabriel relayed the specifics about their encounter that day outside of Grimsby House, including the language Belvedere used which had concerned Annie.

Liam's brow somehow managed to grow more furrowed. "I must say I agree with your dear wife, which only further supports my own conclusion. The man is a bully. Out for nothing more than his own power over you, and at some point, you've taught him he can get away with as much."

The words were so blunt it was a moment before Gabriel realized what Liam had said. "I beg your pardon."

Liam leaned forward again, his voice steady. "Whether we realize it or not, we teach those around us how we should be treated. At some point in your shared history, Belvedere learned he could bully you. He's gone so far as to assume he could treat you like a child." He straightened. "And if your dear wife is correct, a naughty child at that."

Without warning, another memory of Belvedere surfaced, one from nearly six months after the death of his father. The one and only time Belvedere had struck Gabriel with his cane for returning home later than he had said he would, delayed by a snarl in traffic and nothing more. Only now with time did Gabriel see what Annie and Liam saw. The oddness of Belvedere's actions.

"I have never been a naughty child, and I certainly am not one now," Gabriel said.

"Belvedere doesn't believe that," Liam returned.

"What are you suggesting I do? The man is a menace."

"And he will continue to be as long as you do not respond with a sign of strength. It's a wonder you haven't already called him out." He tapped the arm of his chair. "But it's not that which worries me. The thing about bullies is they'll keep testing their power, looking for vulnerability in their victims." He looked straight at Gabriel. "I'm afraid Belvedere might try something terrible if only to test you. Bullies never know when they've gone too far, and what I know of him, Belvedere won't realize it either."

"What do you think he'll do?"

"I don't know." Liam's voice had turned quizzical. "But you must watch out for yourself, friend. I didn't like the man on sight, and I don't like him any better from what you've told me about him. You'll need to keep your guard up."

Gabriel set down the newspaper he hadn't realized he was

still holding. "I don't like waiting to see what he might attempt. I prefer to be on the offensive."

Liam nodded. "I can understand the feeling, but in this case, the man is guilty of nothing more than being a nuisance. You must hold your anger and stay vigilant."

"And what of Annie?" He wasn't sure when it had occurred but over the course of the past several weeks of his marriage he'd come to understand there was a certain pause when it came to his thinking now, and in that pause, his wife resided. When he accepted a social invitation, when he promised to join a gentleman for a drink at his club in hopes of gaining his support for the drains bill, even when he decided to work late in the library, there was a pause in which he was forced to consider how his actions would affect his wife. It was new to him, and at first he found the hesitation chafing, but now…well, it felt nice.

There was someone else whose life intersected with his.

He thought the very idea of such a notion would weigh on him like iron chains, but it didn't, and he wondered if that was because it was Annie, and she could never possibly weigh him down or hold him back.

And she didn't.

She'd slipped seamlessly into his life as if she was always meant to be there. They seemed to match each other's rhythm, and by doing so, transitioning to married life had been like slipping into a warm ocean instead of hurtling off a cliff.

He closed his eyes against his wandering thoughts.

"What is this charitable endeavor she has undertaken?" Liam asked.

Gabriel opened his eyes. "She's providing books and reading material to the residents of the Merchant Ship-building Company's factory housing."

"How is it she's stumbled upon that? Don't society ladies usually stick to quilting bees and church outings?"

"I'm happy to say Annie is not like other society ladies."

"Thank God for that," Liam said, getting to his feet. "I don't think Belvedere has it in him to go to the East End, Gabriel. But as you have taught your duchess to defend herself, the only thing you can hope for is that she stays vigilant as well." He tugged at the cuffs of his shirt. "I would ask though if the need arise you come to me for aid, Grimsby. I don't like the idea of you facing off against that ghastly man by yourself. His mustache alone is terrifying." Liam gave a dramatic shiver. "Now if you'll excuse me, I must go make a woman mad with jealousy."

"Only one woman?" Gabriel asked.

Liam's grin was quick. "Well, at least one on purpose, I suppose," he said and turned away with a goodbye salute leaving Gabriel feeling more lost than when he'd first sat down.

# CHAPTER 12

"I thought you said we were delivering one book," Eloise mumbled as she handed out yet another book.

"It got out of control rather quickly, I will admit," Annie muttered in response as she lifted another crate of books onto the table.

It really had gotten out of control. When she'd returned with the books on arthritis remedies for Mrs. McQuiggan, the name of the tall red-haired woman she'd learned, and the reading primers for Molly, Mrs. Stevens, others had moved into the Sagamore by that time and had their own requests.

There had been land cleared at the back of the building for a tenant garden, and as the tenants had never had such a luxury, there were calls for books on horticulture and even one ambitious woman who had asked for anything on constructing a greenhouse. There were mothers who wished to begin teaching their children reading and writing and even one mother who had asked for a text on teaching a child French so she could communicate with her great-grandmother. The flats at the Sagamore were filling up, and with each new arrival came a new request for knowledge, one Annie was only too happy to fulfill.

She'd opened an account at the bookseller on Oxford Street, and she was fairly certain she would be keeping the man in business for some time to come. What the bookseller couldn't order for her, he sourced from other shops. Some books were acquired from private libraries and others from estate sales and auctions.

Her collection of books to offer the residents of the Sagamore had grown so much, she'd been forced to ask Mr. Timmons for space in which to conduct the weekly exchange of books. He'd been only too happy to help, offering her a room at the back of the building on the main floor. She wondered what the space had been meant for, but as she was busy procuring tables on which to distribute the books and the crates necessary to move them all, she hadn't thought to ask him. She was simply grateful for the space.

Women filtered in and out of the room, perusing the titles laid out on the tables, or if they had a specific request, they marched right up to the queue that had formed in front of Annie. The room buzzed with conversation, and Annie was forced to lean across the table to hear some of the requests. When she didn't have a book that would work, she made note of it in a notebook Gabriel had given her in which she also kept track of books lent and returned.

She paused, writing down the request for a book on the phases of the moon, and fingered the creamy page of the journal, her heart warming when she thought of her husband. It was strange really, to have such happy thoughts interrupt her days, but it was happening more and more often recently. They'd been married for more than a month already. It seemed impossible, but it was the truth. Perhaps it was because things came so naturally between them.

Except he hadn't touched her once since that shattering kiss on their wedding night.

A tightening came to her stomach, and she willed it away. A friendship was what she had told Gabriel she wanted, and it was what he was giving her. Even if she wanted more, she must be happy with what she had. After all, it was far more than she ever expected to have.

A woman who seemed impossibly young for the amount of children who clung to her approached the table next and blew out a breath to lift the fringe that stuck to the sweat on her forehead. "I need books on colors and such. The children haven't any schooling, you see. Not with how often their da moves for work, and they're terribly behind." The woman's eyes held a haunted look Annie was coming to recognize. It was the look of a woman who was drowning under the responsibility of raising a child, sometimes many children, and hoping and trying for the very best for them even as they felt as though they were failing.

Suddenly Annie wondered if she would ever have children. Her heart ached, and she shoved the thought aside. Now wasn't the time for it.

Before Annie could response, Eloise said, "I've something for that." She bent and lifted a crate onto the table Annie hadn't seen before. "I mentioned what you were doing here to a few acquaintances, and the Duchess of Ashbourne had these delivered to the house this morning."

Annie shifted the crate just enough to read the title inside. She looked up, startled. "But this is a set of the duchess's own books." Annie shook her head. "What did you say?"

Eloise shrugged. "I said you were starting a library." She turned away then to help a woman who was looking for a book on baking cakes.

Annie's mind went utterly blank as she watched her sister disappear into the crowd of patrons who had gathered to find books. It was a moment before she shook herself free of the hold her sister's words had placed on her enough to remember the woman looking for children's books. She smiled and turned the crate toward her.

"You should find something helpful in here," she said, but her voice was soft as her mind remained somewhere else.

The woman took her time sorting through the Duchess of Ashbourne's books, and it gave Annie a moment to take in the room around her.

She had brought a footman from Grimsby House to help her with the crates of books, and even the tiger had carried in several crates, staying long enough to help set up the tables as well. She'd been so immersed in the business of what she was doing, she hadn't the distance to see *what* she was doing.

Eloise was right.

She'd created a library.

What had started as exercising her ability to help one woman had turned into all of this. It wasn't *just* a library though. Like all libraries, it was greater than the space it occupied. It was the coming together of people. The residents of this building emerging from their flats to become more than just occupants. They were becoming neighbors, forging bonds, and strengthening ties. They were coming together.

Because she'd brought one woman a book.

The answers she had been seeking weren't *in* a book. They *were* the books themselves, and now she was witness to that very thing.

Something sprang loose in her chest. It was as though it had a true sound to it, like a lock shattering under the weight of the hammer, her very soul leapt free. This was what she was meant to do. Books. The answer had always been books. She'd been through any number of books through the years, had turned to them in her greatest moments of trouble and sorrow.

And now they had come again to lift her up and into her new life. Her future. This.

She didn't know how long she'd been staring at the room, but she suddenly became aware of two people standing in front of the table before her. She started, realizing one of them was a man. The room was filled with women as the men were on shift at the ship building company, and she was surprised to see one standing before her.

She could only assume the pair were man and wife, the way the woman clung to the man's arm.

"Excuse me, Lady," the woman spoke first.

When the tenants had started addressing her as Lady as if it were some sort of professional title, she wasn't sure, but she was coming to like it better than her proper title of Your Grace. She would never apologize for it because Lady was hers and hers alone, and there was something precious about that.

"My husband is in need of a book." The woman's voice matched her stature, small and unassuming.

Annie smiled encouragingly. "Of course. What is it you are looking for?"

It was then Annie noticed the crutch the man held under one arm and how his wife's grip on his arm seemed to be tighter than mere connection. She was working to hold him up.

Annie glanced up, searching for the footman she had brought with her in case this man should require aid when he said, "The name's Tanner, ma'am. I'm a joiner at the company." He paused, licking his lips wearily. "A few months back the scaffolding I was on collapsed, and I fell."

His diminutive wife surged forward at this. "It was the metal platers that done it. They didn't raise the scaffolding right proper. I'll tell you till I'm blue in the face. It's the metal—"

"Hush now, Betty. No use getting upset over it." He pulled his arm free of her grip to wrap it around her shoulder reassuringly, and she fell silent. "The problem is, Lady, my leg never healed right after the fall, and now I have troubles keeping up with production. If I can't keep up, they'll let me go. My only chance is to apply and test for a position in the office. It's not typical for a worker like me to move into the office, but I've had some schooling, and I can read and write. I'm real good with maths, and I was hoping to learn something about accounting so I can try for a position what's opening up. They require applicants to take an exam on accounting principles. The Merchant Shipbuilding Company doesn't hire just anyone, you see. I need to know something if I hope to get the position." Here his eyes moved to his wife, and Annie watched his hand tighten on her shoulder.

Involuntarily her mind flew back to that night in the garden when Gabriel had put his arm around her, saved her, brought her to this new life.

She gave herself a mental shake. "You require a book on accounting principles, Mr. Tanner. When would you require to have the book by?"

Mr. Tanner looked down as if suddenly shy. "I'll need it by next month, ma'am, if I'm to have time to study before the test.

Annie smiled. "Very good. I promise I'll have something to you in four weeks' time. Will that do?"

She might have been offering them the Crown Jewels by the way their expressions opened in unison.

"Oh ma'am, that would be right kind of you. May we give you something for your kindness?" He steadied his crutch under his arm, his hand moving for his pocket, but Annie stopped him.

"No, we take no coin here. We only ask that you use the knowledge we can give you to better your life." She wasn't sure where the words came from, but suddenly nothing was truer.

Mr. Tanner stilled in his movement, and he slid a glance to his wife whose lips had parted in disbelief. She looked to Annie.

"You don't require payment?" she asked, her voice soft again.

"No, we do not," Annie said firmly. "Libraries should never require a fee. They are open to all."

The small woman looked about them. "Is that what this is? A library?"

"Yes," Annie said without hesitation. "Yes, it's a library."

The small woman's eyes lit as they roamed the tables around her. "Would you mind if I have look?" she asked, not quite meeting Annie's gaze as if Annie might refuse her.

"I hope you would," she said, and with that, Mr. and Mrs. Tanner floated away, their eyes taking in the titles on the tables around them even as the next person stepped up to the table, a request already spilling from her lips.

* * *

GABRIEL WAS SO ABSORBED in his own thoughts he didn't notice his wife straightaway.

This was entirely his own fault. He'd had several meetings that day with various members of the House, attempting to gain their support for the drains bill but had met with only moderate success. He was going over the meetings in his head, looking for ways he could have shifted the conversation to better sway the target, so he was already to his desk, his jacket tossed haphazardly on the chair, his fingers at his cravat when he spotted his wife on the sofa in front of the window.

"Hello, husband," she said without looking up.

Her head was bent over an open text she had perched against her drawn up knees. This was not unusual. In the month they had been wed, he had come to understand his wife spent a great deal of time in the library, reading and researching. So the current tableau of open book and studious wife seemed natural.

What was not, however, was the fact that she was clearly in her nightrail and dressing gown, and it was hardly past supper time.

Every muscle in his body tightened, and although he willed his eyes to move away, they refused, locked on the image of his wife, her thick dark hair in a loose braid down her back, those damnable tendrils escaping to frame her face.

"Hello, wife." He heard his voice, but how he managed the words, he would never know.

He wasn't sure when, but he'd apparently finished unraveling his cravat because the cloth was suddenly limp in his hand. He tossed it aside with his jacket. "You're dressed for bed." The statement was one he hadn't meant to make out loud, but she seemed unfazed by his observation.

"Hmm, yes. One gets quite dusty moving all those books around. I had a bath when I returned home, and it felt wasteful to soil another gown when my plans for the evening involved not much more than this." She paused, worrying her lower lip briefly as she gathered her next words. "It would be lovely to have a dedicated space for the books, so we aren't forced to do so much hauling." She raised her head and held up the book to reveal its title as something related to basic carpentry. "I'm trying to determine if there's a way for us to construct mobile bookcases. Perhaps Mr. Timmons will allow us to keep the books there if we have a means of moving them quickly."

He raised an eyebrow. "And have you experience with saw and hammer then, Your Grace?"

She wrinkled her nose. "No, but I suppose there's a book on that as well." She bent her head to her reading. "How were your meetings?"

He had nearly stepped forward to take a seat next to her on the sofa when he realized his intent and forcibly leaned back against his desk, wrapping his hands around the edge as if to anchor himself to it. "They were less fruitful than I had hoped," he said, scrubbing a hand over his face. "I'm hoping to meet with several of the gentlemen again to acquire a different outcome."

She not only looked up when he first spoke, but now she was setting aside her book and standing, unraveling herself from the sofa. He should have averted his eyes, but he couldn't. First it was her bare feet again, but now the movement afforded him a glimpse of ankle and calf, and nothing had ever been more erotic in his life.

He sucked in a breath and forced himself to look at her face.

Which really didn't help because she was beautiful.

How was he to endure a lifetime of resisting her?

"When is the vote?" she asked, coming around the sofa toward him.

Why did he suddenly feel as though she were a panther stalking through the jungle and he the prey?

He rubbed his face with his hand again and looked to the ceiling as it was his last hope. "Three weeks," he answered.

"And how many more votes do you have left to secure?"

His gaze swung down. She was close, incredibly so, and he found her standing in front of him, arms crossed under her breasts which only served to boost them up as if she were offering them to him.

God, when had he begun to see her like this? Each piece of her enticed him more than the next, and together she was the summation of sin. He had to remember he was supposed to protect her even if it meant saving her from his own lustful thoughts.

But once imagined, he couldn't stop them, the lustful thoughts of all the things he wished to do to her.

"Gabriel?"

Her voice penetrated the fog that had overcome him, and he remembered she'd asked him a question, a question he could not in the least remember then. He shook his head. "It's all just government work. I'd much rather hear about your day. How was the exchange?"

Her eyes roamed over his face for a moment, and he wondered if she would continue questioning him, but then her eyes cleared, and she shook her head slightly. "Oh, it was lovely." She paced away as she talked, and he watched her, or rather he watched the way her dressing gown clung to her buttocks as she moved. "Every week when we conduct the exchange we have more and more patrons." She turned back, and he lifted his eyes quickly, hoping she hadn't noticed. "We must devise a better system for keeping track of the books. I'm using the journal you gave me as you know, but soon we'll outgrow such a rudimentary system." Again she shook her head. "I must seek out a trained librarian. Perhaps she can assist me with devising a system that would work."

It was a beat before he realized she had finished speaking as he'd become unusually mesmerized by her mouth.

What was wrong with him?

He was working too much. That must be it. He was denying himself the one thing he wanted, and with the added stress of the drains bill, he was simply beginning to crack. If he didn't get his mind straight, Bedlam was in his very near future.

"Gabriel, are you all right?"

Once more he was forced to shake himself from his thoughts. "Quite," he said, pinching the bridge of his nose. "Just a lot on my mind right now is all."

It was strange having someone ask after him. His life had been severely solitary before he had wed, and he found this part of marriage the hardest to adjust to. Having someone looking after him, asking after him, ensuring he was comfortable and well. Hell, she'd even asked him if his eggs were too runny one morning.

He met her gaze now and for the first time in his life, he felt the real compulsion to tell her everything that was swimming through his mind. The opposition to his drains bill. His conversation with Liam and Gabriel's growing concern about what Belvedere might try next. For the first time he thought he might be able to unburden himself, share a bit of himself with someone else, but even as he toed the edge of that cliff, he found he couldn't jump.

He crossed his arms over his chest and settled in against the desk. "I promise you, Annie. It's only the strain of work and nothing more. Have you supped? I might ask Mrs. Featherstone to send up a tray. A warm bowl of Cook's—"

"Gabriel, why did you never marry?"

The question nearly had him falling off his perch against the desk. "I'm sorry?"

She licked her lips and took a step toward him. "I know it's not my business, and you mustn't answer if you don't wish to. It's just you never answered me the last time I asked, and I was wondering…why?"

Her eyes had grown wary, watchful, and he couldn't help but think her inquiry was more about her rather than him. Was that insecurity he saw in her gaze? Their relationship had been unconventional from the start, and now they found themselves in a most untenable situation, namely married. She hadn't voiced her thoughts about Overby's attack, only stating the facts of what had happened, and he wondered now if the circumstances surrounding their marriage was giving her pause.

He studied her face a second longer before realizing there was only one answer he could give her. The truth.

"I never met anyone I wished to marry," he answered.

Her eyes didn't change, and they moved over his face as if trying to detect a lie. "Truly?" she asked, confirming his suspicions. "Even when the title would demand you sire an heir?"

He gave a one-shouldered shrug. "The continuation of a title hardly seems important when it comes to marriage." He hesitated then as she worried her lower lip with her teeth, softening her features, tugging at his heart until he thought she might tug down the last of his defenses with it. But standing there, something hardened inside of him.

Seeing her face, open and vulnerable, he suddenly understood he could never tell her the truth. Never tell her about that day when his mother had presented Belvedere to him, and he knew he would never trust another person again with something like his heart. Because seeing her like that, he wished to protect her from the harshness of his youth, from the loneliness that had followed.

He only wanted her to feel happiness and joy and most importantly, hope.

She continued to watch him, clearly waiting for a greater explanation, but he had none to give.

He felt his expression soften. "Do you remember that day you snuck into my home, Lady Anna?"

She blinked, obviously confused by the sudden change of topic. "Yes," she managed after a beat.

"I'd never laughed like that before. Never. With anyone. And when I found you that night in the garden, I didn't think twice about what I did." He paused to ensure she was listening. "I thought someone who could make me feel such happiness was worth spending a lifetime with." He studied her face, and then said, "Annie, are you all right?" Her expression suggested he might have slapped her for all the warmth in it. Her eyes were huge and dark, her skin suddenly pale. "Annie?" He wanted to reach for her, but touching her right then was a very bad idea. Because if he did, he might not be able to stop, and he'd promised himself he would never do that to her again. She hadn't asked for this marriage, and she damn sure didn't ask for a husband to maul her.

Finally she shook her head, but it wasn't in negation to anything he said but more a gesture of disbelief. "If you thought I was worth marrying, may I ask for one favor more?"

This was a bad idea. He knew it. He could feel it in the way the room suddenly crackled with tension. He moved his hands again, placing them back along the edge of the desk, his grip lethal, and he heard himself say, "Anything."

"Gabriel, will you make love to me?"

# CHAPTER 13

*E*loise was right. If Annie wanted more from her husband, she had to be direct with him, tell him what she wanted.

Yet Gabriel held himself so carefully away from her.

This was her decision, and he was making sure she knew that.

His strong hands curled around the edge of the desk at his back instead of reaching for her, touching her. His breathing remained even, his eyes intent on only her face. There was nothing predatory about him, nothing except the heat in his eyes which told her everything she needed to know.

But he still hadn't answered, and embarrassment flooded her. She wasn't sure if it was from how wanton her statement had seemed or how naive it proved her to be. She waited for him to laugh at her, to belittle her, to make her feel less. But he didn't speak. He made no sound at all.

It happened so fast she wasn't sure how it transpired. His arms were around her—no, under her, but how?—and he was lifting her. Her arms flew around his neck to steady herself, to hold on, and then she was there, perched against his chest as his arms held her aloft. He spun them about until she felt the tap of the desk against her calves, and she thought he would set her down directly on the papers scattered there. But he didn't. He held her, suspended, clinging to him.

She became aware of where he held her. His arms were under her buttocks like a shelf on which he had placed her. Her fingers dug into his shoulders, her heart racing too impossibly fast.

Did he plan to carry her to bed? That was terribly far away. He couldn't possibly…

His eyes were blue, achingly blue, and she stared into them, thinking she might drown.

"Gabriel." He still hadn't spoken a single word, and her confidence dipped. His jaw was too firm, and without her knowing, her fingers traveled to the chiseled line there, tracing the outline, feeling the scrape of stubble. "Gabriel," she said, this time out of concern rather than self-consciousness.

"Say it again." His voice was hardly more than a growl.

Her fingers stilled against his jaw. "I…" Her heart gave a tremendous thud, and she knew she couldn't say it again, make herself vulnerable like that again. But there were different words pressing at her lips, the words she felt inside of her, so she said, "I want you."

"Show me." The words were growled, and it sent a shiver straight through her, her muscles clenching in her most private place. How could he do that with just his voice?

"I don't know how." Her confidence plummeted, and she suddenly very much wanted to be back on her own feet. She squirmed, but his arms held fast.

"You do know, Annie. Your body knows. Let it lead you."

His eyes roamed her face now as if searching for something, something she feared she didn't possess.

Tigress.

That was what he had called her.

The idea gripped her, coursed through her, until she could do nothing but believe him.

She kissed him before she could let her thoughts steer her from her resolve. She kissed him like she had wanted him to kiss her these past few weeks. She kissed him with everything she had kept inside because she was unsure of herself and her future. She was unsure no longer. The moment her lips touched his she knew.

*The spark.*

It was an inferno now, and it engulfed her. Her hands plunged into his hair, the need to hold him overpowering all else. He held her above him, and the angle afforded her everything. Her lips devoured his, her hands explored, discovered, took.

Suddenly she was sinking, and her hands went back to his shoulders, but he was only setting her down on the desk as she thought he would. She heard the crinkle of paper, the scattering of pens, and the distinct sound of books toppling to the floor.

His hands were against her back now, his fingers digging, claiming, possessing. Fear flashed through her, but it was gone as quickly as it came because on the back of it was the realization that she wanted Gabriel to possess her. She wanted him to have her. All of her. Because somehow she knew if he took her, she might finally have him in return.

This wasn't about dominance. This wasn't about control. This was giving and taking, having and finding. This was everything.

He pressed her against him, and she felt all of him, back and front, and she'd never felt safer in all her life. She expected him to lay her back, ease her down onto the desk, shove up her nightrail and take her, but he did none of that.

He kissed her like he planned to do it for the rest of her life.

His hands slid along her back, against her sides, up to brush past her breasts, and then he captured her face, holding her between his palms as if this was what he'd wanted all his life. Just her kiss. A sound came, unbidden, from deep within her throat, and she thought that might have been when she fell the rest of the way in love with him. When he held her like that. When he kissed her like that.

When he worshiped her body instead of claiming it.

Her hands had been at his shoulders, but as he continued to kiss her, savored her, her fingers began to wander. She wanted to know what he felt like, all of him. She'd watched him for weeks now, the easy grace with which he moved, the casualness of effort, and she wanted to trace every muscle, find every valley and curve.

She didn't know she was supposed to take. She didn't know she was meant to want him. Not like this. Her earlier experiences with coupling had involved her lying dormant, willing the man to finish and be done with her. But not now. It wasn't until she touched him, until her fingers brushed the warm skin of his neck that she realized what she'd been doing.

She'd been anticipating this moment.

She'd thought about what it would feel like to touch him like this ever since that afternoon on the sofa when their clothes had stood between them. Her fingers traced the curve of his neck, the ridge of collarbone. The sound deep in her throat came again and suddenly her legs were around him, holding him to her as she drew her hands down his chest, feeling every one of his muscles tighten under his shirt, torturing herself by not pulling up his shirt, delving her hands underneath to feel the hotness of his skin. No, now that she was here, now that touching him was free to her, she delayed, driving her desire higher.

He broke the kiss, and a whimper erupted from her before she could gain control of herself. He pulled back just enough and with a hand yanked his shirt over his head, tossing it aside.

Through the entire motion his eyes never left hers, and then his hands were back, cupping her face, and just before he returned his lips to hers, he said, "Do that again."

That place deep inside of her, the one that yearned for him, clenched at the rough demand, but it didn't matter. As soon as he kissed her again, her hands flew to him as if to hang on. The moment her fingers touched his bare skin, it was as though a bolt of lightning surged up her arms. She jolted at the touch, her fingers skittering. She might have moaned his name against his lips, but he was kissing her jaw now, small points of heat, moving, nipping, scraping as he made his way up her jaw to that sensitive place behind her ear where—

"Gabriel." The place inside of her hovered between pleasure and pain, and she wanted it, memories of what he had done to her that rainy afternoon making her desire ferocious. He couldn't go on torturing her like this. He couldn't. Something had to happen. He had to touch her— "Gabriel." His name the only thing left to her.

She laid fully against the desk now, his hands roaming her body as if he meant to memorize every curve and valley. Her breasts ached, but he didn't touch them. She lifted her legs, wrapping them about him more tightly, urging him to touch her like he had that afternoon, but he kept his hands on top of her dressing gown, kneading her hips. He was driving her absolutely mad.

"Gabriel, please," she murmured against his mouth before

sucking his lower lip between hers. "Gabriel, I need you to touch me."

He made a sound then, a sound so primal she nearly climaxed simply from hearing it. She thought he would undo the sash at her waist, but he didn't. Instead he shoved her dressing gown and nightrail up in one fluid movement, exposing her to him in a single rush.

And then he stopped, his hands at her waist where he held her garments in ragged fistfuls. He looked at her, his eyes a cerulean blue, and her heart shattered as she fell in love with him.

This was probably the most inappropriate time to fall in love. In fact, she was sure someone more sensible would tell her it was only lust that was clouding her mind. But this wasn't lust. This was scientific observation.

No one had ever touched her like her very skin could set them aflame. No one looked at her like she was the most beautiful thing to ever have existed.

No one had ever treated her like she mattered.

Gabriel could make her understand her worth with a single look, and this simple understanding wrapped around her heart.

She slid her hands overtop his, and his gaze flew to hers, his eyes searching, and she wondered what he was looking for. She had the odd sense it wasn't something she could give him, but rather something he had to find himself, and she wondered, for the briefest moment, if even after tonight there would be that distance remaining between them.

The moment was brief as he leaned forward and captured her mouth, his hands dropping her garments at her waist to move to his own trousers. She wanted to help him, eager to have him inside of her, but she didn't know what to do, so she kissed him back, her hands cupping his face, pulling him closer. God, everything felt so right in that very moment. Tears pricked the backs of her eyes.

How could something so wonderful have happened to her? She had thought her life over so many times before, and yet now as she lay there, his heavy body pressed into hers, she couldn't help but feel it had only just begun.

And then he was pushing against her. A cry of surprise escaped her lips.

"Gabriel, you're—" The word jammed in her throat, and embarrassment coursed through her at what she'd almost said. But he was—and she was—and— "Gabriel, I don't think you will fit."

She felt his grin against her cheek. "Trust me, wife. It'll work just as it's supposed to."

He touched her then, at her very center, and she arched off the desk. She wished he had stripped her bare. She wished she could feel him along her whole body, but then he slipped a single finger inside of her, and she forgot everything else except the pleasure that spiraled through her.

"You're ready for me, wife," he whispered against her ear. "Tell me you want me."

He moved his hips, pressing himself into her, and she breathed, "Yes."

He slid inside of her in a single movement, and her lips parted without sound, her fingers digging into his back. He was so big, terribly so, but he'd been right. He did fit, and the pleasure was glorious and—

He started to move, sliding in and out of her, forcing her desire to a peak she'd never have been able to fathom. She reveled in it, losing herself to the passion he stoked in her.

"Gabriel, please." She dug her heels into his back, lifting her to him, begging him to thrust harder, deeper, faster. "Oh God, Gabriel, I need you—"

That was when she shattered, her body convulsing around him. He gave one final thrust, his hands hard on her hips as he drove into her, and then they fell together.

# CHAPTER 14

*I*t was late. Too late.

The gas lamps were already lit, and the front steps of the Sagamore were an unworldly orange from their glow. Annie alighted from the carriage as if it were any other day she had visited the building in the past month, but this time she paused and called up to the driver.

"I'll be only a minute," she said, and he nodded in response.

She turned to head to the door but stopped, tension crawling along her neck like a spider, and she hesitated, her feet not letting her leave the safety of her carriage. This was ridiculous. She was simply frightening herself with imaginings. Still Gabriel had given her an incredible amount of freedom to visit the Sagamore to see to their book needs, and it would be unfair of her not to exercise caution, especially at such a late hour.

The book on accounting principles had only arrived that afternoon, and by the time word had reached her the hour was growing late. She needed to get that book to Mr. Tanner. Both because she had promised him and because her own moral code wouldn't allow her to tarry. So no matter the late hour, urgency drove her forward.

She peered down the street that led back onto the main thoroughfare, but the pavement was empty, the sound of traffic on the cross street and the occasional friendly murmur of conversation from an open window the only sounds on the air. It had rained earlier, and the air was musty, the steps still damp as she climbed them up to the front door.

She entered swiftly, shutting the door behind her, and letting the familiar cooking scents and the warmth of the corridor envelope her. The hall sconces were lit, and the wooden floors gleamed as far as her eye could travel down the length of the hallway. There was more noise about the place now than when she had first started visiting the Sagamore, and she smiled, leaning back against the door to enjoy it. Soon the place would be a proper community, and if she simply worked at it, her library would be an integral part of it.

Snatching up her skirts, she climbed the stairs to the third floor and made her way to Mrs. Tanner's flat. She heard a baby crying somewhere at the opposite end of the building, and she paused to listen. There hadn't been a baby on this floor. It was clear a new tenant had arrived, and Annie made a note to call on the new occupant just as soon as she was able.

And likely at a proper time for calling, and not like she was now, skulking about after suppertime. She knocked briskly on Mrs. Tanner's door and used the time it took for the woman to answer to straighten her skirts. She had her smile firmly in place and the book held up in front of her by the time the door opened.

Mrs. Tanner gasped on sight of Annie. "Oh Lady, you

shouldn't have. I've taken you from your husband during social hours."

Annie waved away the woman's concerns as she handed her the book on accounting principles. "You mustn't worry, Mrs. Tanner. My husband has an important bill coming up for a vote, and he's out wooing support." She shook her head, her smile never faltering. "He doesn't expect me to sit at home waiting for him while he's out working for his causes."

It was as if she had told Mrs. Tanner she planned to move to the northern reaches of the Americas to start a nomadic colony.

The woman's soft brown eyes grew wide, her eyebrows going into her gray-speckled fringe. "Oh Lady, I don't know what to say," Mrs. Tanner mumbled as she took the book, passing one hand carefully over its cover. When she met Annie's gaze again, her eyes were damp with unshed tears. "You can't know what this means for us."

Annie couldn't stop herself from reaching out and placing a comforting hand on the woman's arm. "I do, Mrs. Tanner. I know your husband's test is coming up, and he'll need all the time he can get to study if he wants that promotion, and I know he does." She squeezed Mrs. Tanner's arm. "You mustn't worry. I know he'll do it. This will help him reach the next step in his career." Here Annie tapped the book Mrs. Tanner held so preciously between both hands.

"Do you really think so?" Her voice wobbled with the tears she still had not shed, and Annie's heart squeezed at the sight of the hope in the woman's eyes.

"I know it," she said softly.

A single tear fell from Mrs. Tanner's eye as she said, "Lady, would you mind if I were terribly bold?"

The question was so unlike the mild-mannered woman it surprised Annie momentarily. "Of course not," she said finally, and before she could react, Mrs. Tanner stepped forward and wrapped both arms awkwardly around her.

Annie attempted to embrace the woman in return, but Mrs. Tanner had wrapped her arms over Annie's, and the embrace was more of a stumbling together in emotion, and nothing had ever warmed Annie's heart quite so much.

When the woman finally stepped back, tears stained her cheek, but her mouth tipped up in a shaky smile. "I will be forever in your debt, Lady. Forever."

Annie squeezed the woman's arm one last time. "Think nothing of it," she said. "It's just what a librarian would do, isn't it?"

Mrs. Tanner's smile wobbled on a laugh now. "I suppose you're right."

They exchanged goodbyes, and Annie nearly floated down the stairs, her heart was so light.

She had been right. It wasn't something in a book Annie had been seeking. It was the books themselves, and now she could finally share their power with others who might need it. She felt invigorated, her very blood tingling with excitement. She would call on Mr. Timmons the very next day and discover the intention for the room she had been using for her makeshift library these past weeks and see if it might be commandeered permanently. After all, an educated worker was a valuable worker, wasn't it? Surely the Merchant Shipbuilding Company would agree.

More than anything, she couldn't wait to tell Gabriel.

Things had changed between them in the past few weeks, and although she would say it was for the better, she couldn't help but feel there was still something standing between them, and she couldn't help but feel the guilt lay at her feet. After all, it had been her actions that had forced him to marry her.

She had reached the bottom of the central staircase and taken three steps when she realized something was wrong.

She hesitated, and later she would wish she hadn't. If she had kept going, nothing might have occurred. She might have slipped from the Sagamore, regained her carriage, and gone home to her husband, but that was not what happened.

Three steps from the staircase she realized the sconces at this end of the corridor had been snuffed out. Darkness engulfed the corridor, throwing shadows in unsettling angles across the floor. She could hardly make out the door at the opposite end, and the sight of it, hazy in the darkness, sent her heart galloping, her euphoria of moments before vanishing.

She whirled around, knowing the attack would come from behind her because her assailant would know she would head straight for the door. Her heart gave a single thump when the man separated himself from the shadows. The sconces at the other end of the hallway meant the man was backlit, and his face remained in darkness, but she knew him. His mustache protruded from his silhouette, and his gait was uneven as he slinked toward her.

Belvedere.

"Lady Anna." He drawled her name, stretching each syllable as if savoring each sound. "That's what you prefer to be called, isn't it? Lady Anna." He inched his way toward her as if he were savoring that too, closing the distance between them, stalking her. "What a funny thing when you have the title of duchess at your disposal."

He was hardly more than six feet away from her, and like that night in the garden with Overby, she couldn't make her feet move. The door was at her back. She had only to pick up her skirts and run. This couldn't happen again. This fear that gripped her, that robbed her of her own free will.

"But perhaps you prefer Lady Anna because it reminds you of who you are." He stopped along with his speech, his eyes boring into her through the semi-darkness as he uttered the words that sliced through her heart. "It reminds you of the slut you are." Even in the dim, she saw his mouth kick up on one side as he sneered. "Oh, I know you're a slut. We all do. That darling dead husband of yours told everyone the trouble he had with you. Couldn't keep your legs together, could you?"

It was a lie. It was all lies. Roger had spread lies about her. It wasn't enough that he had controlled her physically, he had controlled how others thought of her too. It wasn't fair.

It. Wasn't. Fair.

She wasn't sure when her fingers curled, anger surging through her, forcing her fingers into her skirt, pulling at the fabric until her hem lifted, higher and higher until it was above her boots. Each movement was small and deft, and had she been thinking clearly, she knew such stealth movement would be lost in the dark, but her conscience was thick with hatred, hatred for Roger who had done this to her. Who made these men think they could have their way with her.

It was clear what Belvedere wanted from her. It was in the way he stalked her, the way he had turned off the sconces at this end of the corridor, trapping them in darkness. It was in the way his eyes roamed her body, assessing the thing he would take.

She was not a thing, and her fingers continued to curl, easing up her skirts. She willed her breath to steady, willed her heart to stop racing, willed her mind to clear as he continued to slink toward her, his sneer firmly in place on his blasted face.

"Does Gabriel know you're a whore, Lady Anna? Does he know what you freely give to other men?" Four feet away. "Does he know he's been cuckolded?" He laughed then suddenly, enough to startle her, her grip slipping on her skirts, but she forced herself to regain focus, pulling at the fabric with her now trembling hands. "I like to think of Gabriel being cuckolded. It's only what he deserves."

Two feet.

She licked her lips. "Promise not to tell him?" It took all she had to force a mewling tone into her voice, soft and husky. She saw the hesitation in Belvedere's step, the way his eyes twitched from side to side, the sneer wobble. But then he seemed to regain himself, his eyes hungry now.

"Of course I won't, Lady Anna."

His breath smelled of garlic and stale beer, and that was when she picked up her booted foot and drove it down on the arch of his foot. He had hardly given a yelp of pain before she had her leg up, the kick meeting its mark squarely between his legs. He doubled over, his hands reaching, cradling, and it was simple to shove him away. He landed with a backbreaking thud on the hard floor, his cries cut off by the obvious pain he was in as he writhed on the floor, his chest still as if she'd knocked the air out of him as well.

She didn't wait to see what other damage she had wrought. Skirts still in hand, she ran for the door, and the safety of her driver. She was on the front stoop, the door in one hand when Belvedere's voice reached her.

"You would run away so easily. You're a coward and a slut."

She wasn't sure why his words should stop her, but suddenly she was tired of letting other people determine her character, so she turned back, the truth on her lips.

She gave a one-shoulder shrug as she said, "You're not my demon," and with that, she slammed the door on him.

It was raining again. She pressed her hand to the glass as if she could touch the raindrops that marked it.

She had bathed and changed when she'd returned home. Belvedere hadn't touched her, and yet she could feel his slimy hands on her. Perhaps it was just the memory of his voice coiling out to her, wrapping around her like a python readying for the kill.

She had donned a morning gown for comfort, not wishing to feel so exposed in only nightrail and dressing gown. She didn't wish to feel quite so vulnerable when she told her husband what had happened.

She retreated to the one room that gave her the most comfort in Grimsby House, going to the single window that had witnessed so much change in her life. Touching the glass now, feeling its coolness against her fingertips, she couldn't help but notice how her feelings about the encounter weren't so much about her, but rather about how Gabriel would take it when she told him what had happened. For two years, she had feared her husband's anger, feared what he might do to her physically. And that night she'd faced an opponent who had meant her the most grievous harm and standing there she felt nothing for herself. Her body still radiated with the memory of it, yes, but when she prodded around her feelings, there was nothing.

No fear. No apprehension. No worry.

She'd defeated Belvedere physically without question when she knew only months ago she wouldn't have been capable of the thing. Had Gabriel given her that? Had he given her that strength? Or had he simply restored it?

But if she truly had her strength returned to her, why did she fear Gabriel's homecoming?

Their relationship had changed so much over the course of the past few months. From acquaintances to friend to lovers, each a degree deeper than the last, and yet she still felt as though he were apart from her. They may have embraced each other physically, but there was a space that yawned between them that she couldn't seem to breach.

She stepped away from the window, seeking the comfort and warmth of the fire, her mind in turmoil as she once again went over the course of her marriage. Was Roger right? Was there something wrong with her? Was that what prevented her marriage to Gabriel from becoming something more? She could have dismissed it if Roger's was the only voice in her head, but now others had repeated his words, and they were like an echo, accusations playing in round over and over again.

Despite the rain and the crackle of the fire, she heard the front door open below her. Gabriel had gone out to attend a function at his club that would allow him to mingle with those whose support he still needed for his drains bill. She had welcomed the respite from social obligations as it had allowed her to deliver the book to Mrs. Tanner, but her elation of only hours earlier was now tainted by what Belvedere had done.

She listened, but her husband's footsteps were muted by the house itself, and so she could only wait until the library door opened moments later and her husband appeared.

She forced a smile before she turned about, only to find him weary and worn, the stress of the day apparent in his expression.

"Oh Gabriel, what's happened?" she asked, rushing forward, her own news momentarily forgotten.

Instead of answering, he pulled her into his arms, setting his chin atop her head as he was wont to do. "There are parts of my duty that I find entirely vexing, Annie, and a night spent with overprivileged gentlemen with arcane ideas about class and welfare is one of them."

"Was it truly so terrible?"

He eased her away, and she looked up to find his expression grim. "The Earl of Wansdale informed me anyone of the working class should be kept in barracks behind a soaring wall so he wouldn't be forced to look upon them."

"No," she breathed.

"Yes," he replied and let go of her, wandering over to the drink cart in the corner and pouring himself a glass. He gestured with it to her. "I trust you had a pleasant and restful night in."

She swallowed, gathering her courage. "Actually there's something I must tell you." And she did before she lost her nerve. She told him about the book, the Sagamore, and finally Belvedere. Through the entire recitation she imagined what he would say. That he might forbid her from her work at the Sagamore, that he may forbid her to leave the house entirely.

She hadn't once thought of any of this since Belvedere attacked her, but seeing Gabriel now as realization sank in, as her words continued to tumble out, her strength, of which she was so sure only minutes before, wavered.

It was only in that moment that she remembered who he was.

Her husband.

And by law, he could do anything he wished to her. Would he punish her for another's actions? Would he suddenly realize what Roger had known all along?

When she finished, he still hadn't moved or spoken, not even to ask a question or seek clarification. He held his untouched drink in one hand, and she realized she hadn't even given him the time to remove his coat. Still he didn't speak, and the silence grew until it held weight, pressing in on her until she knew it would rob her of breath.

"I'm sorry, Gabriel." The words spilled out of her, an apology the only antidote she knew for silence. It stung, saying these words to him. They were the very ones she'd said to Roger to deflect a blow.

Her heart shriveled, hope receding, but Gabriel didn't strike her. Of course he didn't. He carefully set down his glass and came to her, taking her shoulders in his hands as he so often did.

"Are you hurt?" It was the first question he had asked, and there was something strange about his voice. It wasn't him. It wasn't Gabriel, her husband, the man she loved so much she was afraid to tell him.

The person in front of her was someone else entirely, and just from the sound of his voice, something shifted inside of her. She felt it, like the click of a door or the snap of a trunk closing. The man she had believed him to be had become the man she knew and understood, and now he had changed again.

"No," she said carefully, shaking her head. "I never gave him the chance to hurt me." She chose her words carefully, sensing each one had the power to explode the delicacy that hovered between them.

Gabriel let go of her and walked away, not back for his drink but in the opposite direction. He only stopped when he reached his desk, the very desk on which he had first made love to her. Was that only a mere few weeks ago? How had so much happened so quickly?

He leaned against the desk now, his hands fisted against the blotter. She watched him breathe, watched his back expand and contract with each controlled breath.

"Gabriel." She spoke his name, but she wasn't sure it was a question. It was more that it was the only safe thing to say in that moment, and she wanted to know if he was all right.

But of course he wasn't all right.

He straightened and turned, and she sucked in a breath as she took in his face.

Her husband was gone.

Gabriel was gone.

She didn't know who this man was who stood before her, but it wasn't Gabriel. It wasn't the man who had covered up her husband's death to save her from scandal. It wasn't the man who had shown her friendship. It wasn't the man who had given her pleasure. It wasn't the man who had made her hope for love again.

It was a stranger.

"You should go to bed. You need your rest."

He was dismissing her. He hadn't asked her any other questions, only the one, and she was supposed to…what exactly? Disappear?

She took a step forward. "Gabriel, we must talk about this. I know it's upsetting, and Belvedere may try—"

"Go to bed." His voice held an edge, growing quieter with each word.

"But Gabriel—"

"This doesn't concern you, Anna." His eyes were hard and empty, and in them she saw nothing but emptiness.

But then he did the very thing that could convince her, convince her of the truth she hadn't been able to see on the other side of her own lies, the ones Roger had convinced her were true.

He turned away from her.

He turned away, leaning once more against the desk, head down, hands fisted.

It was like someone had lifted a blindfold from her eyes, and after too long in the dark, she was forced to squint against the light.

She had spent the hours between the attack and now thinking of what she had done wrong, of how Gabriel would react, of what she could do to stop this from happening ever again. She had been so focused on herself because she'd been taught to understand that the fault would always lie with her. Roger was so quick to blame her she had accepted it as truth. She hadn't considered that maybe someone else's behavior could be to blame.

But standing there before this stranger who was supposed to be her husband, she knew.

The reason for the space between them was not her fault. It was Gabriel's. The image of his mother, her coldness and condescension. Belvedere and his treatment of Gabriel. The way Gabriel had so carefully shut down any whisper of scandal when Roger had died, how he had orchestrated their union, how he shut her out.

Gabriel hadn't just erected a wall between himself and everyone else. He'd built an unscalable fortress, and she was on the wrong side of it.

Roger had taught her to assume blame, assume it was her fault, and she'd repeated the same thing in her next marriage. Standing there, the gulf between herself and her husband growing ever greater, she knew.

She was done being the keeper of another's behavior.

This wasn't her fault, and it wasn't hers to unravel. Gabriel's seclusion was all his own.

Just as she had to have been the one to see it, so too Gabriel would need to see his own faults from himself. She couldn't make him see it just as no one had been able to force her to see how she accepted blame without reason.

She gathered her skirts in one hand, holding them carefully out of the way of her slippers. "Good night, Gabriel," she said and left.

# CHAPTER 15

Gabriel had never called on Ardley before, but this wasn't a conversation to be had at the club or at the side of the ballroom where others might overhear.

He waited in the foyer of Ardley's townhouse as the butler went to see if the duke was in. It wasn't below him to have a look around while he waited, noting the marble floors, the gilt frames on the portraits that marched up the wall to one side of the sweeping staircase with its brass and wood balustrade. The space exuded wealth while remaining tasteful, and Gabriel thought it reflected the duke's character very well.

He was only standing there for less than a minute when the duke himself tumbled through the front door. Tumbled, in fact, because he was brushing dust from his riding pants and slapping at a particularly brutal patch of mud on one thigh with his riding gloves as he muttered something about hellions of the opposite sex.

"Ardley," Gabriel said before the duke could utter anything he might regret as he was focused on his riding breeches and hadn't noticed Gabriel yet.

The duke moved only his eyes up, still bent as he tended to the dust Gabriel now realized covered him from head to toe as though the man had taken a spill.

"Grimsby," Ardley said as if he'd discovered a Rembrandt hanging amongst the family portraits. "What are you doing here?" The question wasn't an accusation, not coming from Liam. There was a hint of confusion in his voice as if he'd misplaced Gabriel and felt bad about it.

"I wish to speak with you about a delicate matter of some urgency."

Liam finally straightened and tossed his gloves to a side table. "A delicate matter? You've married the Wexford widow. There's nothing left to be done, man."

Gabriel couldn't help a smile at Liam's confusion. "I'm afraid this has to do with Belvedere."

Liam made a snorting nose that suggested his dislike of the man and tossed his hat aside with his gloves. "I was worried you'd say that. We'd better go into my study then."

He gestured for Gabriel to follow him, and they passed the butler returning from the depths of the house, a bewildered expression on his face that led Gabriel to believe he truly hadn't known the whereabouts of his master.

"Cotton, please have a cart sent up, would you, old man?" Liam called behind him as he swept into the study.

Gabriel heard a muttered, "Very good" from somewhere behind him and assumed the butler was off to fetch a tea cart.

"This really isn't a social call, Liam," Gabriel said as the duke made his way to the opposite end of the room. Gabriel took a moment to look around him and found the duke's study as well appointed as the foyer had been with rich carpets in muted hues, polished wood, and heavy drapes.

"The cart isn't for you," he said, pulling off his jacket and tossing it on the back of a chair as he passed. "I'm famished."

He stopped and whirled about, his cravat swinging wildly in the hand he pointed at Gabriel. "Have you ever raced a woman on Rotten Row?" Gabriel was so startled by the question he didn't have a response at hand before Liam went on. "Vexing creatures. All of them. A gentleman only wishes to engage in simple sport, and a lady is the first to inflate it to monstrous proportions." He chucked the cravat onto his desk before circling it to collapse into the chair behind it. He waved a hand as if the anger had left him. "Go on then. You said this was a matter of some delicacy."

Gabriel approached the desk uncertain of how to begin. He wished to ask a favor of Ardley, but he sensed it would be good of him to inquire as to the cause of Liam's unrest. He thought, perhaps, that was what a friend would do. He took a seat in front of the desk and eyed his new friend.

"I take it you raced a lady on Rotten Row," he said, hoping to pluck some answers from Liam without having to prod insensitively.

Liam waved that hand again. "It is irrelevant, Gabriel. The woman is a menace, and I should have known better than to challenge her. I shall remember in future to keep my dealings with her to a minimum."

Gabriel could recall with excellent clarity that night when Liam had upset a group of giggling debutantes with a mere look and found his current state perplexing. How could a man with such clear control over the opposite sex be so lost after a mere horse race with one of them?

"I think you'd better tell me what happened," Gabriel decided to say, but Liam was prevented from answering with the arrival of the tea cart.

Liam stood as soon as the maid who had brought the cart left and helped himself to a generous plate of sandwiches and a cup of tea. He gestured for Gabriel to help himself but didn't wait for the other duke to respond and instead slunk back to his chair where he finished off two sandwiches before speaking.

"I've never had a female trouble me the way this one does, Grimsby." Liam shook his head and downed nearly the entire cup of tea. "It puts me in a mind to swear off my whole system. Be done with the lot of them." He sat forward, clunking his cup down on the table so swiftly tea sloshed over the rim. "What is it like being married? Are women more agreeable once they're wed? Is it something in their brains that requires an attachment to make them docile?"

Gabriel blinked. "I don't think I should answer that."

Liam scoffed and wiped a hand across his desk as if to dismiss the matter. "You're probably right. I should let the whole thing go, shouldn't I? She's hardly worth my time." He drank the last of his tea and sat up in his chair. "Right then. Out with it, Grimsby. What is it you'd like to speak with me about?"

"I'd like to ask you to be my second."

Liam didn't answer right away. Instead he looked into his empty teacup as if wondering what it was he had consumed. "Did I hear you correctly?" he finally asked. "You're asking me to be your second?" He looked about now. "What year is it exactly? Are we still defending our honor through physical harm?"

"Belvedere attacked Annie, and he must pay for it." Gabriel heard the steel in his voice, heard the undercurrent of hatred, and yet he could not feel it. Since Annie had told him what had happened, he'd been oddly numb. "You said if I should ever need help, I should come to you."

"Is she unharmed?" Liam's voice had gone quiet.

"I taught her how to defend herself, and she was able to get away, yes, but that doesn't mean he won't do it again."

Liam leaned back in his chair, his agitated mood of moments before seemingly gone, and before Gabriel was a man he'd never witnessed before, one of calm movements and objectively sterile calculation. "And you would resort to murder to prevent it from happening again."

"It will be a challenge to first blood. I've already run the man out of the country and ruined his reputation. A duel is all that is left to me."

"Have you thought about going to the authorities?"

"The Metropolitan Police?" Gabriel shook his head. "What could they do? It would be Belvedere's word against Annie's, and my mother and any number of her acquaintances would vouch for Belvedere." He shook his head again. "I won't take that chance."

"What does Annie say about this course of action?"

For the first time, Gabriel felt something. It was a shifting inside of him, one he cared not to name. "She doesn't know about my plan."

Liam sat up. "She doesn't know because you haven't told her."

The words were not a question, and they were spoken in the same sterile voice Liam had assumed at the first mention of Gabriel's request, but Gabriel heard the accusation plainly.

"It's best if she doesn't know about this." Again, Gabriel heard the words in the voice he had assumed since the night Annie had confessed to him what Belvedere had done, and yet he could not summon the proper emotion to go with the words. It was as though by keeping himself detached he wouldn't know the truth of what he was doing.

He was keeping things from his wife.

Their marriage wasn't one built on love. He knew that. He had offered for her to protect her from the scandal that was inevitable after what Overby had done. There was no romanticizing that.

But something had changed over the course of the past

two months. A lot had changed. The idea of keeping things from Annie made him physically ill.

Perhaps because he was falling in love with her.

Despite his best efforts not to, he had allowed his emotions to get the better of him, dictating his actions when it would have been better had his brain been in charge. But it was impossible to resist his wife, and now he was sitting in front of the Duke of Ardley and asking him to be his second in a duel because Gabriel was nearly absolutely certain he would do anything to protect Lady Anna Bounds.

Including die for her.

Liam had grown quiet again, and it was so unlike him Gabriel shifted in his seat, feeling the tension crawling along the back of his neck.

Finally Liam nodded. "I will do everything in my power to protect you, Grimsby. You know as much." He paused, but Gabriel didn't speak, knowing Liam well enough now to understand these small pauses were his way of gathering his thoughts. "I just want to ensure you understand how keeping this from your wife undermines the foundation of your marriage."

The words were so insightful Gabriel had trouble believing they came from a man who had a system for flirting with debutantes. He shifted again in his seat, but he never let his gaze drop from Liam's face.

"I must do this, Ardley, to protect Annie." It was neither admitting nor denying the truth of Liam's words, but it still left him feeling hollow.

Annie need never know of his plans or of their outcome. He would challenge Belvedere, quietly wound him and exact his revenge. Honor restored he would banish the man to the Continent once more and be done with him.

Liam nodded as if accepting Gabriel's statement before asking, "When is it you plan to issue your challenge? I shall make sure I am in attendance to arrange matters with Belvedere's second."

Feeling on firmer ground now, Gabriel said, "I plan to confront him at the Summer Solstice Ball. I want it to be public enough that he can't squirm away yet not so public as to take out a column in *The Times*."

Liam nodded. "I shall be there then." He stood and offered Gabriel his hand.

Gabriel stood as well, taking Liam's hand into his own. He felt the solidarity in his friend's grip, yet he couldn't help but feel as though he were treading in the entirely wrong and dangerous direction. He gave himself a mental shake. He couldn't let such thoughts intrude. He had to remember he was doing this for Annie.

"Till the Summer Solstice Ball then," Liam said and let go of his hand.

"Until then," Gabriel said and left, feeling his resolve none the firmer, Liam's warning ringing in his ears.

* * *

SHE SENT a note to her mother, sure she would relay the information in it to Eloise and Grandmother Bitsy, and then she went to the library to hide.

It was difficult, the emotions she felt in that room now. She pulled the quilt around her as she nestled onto the sofa, her eyes unseeing even as she stared out the window opposite, watching the sky grow dark. She should be getting ready for the Summer Solstice Ball, the height of the social season. She should be fixing her hair and dabbing lavender water behind her ears. Gabriel should be waiting for her in the foyer, looking resplendent in his evening wear. He would smile up at her as she descended the stairs, one gloved hand sliding along the balustrade as she did so. When she reached him, he would tell her she was beautiful, more beautiful than anything he had ever witnessed, and that he loved her more than anything.

But he hadn't said those words, and he wouldn't be saying those words because they hadn't spoken to each other since he had dismissed her from this very room a week ago. And she was not getting ready for the ball. She had sent a note with her regrets to her mother so the woman wouldn't worry, as she was sure her mother would be expecting her there, and Annie had every intention of remaining ensconced on that sofa for the remainder of the evening.

She had pulled a stack of novels close to her on the low table before the sofa, and Mrs. Featherstone had brought in a tray of tea without having been asked. There was something quietly motherly about the housekeeper. Annie had been so preoccupied with her work at the Sagamore, she hadn't had time to work closely with the woman yet. But there was hardly a need to as Grimsby House was run with a cool efficiency that matched its master's demeanor.

It was terrible how a simple shift in perspective could cause everything to make a lot more sense.

The world had become an absurdly bright and open place since she'd realized everything was not her fault. When she had shed the idea that she was to blame for everything, her situation and her surroundings had become a great deal clearer. It was as though her own bias had stained the world around her, making it darker and more foreboding than it actually was.

Was this the return of the strength she had known she'd possessed all along?

Or was it simply a matter of opening her eyes?

She couldn't be sure. Perhaps it was a bit of both. Because there was nothing more difficult than seeing oneself for who one truly was.

Whichever it was, it wasn't worth thinking about when Mrs. Featherstone had brought her an entire plate of Cook's butter biscuits.

She'd just picked up the plate when there was a soft knock at the library door. For an instant, her heart thudded, thinking it might be Gabriel, but he had left hours ago. Mrs. Featherstone had casually mentioned it five or six times in the past few hours and how His Grace would not return in time to escort Annie to the Summer Solstice Ball. Annie had finally put the woman out of her misery by stating her intent to remain in that evening.

Mrs. Featherstone's small features hadn't even twitched at the suggestion. If anything, Annie would have sworn there was the tiniest of grins tugging at the woman's small mouth. It had made Annie wonder what the servants were saying about her. She had, after all, invaded the duke's home against all propriety only to become his wife weeks later. What on earth did they think of her?

"Come in," she called and took a generous bite of the butter biscuit.

Rives stepped smartly just inside the door. "Your Grace," he said, extending a silver tray with a card on it.

"Who is it, Rives?" she asked before the man had a chance to make his way to her so she could read the card. The fact that anyone should be calling on her at this hour was alarming, and she couldn't wait for the butler to take the six steps required to reach her.

Rives was nonplussed as he replied, "The Duke of Ardley, ma'am."

She set the plate of butter biscuits aside, dropping her feet to the floor. "Show him in please."

Her mind went utterly blank. Even though her heart pumped furiously as she tossed aside the quilt that had become tangled around her shoulders it was as if there wasn't enough blood to reach her brain to form any kind of conclusion as to why the Duke of Ardley should be calling on her at such an inappropriate hour.

She'd only met the man once at her sister's introduction ball, and that was more than two months ago now. It was hardly a relationship which excused the late hour, and this only sent her heart into a whirl. She pressed her hand to her chest, hoping to slow it while she shook the wrinkles from her skirts.

"Ma'am," Rives intoned from behind her, and she spun back to face the door. "The Duke of Ardley."

She blinked, unsure why she should be so startled, but she hadn't anticipated seeing the duke in formal evening wear. The man was handsome, classically so, and it was no wonder society was in such a fury over him. But what was he doing in her library?

"Thank you, Rives," she said, dismissing the butler who slipped through the door, closing it discreetly behind him. Then to Ardley, "Your Grace." She curtsied as was proper, but the duke was already striding toward her.

"I apologize for my unannounced visit, Your Grace, but I felt you should know that tonight at the Summer Solstice Ball your husband plans to challenge Brogden Belvedere to a duel."

Once more she found herself blinking, her heart racing even as her mind emptied. "I beg your pardon."

He stood in front of her now, his face utterly relaxed when his words conjured anything but a state of calm. "Your husband plans to avenge your honor through the drawing of first blood. Frankly, I don't trust Belvedere to stop at first blood, and if you should like to not return to widowhood in the coming hours, I suggest you accompany me to the ball."

Her mouth opened, but she could drive no words forth until— "How did you know to find me here? I thought it would be assumed I would attend the ball. It is the most fashionable event of the season."

Something flashed across his eyes, and she couldn't help but feel he was holding back a grin. "I have my sources," he said. "Now I suggest you get ready. We must leave immediately. I am to meet Grimsby in the ballroom at half nine, and we haven't a moment to lose."

This only served to stall her further. "Half nine?" She shook her head. The time hardly mattered. "Why should you be meeting him?"

"Because he's asked me to be his second."

Until that moment, she had believed Ardley had it wrong. That he was guessing at Gabriel's intentions and was causing her undue worry.

"His second?" She posed the question not for clarification, but as if by saying it herself, it would become real.

Ardley nodded. "When he first came to me with concerns about Belvedere's behavior, I swore to aid him in protecting what was his against the man's ill intentions. And though I pledged to be his second in his challenge, I think this is a much better way of helping him."

"This?"

He nodded, gesturing at her. "Fetching you."

This made no sense to her. "How is fetching me going to help? If Gabriel wishes to challenge the man, there is little I can do." That day in the library when he had turned his back on her appeared fresh in her mind, and she shifted her body ever so much as to not see the desk behind her.

Ardley's brow furrowed. "Your Grace, I have known Gabriel professionally for many years. I've never seen the man swayed by anything when he determines the correct course of action, and yet you have influenced his every decision for the entirety of this season. I don't know how it is that you can get to him, but right now, he needs you. You must make him see the colossal mistake he's about to make."

She shook her head. "You must have it wrong, Your Grace. I don't—"

"Did you have any intention of remarrying?"

The question cut through the space between them like an arrow, and she shut her mouth against her words. She looked down at her feet before meeting Ardley's gaze once more. "No, I did not."

"And Grimsby, did he ever plan to wed?"

The inquiry was too personal, and she chafed at the question, but she realized Ardley wasn't looking for the answer. He was attempting to make her *see* the answer.

Gabriel hadn't planned to wed. Ever. While circumstances had forced both of their hands in this marriage, Gabriel had proposed long before that night in the Tyntsfield gardens.

Her lips parted, a small sound escaping as she assembled the bits in her mind. Gabriel's back to her, his strong shoulders hunched forward as he shut her out. She'd walked away. She'd walked away before she remembered what power she had. Like water finding its way into a crack, she'd somehow managed to penetrate the fortress Gabriel had built around him. She had been wrong. She hadn't been standing on the other side. She'd been standing in it.

And she only must exert pressure to watch the thing crack.

Ardley hadn't moved as she had arranged these thoughts in her mind, and now he only watched her.

"Your Grace, you must excuse me. I must ready myself for a ball." She gestured behind her. "Do help yourself to Cook's butter biscuits while you wait. I shall return as quickly as I can."

She didn't wait for his response. Picking up her skirts, she all but ran through the library doors in the direction of her rooms. If Gabriel planned to ruin his life tonight, she would hold nothing back in stopping him. No matter the consequences to herself or her peace, she would need everything she had to get his attention. And she knew just what would work.

She burst through her bedchamber door seconds later to find the room already occupied. But not by her lady's maid as she might have anticipated but by Mrs. Featherstone herself.

The diminutive woman stood on the threshold of the dressing room as though she had just stepped out of it.

"Mrs. Feathersone," Annie said, slightly breathless from her run. "I must change for the ball."

A true smile came to the woman's lips, the first real expression she'd ever witnessed on the woman. She turned ever so slightly to reach behind her into the dressing room she had now clearly just vacated. "I thought you might change your mind, so I had this aired for you."

When she turned back around, she held aloft the sinful red gown.

# CHAPTER 16

*W*here in Hell's teeth was Ardley?

Gabriel had sent instructions for the duke to meet him at the Summer Solstice Ball at half nine, and the man was late. Like all balls, the festivities were just getting underway at that hour, but the ballroom was filling quickly. The faint tuning of a violin could just be heard over the buzz of conversation, the clinking of glasses, and the odd punctuating giggle.

The room wasn't so full yet that he couldn't see to the end of it, but he'd arrived early and had watched every single guest enter the room, waiting for Belvedere. The man had shown up a little past nine, Gabriel's mother on his arm, which was of no surprise to him. He had no qualms with issuing his challenge in front of his mother. In fact, a part of him would likely enjoy it.

A gaggle of debutantes passed by him sporting every shade of white imaginable, and he thought it a terrible lost opportunity for Ardley. He plucked his pocket watch from his waistcoat even as he turned to the door. Where was the blasted man?

There was nothing for it. Gabriel had no wish to waste any more time, and he couldn't count on Belvedere refraining from wandering off. There were any number of lambs he could prey on at the Summer Solstice Ball. It mattered little who one was when it came to the midsummer fete, and anyone with a smidge of pedigree was in attendance. Belvedere was a prime example of that.

The ballroom was rectangular with a gallery above for those who wished to observe the festivities rather than participate in them. The night's theme was likely Shakespearean, *A Midsummer Night's Dream*, it looked like. It was terribly on the nose, but it was exactly this kind of theming that thrilled the *ton*, so who was he to disparage it? Anyway, he wasn't there for the decorations.

Belvedere began to circulate. With Gabriel's mother on his arm, he turned in the direction of the staircase that would lead up to the gallery. That was where the real wealth lay. The debutantes and wife-seeking gentlemen would all be dancing, but it was the older sect that would be in the galleries, happily ensconced with their cronies and sitting out the main entertainment in favor of gossip and prattle. It was ripe for Belvedere's scheming.

He followed at a distance, taking the stairs more sedately than was his habit, but he did not wish to issue his challenge with Belvedere standing on a stair above him. He tried not to think of Annie, of how she'd hardly spoken to him since that night in the library. What had he expected? He had shut her out as she seemed to have shut him out.

She hadn't spoken to him since the day of her attack, and it only served to fuel the fire inside of him. He would not allow Belvedere to ruin the one thing Gabriel had ever cherished, the one thing that had been his.

The wife he loved.

He knew he loved her. Despite everything he had done to stop himself, he'd fallen in love with her.

And Belvedere had threatened her.

He reached the gallery to find Belvedere and his mother several feet ahead of him along the gallery. The space was large and well lit with chandeliers and wall sconces. Seating arrangements dotted one side while an intricately carved railing made up the other. It wasn't overly crowded yet, and he was glad he wouldn't have quite so much of an audience for this. This was between him and Belvedere, and he wanted it over with as quickly as possible without so much gossip getting in the way.

Vaguely he noticed a tall woman detach herself from the group to his right, and too late he realized it was Lady Stoke Bruerne, Annie's mother, and—oh hell, Eloise too. Lady Stoke Bruerne raised a hand as if to get his attention, but he ignored her, plunging forward.

"Belvedere." His voice cut through the quiet hum of the gallery, and he watched, aware his heart had picked up its pace as Belvedere stopped, his cane skidding along the carpet as his footfalls were unexpectedly interrupted by the sound of Gabriel's voice.

His mother turned first, the dowager duchess's gaze zeroing in on him before she'd turned completely around.

"Gabriel. What is the meaning of this?" She made to step forward, but Belvedere held out a single hand, the light catching the ruby of his signet ring on his pinky finger.

"Elizabeth, I'll handle this." Belvedere's voice was soft as velvet and his smile slimy.

Gabriel held his ground. "Belvedere, I—"

"Grimsby."

If Gabriel's voice had cut the air, this one exploded it.

He didn't move. He couldn't. Every muscle in his body seized at the sound of her voice, at the authority laced through it, at the command it held. But he didn't need to move.

There was the swish of silk, the pad of a footstep, and then there she was.

Oh Lord, there she was.

He blinked, sure something had gone terribly wrong with his eyes.

His wife stood before him, his beautiful wife in a gown of fiery red silk that clung to the very curve of her shoulder as if the entire thing might suddenly fall. It was daring and alluring and—dear God, his wife was the very definition of desirable. He had to get her out of there. No one but him should see her like that. He made to move, to usher her outside and into a carriage, or at least into a cloak, anything to keep people from seeing.

"Annie, listen—"

"No. You listen to me." Her voice was steel and loud—forcibly loud—and he was rendered useless, every thought leaving his brain, every word slipping from his tongue.

But he didn't need to speak because just then a startled gasp interrupted their duel. They both turned to find Lady Stoke Bruerne, eyes wide, hand still raised as if she meant to get Gabriel's attention, Eloise frozen at her side, Grandmother Bitsy toddling forward.

"Oh Annie, you're back," Lady Stoke Bruerne whispered, her eyes growing wet, her lips trembling as she absently took Eloise's arm.

Eloise's eyes were equally wet, but her smile was bright and sure as she nodded. "I knew you'd find your way back, sister."

Grandmother Bitsy had made her way to the front by then, and pumping one fisted hand, she said, "Get him, Annie. Get him!"

He looked back at his wife in time to see a soft smile just

disappearing from her lips before she rounded on him again, her eyes hardening. She had no smile for him.

"You're being an idiot," she said. "You would throw away your life for a coward. Don't you realize that?" She flung her hand behind her, her finger pointing directly at Belvedere. "That man is a coward, Gabriel. He preys on vulnerable women and tries to gain power from children. He is the very definition of the word."

Belvedere let go of Elizabeth's arm, his hand tightening around the head of his cane. Gabriel kept one eye on him and one on his wife, not trusting the parasite so close to something he loved.

"And you would give him the rest of your life by challenging him." This caused a flutter of whispers through the crowd, ladies shifting uncomfortably in their seats, gentlemen exclaiming under their breaths. Lord Stoke Bruerne stepped forward, taking his wife's other arm as his gaze focused uncomfortably on Gabriel.

Annie took a step closer to him. "You're not angry with Belvedere, Gabriel. The man is so insubstantial he couldn't anger a fly. You're angry at your mother."

He blinked, wondering if the carpet beneath his feet had shifted somehow, and that was why he was suddenly feeling upended.

"Your mother tried to replace your father with Belvedere. That's why he treats you the way he does, why he speaks to you like that." She shook her head, a line appearing between her brows. "Gabriel, you never had time to grieve your father. You should have been given that, and your mother took it from you. You hate the man she tried to put in your father's place because he's the obstacle keeping you from the emotions you had every right to feel."

He shook his head. "No, that man deserves—"

"Nothing." She put her hands on his arms as she said the

word, and she was so close now he could smell her lavender soap. "That man deserves nothing, Gabriel, and I won't let you give him anything more. He's taken enough from you."

The warm light from the chandeliers gave his wife an ethereal glow, but he thought perhaps that glow came from inside of her. Her mother and sister were right. Something had happened to her. He didn't know when, but it had happened, and now he witnessed the aftermath.

Anna Bounds was no longer the scared widow he had sought to protect, the survivor of an abusive marriage, the lost soul trying to find her way in the world. The creature before him didn't require protection.

She was protecting *him*.

Once more it was as though the very ground shifted beneath his feet. Everything he had once clung to, everything he once let guide his life, was gone, evaporating even as he held it in his grasp.

Annie was right.

A pain had opened up inside of him, a pain so great he pictured a hole spreading in his chest, a hole into which he could fall and never be seen or heard from again. The pain grew, morphing, eclipsing, contracting, and vibrating. The past twenty years of his life came to a single point, and she was standing in front of him in the fiery red gown of a goddess.

But she was his goddess, and with that thought, the world righted itself, and he could once more breathe.

"You're right." They were the only words that needed to be said. There were other words he wished to say to her, but not here, not now. "You're right, Annie. I should have listened to you."

Her lips parted as her eyes searched his face, and he wondered what she would say, but she didn't get to say it.

Because just then his mother pushed past Belvedere, her bony jaw jutting forward as she marched up to them.

"Gabriel." She spoke his name as if it were a bullet. "You are a disgrace to the family. I'm ashamed to have born you. I can only hope God will forgive me for my selfishness." Her attention turned to Annie who had turned to face her. "And you. You're clearly the whore your first husband knew you to be."

Everything inside of Gabriel turned to steel, his fingers curling into a fist involuntarily. But then…Annie didn't move. Her expression didn't change. She didn't even flinch. The words struck her like a blow, and she took it without so much as a blink of her eye.

"I'm not a whore actually. I'm not any of those things my first husband claimed." Again she threw out a hand, her finger pointing squarely at Belvedere. "For anyone who would like to know, that man there, Brogden Belvedere, attacked me at the Sagamore, a housing unit for the Merchant Shipbuilding Company, while I was there completing charity work. If Gabriel hadn't taught me to defend myself, he would have violated me." Her hand swung in another direction, and Gabriel realized with a jolt Viscount Overby was attempting to slink away. "Viscount Overby attacked me in the Tyntsfield garden that night. I slapped him, and he fell into that hedge. Gabriel offered to marry me to protect my reputation, but he shouldn't have been forced to. Overby should be the one punished for what he did. Not me." She eyed the gathered crowd, and Gabriel followed her gaze, noticing they had drawn quite a lot of onlookers. The gallery was almost crowded now, but one man stood out. He stood out because of the ridiculous grin on his face.

Ardley.

Annie's sudden appearance made perfect sense now, and

something warm and unfamiliar twisted inside of him at the sight of his friend.

"Is there anyone else who would like to tell me something my first husband said about me? I'd love to hear it." Annie's chin was up, her voice cutting, but no one uttered a single word.

No one except Elizabeth Phelps.

"You can defend yourself all you wish, but you are still married to the most worthless son a mother could be cursed with."

Annie turned on her, and Gabriel braced himself for the worst, but Annie's voice was sickly sweet as she said, "Do you know we met once a few seasons ago? It took me a while to recall where though as we were never properly introduced. I was Lady Anna Bounds before I married anyone. Perhaps you remember my sister. Gwendolyn."

The first tick of apprehension gripped the back of his neck. His hands seemed to float up of their own accord, reaching to stop his wife, but there was no stopping her. He knew that.

Gabriel's mother looked as though she'd swallowed a frog. "Gwendolyn Bounds, you say?" She shook her head, but the movement was half-hearted, and she waved a hand as if to dismiss Annie's word. "I'm not sure—"

"You said her face looked like the etching of a cobblestone street."

*Oh no.*

"So what if I did? It's only the truth," his mother hissed, spit flying from her lips as her eyes narrowed in cold hatred.

Annie smiled then, a smile he would remember for the rest of his life. It was filled with satisfaction, with pride, and with strength.

It was the smile she wore when she punched his mother squarely in the face.

* * *

"Ow! That hurts." She tried to tug her hand out of her husband's grasp, but he held it firmly in his own, so she was forced to meet his gaze as she said, "You're a terrible teacher, you know. You never explained to me how much it hurts to punch someone like that."

"Had I known you were going to rush off and punch my mother, I would have explained better."

She stopped struggling and let him apply the salve Mrs. Featherstone had brought up from the kitchen supply. They were nestled on the sofa in the library, her beautiful red gown getting mercilessly wrinkled, but she didn't care. She had stopped Gabriel from making a terrible mistake and vanquished not only herself but her sister in the bargain. Even though she hadn't danced in her beautiful dress, she still counted the night a success.

"I won't apologize for that," she said, watching his face carefully for a reaction, but she needn't have.

He laughed, heartily. "I'm not asking for you to apologize. The woman deserved it."

She placed her other hand over the one he was using to spread the salve on her bruised knuckles, making him look up and meet her gaze. "I meant what I said, Gabriel. Your mother shouldn't have done what she did. She should never have tried to replace your father, and you should have been given the freedom to mourn him."

His hand stilled against hers, his eyes dropped back to what he was doing, and his words were slow and careful as he said, "I don't wish to mourn him. It's been so long since he died." He looked up again, and she was startled by the fierceness in his eyes. "I'd like to talk about him. I'd like to tell you stories about him, things he did, his habits, his triumphs, his foibles. All of it. I want someone else to know him who will never meet him."

Her heart squeezed at the earnestness in his eyes, and she said, "I'd like that very much." She had taken another breath to hold back the tears as she added, "And maybe one day, you could tell our children about him too?"

She waited, her heart hammering inside of her as if her very existence depended on what he would say next. She knew just because she had punched out his mother and stopped him from challenging Belvedere their problems weren't magically spirited away. It would take a lot of dedicated work to tear down the fortress Gabriel had built around himself, but she was willing to do it, even if it meant going one brick at a time.

He looked at her for so long she was sure he wouldn't answer, but then a soft smile flirted at the corners of his lips. "Only if I get to tell them about their mother's right hook."

Relief flooded through her, and she drew in a deep breath. "I've only punched one person."

"So far." A hint of laughter was in his voice now, and her tension eased further.

He rubbed the last of the salve into her knuckles and carefully wrapped her hand in a loose linen dressing. "I think you'll live, Your Grace," he pronounced, setting aside the jar of salve and wiping his hands on a towel Mrs. Featherstone had brought up with a small tray of tea and biscuits.

Apparently the housekeeper thought a round of sparring required sustenance.

And then Gabriel was kissing her, his big hands cradling her face, the roughness of his palms against her skin so familiar she whimpered at his touch. He backed away, concern flaring in his eyes.

"Did I hurt you?" he whispered.

She shook her head, her hair rustling between his fingers

as she was quick to reassure him. "No, not at all. It's just been too long since you kissed me." Heedless of her bandaged hand, she gripped the front of his jacket, pulling him to her.

He kissed her, long and deep, pushing her back into the cushions, tangling her legs with his as she tried to hold as much of him as she could. Unbidden came the memory of that day she'd awoken on this very sofa, the rain soft on the roof, and she nestled in his arms. She had been so adamant about protecting her widowhood then, and the very idea had her going cold inside, thinking of what might have happened had she not gone into the garden that night.

He seemed to sense her shifting thoughts, and he eased back, his eyes studying her. "What is it?"

She licked her lips, regretting the loss of his kiss. "I was just thinking how terribly much I wanted to remain a widow." She tried to smile, but it faltered, and she touched his cheek, her touch gentle as she tried to reassure herself he was real. "I would have missed this. I would have missed you."

He took her hand into his and pressed a kiss to the palm. "Annie, there's something I need to tell you."

She stilled, her breathing slowing as if to preserve her energy for what was about to come.

Her husband looked directly at her and said, "I love you, Annie."

She waited, blinked. "That's it?" She hadn't meant the words to come out so strangled but...well, with everything they had been through she'd been expecting a great deal more.

"Was there something else you wanted?" His brow furrowed, and she shook her head.

"No, it's just..." But she didn't know what to say because there was nothing to say. Nothing except—"I love you too, Gabriel. I love you so terribly much." She tugged her hand to pull him toward her and kissed him, slowly, deeply, savoring every second of just being there, with her husband, in the home that was now theirs.

It was some time later when Gabriel pulled away, holding her back when she tried to kiss him again. "Annie, I also owe you an apology. I shouldn't have treated you the way I did after you told me about Belvedere. I—"

She placed two fingers against his lips. "I don't want your apology, Gabriel. I want a promise instead. Promise me you'll never let what your mother did to you dictate how you react in future. Promise me."

His eyes darkened as he took in her face, and slowly a smile came to his lips. "I promise," he said and finally kissed her again.

She wasn't sure how much later it was when he nuzzled her neck, murmuring, "I'd also like to talk about this dress, Your Grace. I don't seem to recall you wearing it before."

She couldn't stop the giggle as his hand slid up her torso, skirting the curve of her breast to find the scrap of sleeve that clung to her shoulder. "Oh I think this gown is rather boring, don't you?"

He pulled back, and the look on his face was devastatingly comic.

"I'd much rather discuss the migratory practices of the short-eared owl." It was all she could do to force the words out with a straight face.

There was a beat of silence, and then his face transformed into a grin, right before he growled and lowered his head to capture her lips in a toe-curling kiss.

# CHAPTER 17

*ome months later...*



"You're not peeking, are you?"

She frowned. "I don't see why this is necessary."

Gabriel tucked her arm more firmly through his. "Don't ruin the surprise."

She was helpless to hold the frown at the sound of excitement in his voice.

"There are stairs here. Three of them. Go slowly."

She held on to his arm as she felt around with her foot for the first stair. The day was cool, summer melting into autumn, and the play of wind across her cheeks was speckled with the smell of salt and damp, a familiar aroma that had her smiling. She took the stairs from memory then, her feet knowing exactly how far apart each cement tier was.

Next came the click of the door, and she pictured its blue paint as her shoes tapped onto the wooden planks of a long corridor.

A smile found its way to her face as her husband led her down the corridor, and her mind wandered, conjuring all the possibilities for why her husband had brought her to the Sagamore and why he was being so secretive about the reason for their visit.

The building was unusually silent around them, and her ears strained to pick up a sound. She thought they were likely halfway down the corridor when she believed she heard a snicker of laughter, but the sound was brief and might have been a figment of her imagination. But...

Did they have an audience?

Were the residents of the Sagamore included in whatever her husband was about?

She knew when they reached the end of the corridor, and her feet automatically turned for the door that would lead into the room she'd been using for months now. Only—

The air was different. She could sense it straight away. There was a woodsy smell about it with the tang of fresh paint and stain, and she wanted nothing more than to force open her eyes and see what was happening. But Gabriel still held her arm, and she clung to it, willing herself to keep her eyes shut for him.

When she was certain she was in the middle of the room, he stopped her. He placed his hands on her shoulders and turned her until she thought she might be facing the corner by the door.

"All right, you can open your eyes now."

She had never heard such careful expectancy in his voice, and she knew whatever it was that she was about to see meant a great deal to him. She prepared herself to have the appropriate reaction, so he could see how much she appreciated whatever it was he had done, but when she opened her eyes, her mind went absolutely blank, and she forgot how to even breathe.

She couldn't have said what her reaction was. She couldn't have said what her name was.

Because there in front of her was a library.

A real library with gorgeous maple bookcases running the length of every wall, tucked into every nook, and stretching clear to the ceiling high above her. Each shelf was filled, and not a single crate remained on the floor of the room. A small desk was pushed under the window in the far wall, and on it sat her ledger where she kept track of the borrowed books along with a blotter, pens, and ink. But it was the small ladder waiting patiently in the corner that drew her. She went to it, and with two fingers pushed it along its brass rail. It seemed to float along the floor, making no noise as it traveled the rail.

She watched it as it glided, easing to a stop two bookcases away, and she felt her smile more than realizing she was doing it.

But while the library was grand, it was the man standing in the middle of it, his arms at his sides, quietly watching her that made her heart pound with love.

"Gabriel Phelps, did you make me a library?"

There was the definite sound of snickered laughter from the corridor beyond, and she knew with certainty the residents of the Sagamore, the ones she had helped become a community, were listening, and her smile grew wider.

His smile was sheepish as he looked down at his feet before replying, "I arranged for a library to be made for you. I thought it would help you in finding your way."

She shook her head and slowly approached him. "As it happens, I was never lost," she said. "It's only I had forgotten who I was for a time, but I've remembered now."

She stood in front of him as he asked, "And who is that?"

She smiled as she said, "Lady Anna Bounds." She paused, studying his beautiful face, every line and plane she had once thought harsh and commanding that she now found familiar and endearing. She waited for as long as she could, watching him take in her words before she added, "Your wife."

She would never grow tired of witnessing his mercurial eyes, seeing them grow dark with only her words, and she would never grow tired of the way he growled, of the way he made her laugh, right before he kissed her.

# ABOUT THE AUTHOR

Jessie decided to be a writer because there were too many lives she wanted to live to just pick one.

Taking her history degree dangerously, Jessie tells the stories of courageous heroines, the men who dared to love them, and the world that tried to defeat them.

Jessie lives in New Hampshire where if she is not at her desk writing, she's probably letting the dog out. Again.

For more, visit her website at jessieclever.com.